NO PLACE LII

Kerry Wilkinson has been busy since turning thirty.

His first Jessica Daniel novel, *Locked In*, was a number one ebook bestseller, while the series as a whole has sold one million copies.

He has written a fantasy-adventure trilogy for young adults, a second crime series featuring private investigator Andrew Hunter, plus the standalone thrillers *Down Among the Dead Men* and *No Place Like Home*.

Originally from the county of Somerset, Kerry has spent far too long living in the north of England, picking up words like 'barm' and 'ginnel'.

When he's short of ideas, he rides his bike or bakes cakes. When he's not, he writes it all down.

For more information about Kerry and his books visit:

www.kerrywilkinson.com or www.panmacmillan.com

www.twitter.com/kerrywk
www.facebook.com/JessicaDanielBooks

Or you can email Kerry at kerrywilkinson@live.com

KERRY WILKINSON

NO PLACE LIKE HOME

PAN BOOKS

First published 2016 by Pan Books
an imprint of Pan Macmillan
20 New Wharf Road, London N1 9RR
Associated companies throughout the world
www.panmacmillan.com

ISBN 978-1-5098-0444-3

1 3 5 7 9 8 6 4 2

A CIP catalogue record for this book is available from the British Library.

Typeset by Ellipsis Digital, Glasgow
Printed and bound by CPI Group (UK) Ltd, Croydon, CR0 4YY

Visit www.panmacmillan.com to read more about all our books
and to buy them. You will also find features, author interviews and
news of any author events, and you can sign up for e-newsletters
so that you're always first to hear about our new releases.

NO PLACE LIKE HOME

1

FIFTEEN YEARS OLD

Craig Macklin's footsteps crunched across the mix of gravel and dirt. His white trainers were going to be filthy and he'd have to wipe them clean somewhere before he got home. It wasn't the dirty shoes specifically that would get him into trouble, it was his mother's inevitable questioning and the risk his ever-increasing web of lies regarding his whereabouts could tie him in knots. He could picture her, hand on hip, leaning slightly to one side, single raised eyebrow: 'And just where did you get them *that* dirty, young man?'

She'd been more and more suspicious of him in the past year or so, not that he could blame her, not after the newsagent incident. She had already tried the teary arm-round-the-shoulder approach, telling Craig how she wanted only the best for him. They were now onto the angry approach, with a curfew, intermittent threats of grounding, plus demands to know where he was every second of the day. His dad would shrug and say he was off down the Legion but she definitely wouldn't approve of him skipping school.

Again.

As Craig mentally planned where he might be able to find leaves big enough to clean his shoes on the walk home, Mark continued to stride ahead of him, scuffing his feet, unconcerned about any potential inquest into the state of his footwear. The woods at the back of the school were a haven for skiving students, with trails of cigarette butts leading through the inner crop of trees to the series of clearings out of sight of the main school building. To those who didn't know, it was a muddy patch of grass, but to a certain underclass of students, of which Craig was a part, it held its own mystique. Drugs had been dealt, pills popped, fags smoked and, if the gossip was to be believed, virginities lost.

As if reading his mind, Mark pointed to a leafy bush on the edge of the clearing. 'That's where that Amy girl from year eleven shagged that Kevin kid.'

It was the same thing Mark said every time they passed this particular spot. Craig had never asked any follow-up questions, such as how Mark knew for sure. There was no point; he knew Mark would grin, scratch his chin and then claim he was there. Perhaps he had been, though Craig never quite knew where the truth ended and his friend's bullshit began. As much as Craig wanted to believe there was a shagging bush mere metres from their school, he knew the prickly branches and sodden ground made it unlikely. Still, it was an enticing thought.

Craig continued following Mark across the clearing, past the next line of trees, heading towards a tightly packed clump doused in shadow. He didn't bother to ask where they were going, instead trying to avoid the muddiest patches of land.

Ahead, Mark swung his leg towards a loose stone, connecting and sending it spiralling into the darkness with a thwack of rock on bark, then slowed his pace, turning to face Craig. There was a recent cut across the top of his eye that had started to heal, only to be picked back open. The dark red blood had pooled underneath, scabbing into a bulbous dome of crusty plasma. His hands were in the pockets of his dark school uniform trousers, top button of his shirt undone, rucksack slung across his shoulders. They weren't going back to school any time soon, if at all.

'Whatcha get up to last night?' Mark asked.

Craig shrugged. 'Not much, played a bit of Pro Evo.'

Mark was at Craig's side, matching his speed. They were around the same height, five seven or eight, but Craig felt cowed. Mark had a broader chest, bigger shoulders, thicker jaw, larger hands. He was like a boxer with a natural brawn; Craig was skinny, like an athlete or cyclist but without the speed.

'Dad was arrested yesterday,' Mark replied. 'Got in some ruck down the pub. I think he broke the other guy's nose.'

'What time was that?'

'Dunno, he didn't get in 'til three this morning, going on about the Old Bill not having enough cells down the nick. I think he's got to go back today.'

There was a rustle from the nearby bushes as a grey squirrel dashed from the undergrowth, scuttling up a tree, waiting halfway and staring at them with its dark brown eyes. Mark stopped, crouching to pick up a stone and then launching it at the creature. The squirrel remained still until the stone struck the bark a few centimetres from its head, sending up a spray of dust and chipping. A moment later, it had disappeared in a flurry of frightened limbs up the tree into the shrouded branches.

Mark sent another stone towards the tree but it clattered off a hanging branch and dropped to the ground.

'Does that mean social services will be looking for you?' Craig asked.

'*Looking* is the key word. They can piss off.'

Mark's attention was quickly taken by something red lodged in a nearby tree. It looked like it might be round but the compact branches and leaves were shielding it from full view. Before Craig could say anything, Mark was shimmying up the trunk, grasping towards the lowest branch and then heaving himself into a sitting position. He was surprisingly flexible for his size, sliding along the wood, before stretching up and grabbing what turned out to be a Frisbee. He turned it over in his hands, looking disappointed, and then flung it into the distance with a grunt of annoyance.

Back on the ground, Mark continued walking away from the school, Craig in tow. 'There's all sorts of stuff around here,' Mark said. 'I once found a wallet with a hundred quid inside. Cards, too. The pin number was in there on a piece of paper. I went to the cashpoint and took all the money out. There was, like, a thousand pounds or something.'

'What did you do with it?'

'I've still got it – gonna buy a motorbike off one of my dad's friends.'

'Wow . . .'

Craig did his best to sound impressed, even though he knew it would definitely be the last he heard of either the fictional thousand pounds, or the mythical motorbike. They'd go the same way as the sixth-form girl Mark had copped off with, the Ferrari he'd test-driven at a disused airfield, and the holiday home in Jamaica Mark had been left in the will of some grandparent he hadn't mentioned before or since. Craig knew the truth of what went on between Mark and his father, and if Mark wanted to invent stories to pretend his life was better than it was, then who was Craig to say anything? Besides, Craig didn't have a long line of people queuing up to be his friend. He could put up with a certain amount of made-up nonsense if it meant having someone to hang around with.

They'd only gone a short distance further when Mark was shuffling away again, his attention stolen by a deflated, abandoned football. He booted it towards Craig but the ball was so flat that it barely travelled a metre before sinking into the mud. Mark tried kicking it again but only succeeded in sending a spray of filth across the bottom of his trousers.

He peered down at the mess, grinning. 'Ah, well, can't go back to school now.'

They continued traipsing across the soaked ground, Mark wading through the puddles, Craig edging around them, until they reached a chain-link fence. Glinting, vicious razor wire spiralled around the top, with a red and white sign pinned to the fence directly in front of them, as if someone knew they were coming.

NO TRESPASSING: RISK OF SERIOUS INJURY OR DEATH

Craig's eyes fixed on the word 'death' but Mark was unaffected. He ran a hand through his short dark hair, gazing along the length of the fence. They'd been in the woods before, but never gone this far. On the other side of the barrier was a river of sand-coloured gravel, four sets of train tracks, then more gravel and another fence. Electrical lines were high overhead, lines of pylons stretching into the distance.

Mark dumped his bag on the ground, crouching and unzipping the top, then rummaging inside.

'Shall we nick off to town?' Craig said. 'I think those gippos are putting up the funfair.'

Mark didn't reply, which was ominous. Craig hated it when his friend had an idea fixed in his mind because there was no chance of changing it, no matter how stupid the plan. Mark dropped a pile of exercise books onto the ground as he pulled the bag open further, digging deeper, before removing a pair of hedge clippers. The blades were curved, with thick sharpened edges that looked like they could slice through anything, fingers included. Mark clicked them back and forth, grin widening. Craig tried not to show how uneasy he felt. He was uncomfortable with weapons at the best of times, let alone when Mark was wielding them. It wasn't often present but, sometimes, a glint appeared in Mark's gaze that made Craig wonder if he knew his friend at all.

Mark's eyes twinkled as he turned back to the fence, snipping through the metal as easily as if it was butter. He worked outwards in a circle and then cut back towards the centre until there was a gap big enough to squeeze through. Mark tossed the clipped pieces of metal to the side and then repacked his bag before throwing it through. He ducked under the metal and then turned back.

'You coming?'

Craig wanted to say no. What good was possibly going to come from being on the train tracks, especially with Mark in this mood? He glanced at the sign again, focusing on the word 'death', before doing what he always did: following. As he passed through the fence, Craig stood too quickly, the spiky jaws of the sliced metal raking his shoulders before he ducked again with a grimace and whispered a swear word. Mark didn't notice: he was already on the tracks, peering towards the centre of Manchester, hand shielding his eyes from the late-morning haze.

Craig scuffed his shoes on the gravel, getting rid of some of the mud, glancing to the pylons above. 'Aren't the lines electric?'

Mark shrugged, not turning around.

'Did you touch them?' Craig asked.

'Just step over them.'

'Why?'

'Because it's fun.'

'What's fun?'

Mark hopped over the rails like a human Frogger game until he was on the far side, then hurdled his way back until he was at Craig's side.

The sparkle was in Mark's eye, a darkness of which Craig knew he should have no part. Mark was taking deep breaths through his nose and exhaling through his mouth, puffing his chest out as a grin crept across his face. 'Do you ever think about doing something crazy?'

'Like what?'

'I don't know . . . blocking the line with branches and bricks to see what happens.'

'The train would be derailed. People could get hurt. There was this big disaster in Spain the other week, where—'

Mark was barely listening. 'We'd be the first on the scene to help people. We'd be heroes.'

'But it'd be our fault.'

'So?'

'So, people would find out. They'd ask what we were doing here, wonder why we were out of school.'

Not to mention the guilt.

Mark started to chew on the corner of his mouth, weighing up the options. Craig wondered if he really meant it. Sometimes Mark said things to get a reaction, like swearing at teachers, or asking the year eleven girls about their bra size.

'Hmmmm . . .'

Mark eventually stepped away from the tracks, scooping his backpack from the ground and heading towards the fence. For a moment, Craig thought it was over, and they'd head off to town to find trouble. Instead, Mark paused, turning as the ground started to shake. Craig felt it in his knees first, a gentle wobble that made him stumble slightly. He'd never been in an earthquake but had seen videos and thought it'd probably be like this. In the distance, a rumble was building, making the ground tremor even more. Mark was suddenly alive, dropping his bag again and treading carefully towards the lines.

'I think a train's coming,' Craig said.

Mark didn't reply, stepping over the raised rail until he was in the centre of the track. Craig headed to the fence, squinting towards the city where the silhouette of a train was zipping towards them.

'Mark – it's a train.'

The thunder continued to roar, the vibrations spreading from Craig's knees to his upper body. The train was so loud that he could feel his bones rattling.

'Mark!'

Craig was shouting but could barely hear himself. Mark hadn't moved, spreading his arms into a crucifix pose as he stared at the oncoming train. Craig could see the yellow front, the bluey-purple sides and the word **FIRST** emblazoned across the front in golden letters. A loud horn blared as a screeching began to echo around the trees. Mark still hadn't shifted, arms wide as the train barrelled towards him, wheels screeching, brakes clamped against the metal.

The train was slowing rapidly but there was no way it could stop in time.

The horn continued shrieking, a deafening honk drowning out the squeal of metal on metal. Somehow, Craig could still hear Mark. He was laughing and shouting, daring the train to hit him.

'*Come on!*'

Craig glanced from the train to Mark and back again, holding his breath. He knew the train's speed would be immense, yet somehow it was happening in slow motion. The train was so close that Craig could see the driver, a middle-aged man in a dark uniform, eyes wide, the whites frozen in fear as they settled on Mark in the deadliest game of chicken.

'*Come on!*'

Craig's feet were fixed to the ground, his entire body shaking from the oncoming storm. Fifty metres. Forty. Mark didn't move. Thirty. His arms were still wide, laugh resounding under the booming force of the train. Twenty metres. Ten.

Craig blinked.

The train flashed past, chikka-chikka-chikkaring along the lines as the brakes released. Craig could see rows of passengers through the windows. Some were reading, others gazing into nothingness. One or two stared back at him, turning to watch until the angle became too much. With a heavy gust of wind, three carriages flew past, revealing a grinning Mark on the other side of the tracks. A speckling of dust had sprayed from the train onto his face. Mark stepped back over the rails, still smiling as he plucked his backpack from the ground and took a breath.

'Wow.'

Craig dared not move, fearing his balance would desert him if he tried.

Mark ran a hand across his head. 'You don't know what you're missing. That was *a-may-zing*.'

Craig's voice was more of a gulp: 'What were you doing?'

Mark shrugged.

'Were you trying to kill yourself?'

Another shrug, then Mark poked an accusing finger into Craig's shoulder. 'Kill myself? Why would I do that?' He took another breath. '*That* is what you call living.'

2

Craig hoiked his duffel bag higher on his shoulder, weaving through the crowd and trying not to take anyone out. The bloody thing was ridiculously heavy, although it did contain more or less everything he owned. Piccadilly train station was heaving, hordes of people hurrying across the main concourse doing whatever it was people did in the north west nowadays. Some were in suits, either just leaving work or, perhaps, given the twenty-four-hour society everyone was stuck with, heading in. Others were dressed for a party – short dresses, high heels and fake-tanned legs for the girls; smart shirts and too much hair gel for the lads. More still were wrapped in thick coats, with a handful of blokes sporting ludicrous Christmas jumpers: red, green and hideous, like the contents of a blown broken nose. When did they become fashionable?

It was early evening on Wednesday and Craig's delayed train had taken the best part of four hours to get from Euston to Manchester. Four sodding hours. While Richard Branson was busy fiddling with hot-air balloons, space flights and whatever else he amused himself with, he needed to be told that his trains were a shambles.

Craig slid to a halt as a young girl in a red velvet dress

skipped along the floor in front of him, her apologetic mother a short distance behind, bellowing 'Abigail!'

The station smelled of pastry and burger and there was so much noise that Craig was stunned by the sensory overload. Not only was there the usual low hum of chatter, there was a booming speaker announcement, screaming kids, the rumble of trains and clatter of luggage on hard floor. He peered around at the now unfamiliar setting. Thirteen years previously, he'd got on a train heading for London and now he was back. There were advertising panels everywhere, huge information boards and so many, many people.

Craig followed the signs for the exit, passing through the gaping glass doors onto London Road, where there were even more people hurrying into and away from the station. It was dark and cold, the air crisp and fresh, yet there was glee in the air. Christmas was two weeks away and people were looking forward to the parties and time off work. Craig continued walking down the slope, peering around, looking for the unfamiliar-familiar face that he hadn't seen in person since he was seventeen. He eventually saw the man leaning against the railing close to the bus stop. The scruffy trousers and school uniform were gone, replaced by trendy jeans and a tight-fitting woollen coat. His face was a little chubbier but Mark hadn't grown in height or bulk and his hair was still as short as it had always been. They'd been friends on social networks for a while, as much as two people could be when they'd grown apart and lived at opposite ends of the country. Craig felt a stab of sadness at seeing his old mate: they'd grown up together and then . . . things had happened and thirteen years had passed.

Mark glanced up from his phone, spotting Craig and breaking into a grin: 'Well, I'll be buggered. Look who it is.'

They shook hands, looking each other up and down, seeing how the missing years had affected one another. If Craig was honest, he knew time had been kinder to Mark than it had him. They were only thirty, yet his fair hair was already greying, wrinkles swimming across his forehead. Mark was still baby-faced, with that half-grin that got him out of trouble.

Craig peered along the road, over the throngs towards the city centre. 'I can't believe how busy it is.'

'Isn't it busy in London?'

'Not where I lived, but I suppose so. I never realised Manchester had become so . . . big.'

Mark shrugged in the dismissive way he always had. 'It's Christmas, innit? C'mon – we'll go check out the markets, then we can have our first-ever legal beer.'

He set off, not waiting for acceptance. It sounded fine to Craig, though the thought they'd never had a legal drink together was sobering considering the amount of cider and beer they got through in the old days. Mark continued along the main road, weaving through the masses, before slowing as they reached Piccadilly Gardens. The giant square was surrounded by strings of Christmas lights, with a large tree in the centre of the grassy area. On the far side, three trams vied for position, with hundreds of people bounding on and off, heading into the night. A man on the corner was selling Santa hats and reindeer ears from a cart, with the tones of that bloody Slade song drifting from the nearby Costa.

Mark slowed to a stop, nudging Craig with his elbow. 'Bit different, ain't it?'

'This was a dump when I left, all mud and boarded-up shops.'

'Wait 'til you see Albert Square.'

Craig didn't expect much but the area outside Manchester Town Hall was transformed from what he remembered. Instead of a crookedly paved area where the alkies hung around, swearing at strangers and begging for money, there was a sprawling market jammed with stalls selling hot cider, German sausages, paella, chocolate, cake, Christmas decorations and beer, beer, beer. Hundreds of people were crammed into the area, spilling onto the roads as taxi drivers swerved and beeped their horns in annoyance. There were two-storey cabins built from thick wood, with winter-clad revellers packed on top and inside, eating and drinking; plus rows of high tables for people to lean against. There were so many visitors that there was no chance of Craig being able to wade against the tide with his duffel bag across his back, so instead they cut through the side streets, crossed Deansgate, and headed into the Spinningfields area of the city. As the office blocks soared high above, they were greeted by a giant inflatable snowman, beaming white lights and an ice rink. Mark led the way around the side of the square until they reached a seated area out of sight of the road, surrounded by tall gas heaters that were glowing a cosy orange. Craig finally dumped his bag on the floor, relaxing into a sturdy metal chair and cricking his neck.

Mark was still on his feet: 'Beer?'

'I'll get 'em.'

Craig started to stand but Mark waved a dismissive hand and headed towards a stall close to the ice rink. Craig stifled a yawn, the chilled air prickling his ears until he shuffled further under the heat lamps. There were a dozen tables that were empty except for a couple enjoying a bit of leg stroking a few metres away. The area around the rink was packed with children and parents, the strained tones of Wizzard echoing from the speakers and pissing everyone off. Being Christmas every day would be fine – except for having to listen to the same sodding music on a loop.

Mark returned with a pair of German steins full of frothy beer. He plonked them both on the table and slumped into the seat across from Craig, nodding at the tankards. 'Go on then.'

The beer was almost freezing, the foam thick and sticky. Bloody good, though. Craig wiped his mouth and sighed in satisfaction. It had been a long day and this wasn't a bad way to finish it.

Mark had a second swig, fingers stretched through the large handle, cradling the thick glass. Their breaths spiralled into the air as the heater clinked. Over Mark's shoulder, the couple were in full lip-biting, get-a-room, oh-to-be-young mode.

Craig realised his friend was looking at him. 'I didn't think you'd ever come back from London,' Mark said.

'Mum's been going on about it for ages. She and Dad have been down a few times but they're getting on a bit. Then you got in contact. My old company is restructuring, so I'm on thirty-day gardening leave before I'm made redundant.'

'They're still paying you?'

'Only for a month.'

'What do you do?'

Craig started to make bunny ears with his fingers and then stopped himself. He hated people who did that. 'Logistics management – it's too boring to talk about.'

Mark threw his head back, chuckling, before having another drink. It was incredible that he could still make Craig feel embarrassed all these years on. It sounded like such a stupid job title to say out loud. Mark rolled the words around – 'logistics management' – before finally stopping laughing. 'Who would've guessed either of us would end up doing something like that?'

Craig didn't reply. What could he say?

Mark flicked his head upwards, like an exaggerated tic. He'd always done it when he wanted attention. It was frightening how his smaller mannerisms were the same. 'You back for good?'

'I'm not sure. I needed to get away from London for a bit.'

'Because of your wife?'

It was Craig's turn to shrug. '*Ex*-wife.'

'What happened?'

'Harriet . . . left.'

Craig hid behind his glass, supping, wiping his mouth and then drinking again. He didn't want to think, let alone talk, about it. His mum would have questions, too. It was easy to gloss over things when there was a buffer zone of a few hundred miles, less simple when your mother looked you in the eye and asked why you weren't married any longer. They were nothing compared to the questions he asked himself. He and Harriet had been together for twelve years, married for seven. Had he ever loved her, or was she the person he'd run to because he was tired of thinking about the reason he left Manchester? She'd done them both a favour by leaving.

Mark had already half-finished his drink, his gaze following a short-skirted woman hurrying out of an office towards the main road. 'You staying with your parents?'

'For now.'

'They still in the same place?'

'Yep.' Craig lifted his glass. 'Once I'm done with this, I've got to get out to Salford to see them. They were expecting me . . . well, around now. I told them I was meeting a mate for a drink but the train was delayed.'

Mark checked his watch, something chunky and silver, no doubt a fake. 'It's only half six.'

'Maybe I can get a second down, then I definitely have to go. What are the trams like nowadays?'

'There's never anyone checking tickets. Just hop on and off you go.'

'I meant do they run on time, are they safe . . . ?'

Mark snorted, as if those things never crossed his mind. They probably didn't. When they were kids, it was all about sneaking onto trains and trams, trying not to get caught without a ticket. Surely he wasn't still like that?

Mark was nodding. 'They're fine but a bit busy at rush hour. You don't want to end up standing next to some stinky sod, but there are some tidy girls about.'

Also not what Craig meant.

He downed the rest of his drink, enjoying the buzz, and then headed to the stall by the ice rink. The area was even busier than it had been when they'd walked through. A wooden cabin was doubling as a restaurant and was packed, with rows of excited children outside queuing for the ice rink as a Zamboni zipped around the surface. The hot chocolate stand had a menu of various alcoholic hot drinks, with a line of two dozen people hopping from foot to foot, trying to keep warm. If Craig had been by himself, he'd have preferred a whisky-laced hot chocolate, but he'd look a bit of a tit if he sauntered back to Mark with a pair of steaming drinks instead of two beers.

The poor girl behind the stall was dressed in green lederhosen, with long blonde pigtails, but was doing her best to smile through it. As he paid her eight quid for each drink, Craig hoped she was on more than minimum wage. Even compared to London prices, it was steep. Back at the table, Mark was thumbing his phone, peering up briefly to mutter 'thanks', before returning to the screen. Craig started his second drink, glancing towards the couple over Mark's shoulder. They were in their teens or early twenties, wearing matching red bobble hats. The girl was now on her boyfriend's lap, one hand snaked around his back, the other cupping his chin as they snogged as if their lives depended on it, oblivious to who might be watching.

Those were the days.

Craig was about to have another drink when his pocket started buzzing. He rattled the table leg as he stood abruptly, battling with his jeans until he managed to free his phone. It was his mum, probably wondering where he was.

'All right?' Craig said.

She stumbled, slightly, which wasn't uncommon when she was on the phone: 'Craig?'

'Who else?'

'Are you . . . near?'

'I won't be long, Mum.'

'There were men. They knocked on the door and . . .'

Craig suddenly realised his mother's voice hadn't broken because she was unsure of the technology, it was because she was terrified. A shiver flickered along his spine. 'What happened?'

'Please hurry.'

3

Craig didn't bother telling Mark there was a problem, instead saying they'd catch up soon and that his mum really wanted to see him. He'd been looking forward to seeing how the area in which he'd grown up had changed, but Craig barely noticed any of it as the taxi sped through the streets, dropping him outside his parents' house in Salford. He dropped a twenty-pound note over the driver's shoulder, didn't wait for change, and then hoisted his duffel bag from the back seat, heading to the front door.

He expected splintered wood, damage, carnage, but it was almost as he remembered from the day he left. The green paint on the front door was chipped and faded, the welcome mat gone, the pebble-dashed front as ugly as ever.

It was . . . home.

Craig pressed the doorbell, hearing 'Greensleeves' tinkling from beyond in the same annoying way it had since the dawn of time. The hallway light came on, illuminating an approaching shadow that soon filled the entirety of the rippled glass.

'Who is it?' a solemn voice asked from inside.

'It's me, Mum.'

Three bolts clinked and then a key turned before the door opened a fraction, still stuck on the chain. Craig could see half of his mother's face, wrinkled and aged. It was the first time he'd seen her in person for nearly four years. They spoke on the phone every now and then, making small talk as he danced around his crumbling relationship, before he finally plucked up the courage to tell her that Harriet had left, that the dream of grandchildren was over for the time being.

The door closed momentarily as the chain unclicked, and then Craig's mother revealed herself, arms open. 'I'm *so* glad you're back.'

Carole Macklin was shorter than Craig, dumpy with curly grey hair. Technically, she was unemployed, not quite over the retirement age, although the chances of an employer bringing her in were slim. She'd not worked in more than a decade, a mix of health problems and reluctance on her part.

Craig didn't have room to drop his bag as his mum hugged him, shoving her chin into his chest. 'I didn't think you'd ever come home.'

He patted her back, peering over her shoulder to the empty hall behind. Small slivers of glass were glinting along the skirting boards from where she had tried to clean up. The patchy walls were sun-scarred with chequered dark and light spots indicating where photographs had recently hung.

His mother finally released him, stepping away and welcoming him inside before re-chaining, bolting and locking the front door.

'What happened, Mum?'

She scuttled past him, along the hall, head down, into the kitchen and adjoining front room. Craig left his bag in the hall and followed. There was more damage in the living room, picture frames swept to the side, with thick shards of glass spiked into the carpet. The lampshade at the back of the room had been smashed to the ground, leaving a gauntlet of glass underneath the sullen darkness. Craig waited in the doorway, taking in the room. The television and stereo were untouched, with the damage largely superficial – sentimental items that would take time to clear up, rather than anything overly violent.

Craig's mother was hunched over the armchair, dabbing a ball of cotton wool on her husband's eyebrow. The white cotton revealed blobs of deep red blood, though Craig's dad seemed nonplussed, trying to peer around her towards the television. Dennis Macklin was a few years older than his wife and hadn't worked in at least twenty years. His hair was shoulder-length, grey and tied into a stumpy ponytail, a hippy in the wrong decade. He was wearing a Manchester United shirt that was at least five seasons out of date and didn't bother turning to see Craig.

'What happened?' Craig asked.

His mother continued dabbing at her husband's face. 'There were men who knocked on the door. They pushed their way in.'

'Did you call the police?'

She looked up at him as if over imaginary glasses, not very mumsy. She didn't need to say anything because he already knew the answer. This wasn't the kind of estate where the police were called. Even if someone was trapped in a burning building, the neighbours would think twice about dialling 999.

Craig tried a second time: 'What's going on?'

His mum nodded towards the armchair. 'Sit.'

He did as he was told, wriggling into the uncomfortable brown cord material and trying to remember if this was the three-piece suite they'd had thirteen years back. At least one errant spring was stabbing into his spine. It was faint but there was still the smell of cigarettes, so it probably was the same. The dimpled ceiling had a brown tar-ridden smoky glaze as well. The carpet was different – cream and fluffy – and there were matching curtains, but, aside from the upgraded television, Craig couldn't see much that had changed in the years since he'd left. His mum's well-thumbed Mills & Boon paperbacks still lined the back wall and his dad's landscape photograph of United's 1994 Double-winning team was above the TV, albeit significantly faded.

'Mum?'

Craig's mother ignored him, pressing the swab to her husband's head, muttering 'hold that' and then shuffling into the kitchen. Craig's dad didn't turn away from the TV, which was showing some greyhound race.

His lips barely moved: 'Did you ever get to the dogs down London?'

'I'm not interested in that, Dad.'

'I've always fancied going to Wimbledon.'

Craig rolled his eyes, knowing full well neither of his parents was keen on leaving the Greater Manchester area. On the three occasions they'd visited him in London – including for his wedding – they'd barely left the hotel in which they'd stayed, afraid they'd be mugged. Blackpool was the furthest they went on holiday – and, even then,

23

they spent the entire time complaining about being away from home.

'You could've come down at any time,' Craig replied.

'Too many foreigners. I don't know how you put up with it all.'

Craig bit his tongue, not wanting an argument. When he'd told his father he was engaged to Harriet, his dad's response was that it was 'a nice, white name'. Both of his parents were too far gone in their overt racism for Craig to bother picking fights. The best he could do was shake his head and tut. Even that felt wrong at the present moment considering what had just happened.

His mother hobbled back into the living room carrying a tray with three cups of tea and a box of plasters. A nice cup of tea had always been her solution to everything. Typical Brit. She placed the tray on the floor, scooping two mugs onto the sideboard next to the sofa and then passing Craig the third. There was a faded blue Manchester Polytechnic logo on the side, which, considering the Poly had become a university over twenty years ago, was good going. Even more so considering none of them had attended. They were probably 10p finds from a car-boot sale somewhere.

She removed the cotton wool from her husband's head and carefully stretched a plaster across, before taking a seat next to him and starting on her tea.

'Mum?'

She didn't look up. 'What?'

Craig was struggling to keep the annoyance from his voice. 'You called me, remember. Told me to come home quickly. There's glass in the hall and at the back of the room.'

'I'll clear that up later.'

'I was more asking about *why* there's glass.'

'Oh, y'know . . . I've set your old room up for you, by the way.'

'Mum! What's going on?'

She turned to frown at him, before focusing back on the TV, even though Craig knew she had no interest in greyhound racing. She sipped her tea and licked her lips before starting: 'Y'know Sharon from the hairdresser's? Her brother works at that garage over the back. Liam something. Or Leslie? No, definitely Liam.' She was arguing with herself, twirling her hand as she spoke, gossip mode in full swing. 'Anyway, you remember that cold spell last Christmas? No, course you don't, 'cos you were . . . anyway, it was really cold up here last year. People couldn't get their cars off the street because of the ice. Y'know Mrs Jones next door? She had to get her son out to help her move the car—'

'That wasn't last year.'

Craig's father's interruption was met with a slap on his thigh. 'Course it was.'

'Your memory's going. That was three years ago.'

'It was last year. I remember because she got a new car and it was that one which was stuck.'

'Nope.'

'It was.'

'And you go on about my memory! That was three years ago.'

Craig turned from one parent to the other, barely

believing the bickering. He wanted to interrupt, to tell them to get on with it, but then he'd end up having to take a side and that was the last thing he wanted. It took them five more minutes of back and forth until they finally agreed it had definitely happened, although they couldn't be sure about the year.

'Anyway,' his mother continued, 'the boiler packed up. Leslie came over and looked at it but he said it was too old to be his thing. He knew this other bloke, Liam . . . or was *he* Leslie? Whatever he was called, he came over and poked around but he said he couldn't get the parts any longer, so we needed a new boiler. He said he'd do it at cost, but it was still going to cost two and a half thousand.'

'Why didn't you tell me when it happened?'

She wafted a hand dismissively. 'We didn't want to bother you. Anyway, your father went to see Rodge to see if he could help.'

Craig squeezed his eyes closed, trying not to sigh as the rest of the story came out. Rodge 'the Todge' ran the local pawn shop, Tiger Pawn, but had also been the local loan shark for as long as Craig could remember. The nickname was largely self-explanatory, something which Rodge was so proud of that he openly referred to himself as 'the Todge'. As far as Craig knew, despite the nature of his business, Rodge wasn't a violent man. He must be in his sixties by now, too.

Craig pointed to the back of the room and the glass. 'Rodge did this?'

'Course not. We were fine paying him back in cash for

seven or eight months but then Rodge told us he was stopping.'

'Did the police finally get him?'

Craig got another scowl for his troubles, as if the Todge
was a family friend he'd insulted. 'He told your father that
all outstanding debts were going to be handled by someone
else – Pong, or something like that?'

'Pong?'

'Ask your father.'

Craig didn't speak for a moment. Considering his dad
was sitting next to his mum, he figured his father could
speak for himself.

Apparently not.

'Dad?'

'Don't ask me.'

'Weren't you there?'

'Yeah but it was some foreign name – Pungy, Pingo,
Pongo, Pongy – something like that.'

Craig's mother picked up the story again: 'Anyway, I'd go
to the Post Office every Monday to pick up my money and
then go to Tiger Pawn to pay off what we owed. It used to
be Rodge, but now there's this Chinese girl there. She takes
the money and signs my book but the numbers are all different.'

'How do you mean?'

She wafted a hand towards the bureau at the back of the
room underneath her books. It used to be – and presumably
still was – where they kept all the bills and letters. Craig
crossed to it, watching carefully for shards of glass. The
bureau would probably be worth a bit as an antique if it was

27

done up but the wood was scarred by years of neglect. Underneath the main lock, 'cRaIg' had been scratched into the wood, a remnant from when he'd been eleven or twelve.

Craig opened the drawer and hunted through the pile of letters until he found a yellowing scrap of paper. Columns had been drawn in black biro, with 'MACKLIN' etched across the top. The left-hand space had a list of payments, with dates and initials, with a total owing in the right column. There were eight months of payments, each neatly chronicled by Rodge, and then three more of equal amounts signed off in different handwriting. For the past three months, instead of decreasing, the amount owed had increased to the point that it was almost at the original £2,500.

Craig returned to his seat, trying to work out what had gone on. 'Did they increase the interest?' he asked.

'Something like that. She said we have to pay £170 a month now, instead of £100, but we don't have it.'

'In a month or two, you're going to owe more than you borrowed in the first place.'

His mother shrugged. 'That's what the men who came here tonight said. I told them we don't have the money but they just said, "find it".'

Craig continued scanning the numbers. 'Who's Pongo?'

He winced at the name, knowing it definitely wasn't right.

'No idea.'

'Didn't you say they'd taken over Rodge's debts?'

'Right.'

'Did you recognise the men who came here?'

Both of his parents were fixed on the TV. His mum

answered: 'There were three of them – Chinese-looking. Maybe Japanese. I can't tell the difference.'

Seriously?

Craig watched them for a few seconds, wondering if either of his parents would add something else. Considering how scared she'd sounded when she called him, his mother seemed ridiculously calm now. He wondered if she'd phoned simply to get the men out of the house. This wasn't the triumphant return home he'd been hoping for.

Craig slipped his phone from his pocket as he stood. 'I'm going to call the police.'

He finally got the reaction he wanted, both parents flying up from the sofa, his mother grabbing his arm, father staring at him sternly.

His mum did the talking: 'Don't be so silly.'

'You can't have men coming round here smashing things up, and you can't have loan sharks increasing the interest so you can't afford it. All of that's illegal.'

Craig's mother gazed at him sadly, not angry, merely accepting. 'You know what it's like round here.'

They stared at one another for a few moments before Craig put his phone away. 'Fine – but I'm going to the pawn shop tomorrow to see if I can find either Rodge, or Pongo.'

Mr Macklin retook his seat, not looking up. 'It's something like "Pung-You".'

Craig's mother didn't sit, but stroked the back of his hand. 'I don't want you causing trouble.'

'I'm not *causing* trouble, I'm going to ask a few questions.'

'Fine – but don't go by yourself.'

'I'm an adult, Mum.'

'Still . . .'

Craig unlocked his phone's screen, scrolling through the list of contacts. There was only one person he could ask to be at his side, the same one who'd been there throughout his childhood.

4

EIGHT YEARS OLD

Craig sat on his schoolbag watching the other kids play football. The sun was warm on his arms and his mum was always fine with him staying out when it was light. He told her that he was playing football with friends but the truth was that he didn't really have any friends. He wasn't even *playing* football; watching was as close as it got.

Patrick Henderson was the biggest kid in his class, towering over the rest as if he'd somehow wound up in the wrong year. He dominated everything energetic, whether football, soft tennis, tag, British Bulldog, or actual PE lessons. His dad had some job abroad and his family were rich, meaning he had the best of everything, including the brand-new United kit every year. He was the one who brought a football to school – a Mitre one that always seemed to be clean – so he was the person who got to decide who was allowed to play on the fields afterwards. Craig was thin, short, 'ginger' and 'gay', so he wasn't allowed to join in. On the rare occasion he did, Patrick or one of his friends would clatter him anyway, deliberately launching themselves over the top of the ball in an attempt to break his leg.

Despite that, Craig still preferred watching the other boys kick a ball around than going home to find his dad chain-smoking, drinking, and watching the dog racing. Sometimes, Patrick would have to go home early and he'd leave the ball for the others. When he got his chance, without the underlying threat of being crippled, Craig wasn't that bad. His size meant he could skip away from tackles and slalom his way out of trouble. He didn't have a lot of strength in his shots, but that was because he didn't have anywhere to practise. The back yard at home was covered with various lawnmower parts, and he couldn't afford a football anyway.

As Craig daydreamed about being allowed to play, he heard Patrick's voice bellowing at him, distinctive because it was so low compared to the others.

'Oi, Gayboy, now's your chance.'

Craig glanced up, watching the football bobbling across the uneven grass towards him. The other kids were all watching, wanting it back after someone's errant pass. Craig hoisted himself up, straightening his school trousers.

'Forget your trousers, Gaylord, just kick it back.'

Craig took a short run-up, wanting to sidefoot the ball directly to Patrick. Perhaps then he'd acknowledge that Craig could play a bit. He realised he'd messed it up as soon as his foot connected with the ball. The surface was bumpy from the rugby season, creating low but solid ridges across the pitch. Instead of fully kicking the ball, Craig booted the ground, only partly connecting with the top of the ball, sending it trickling towards the other boys.

Following Patrick's lead, they all burst into laughter, pointing and doubling over. Craig's second attempt was perfect, passing the ball exactly where he wanted it to go, but it was too late. Patrick trapped the ball but was laughing so hard that it looked like he was in pain.

'You little cripple. What a spastic.'

Craig sighed, and returned to his bag. He'd heard it all before and wasn't bothered by the names. They could call him what they wanted – it was *still* better than going home. He slumped back onto the grass and took out a battered paperback with a picture of a castle on the front. It had cost him 20p in the charity shop. He ignored the jeers and tried to find his page, before he heard a fizzing sound. He glanced up just in time to see the ball flying towards him, ducking out of the way as it zipped past, nestling in a nearby bush.

Patrick was bellowing at him: 'Oi! Go get that.'

Craig dropped the book into his bag and stood, heading for the bush. As soon as he reached the ball, he knew there was trouble. It was wedged underneath, impaled between a pair of spindly, sharp branches. He crouched and pulled it out but it was already deflated.

Craig held it up: 'It's broken.'

Patrick started walking towards him, standing tall and puffing his chest out. 'What did you do to it?'

'Nothing.'

'Don't lie, you little gay.'

'I'm not lying.'

Patrick had broken into a run, fists balled. Craig knew what was coming, so he dropped the ball and broke into a sprint. Patrick had longer legs and was faster than him, but Craig was only five minutes from his house and knew the back alleys as well as anyone – that's if he could get across the field before Patrick caught him. The backpack juggled on his back, the books and his empty lunchbox bouncing as he ran, but he had a decent head start.

'Oi!'

Patrick was growling behind him as Craig risked a glance backwards. The rest of the boys were chasing too, eight or nine of them, howling like a pack of wolf cubs. Craig stumbled across another ridge but kept his footing, heading towards the far side of the football pitch where there was a stile. As he crossed the white line at the edge of the field, Craig was starting to feel out of breath. He could hear Patrick closing but was close enough to the stile that he should be fine.

The mistake came as he peered over a shoulder a second time. As Craig focused in one direction, he stumbled across another crest in the dirt. He tried to regain his balance but a second mound proved too much, his feet clattering into one another, leaving him sprawling face-first to the ground. The dried mud scratched his cheek and a root tore at his sleeve, ripping into his flesh as his bag thudded into his back. Craig half got to his feet but Patrick hammered into his side, rugby-tackling him to the floor. By the time Craig knew where he was, Patrick was straddled across his middle, knees pinning Craig to the floor. Patrick's lips were curled into a snarl, teeth bared as he panted.

'You owe me a football, you little gayboy.'

Craig was trying to wriggle but Patrick was too strong. The other boys skidded onto the scene, creating a semi-circle around them. Patrick glanced around for support, turning back and grinning, then slapping Craig across the face.

'Whatcha gonna do, Gay-o?'

Craig continued trying to squirm but couldn't move. Patrick slapped him a second time. Pink and green stars swarmed, fading into grey before Craig could see again. His cheek was burning with pain.

'Come on,' the larger boy sneered, 'do something.'

Before Patrick could say anything else, there was a thump and, suddenly, Craig was free. It took him a moment to realise what had happened: Patrick was now on his back a short distance away, with another boy on top of him. The rest of the crowd were watching in stunned silence as the newcomer reeled back and punched Patrick across the jaw with as much brute force as he could manage. There was a vicious crack and then a splat.

'Like picking on little kids, do you?'

The boy's voice was a venomous, aggrieved roar, dripping with menace that belied his age. It was only when the second punch sent Patrick's head rocking sideways that Craig realised he recognised the boy – Mark something. They were in the same class but had never spoken. Mark didn't seem to talk to anyone, other than to confirm his name at registration. He sat in the back corner and never put his hand up.

Whump!

Patrick's head cannoned into the ground, bouncing up to be met by another blow. There were no slaps, only full-blooded punches. Patrick's eyes rolled back into his head as Mark stood, turning to the assembled crowd, fists raised. 'Any of you want some?'

There were no takers as the rest of the boys continued backing away.

'Thought so.'

Mark turned back to Patrick, staring down at him and then taking a run, before kicking the taller boy ferociously in the ribs.

He got onto his knees, face a few centimetres from Patrick's: 'If I *ever* see you picking on a smaller kid again – any kid – I'll be coming for you. D'you get me?'

Patrick groaned something that might have been 'yes', before Mark stood and booted him one final time. Mark was barely taller than Craig but held himself completely differently, as if fighting was second nature to him. There was blood smeared across Patrick's lips, more still on Mark's fists. He started walking towards Craig, wiping his hands on his trousers.

'You all right?'

Craig managed to cough a reply. 'Yes.'

'C'mon then, let's leave this lot alone.'

5

NOW

Craig awoke early, taking a few seconds to remember where he was. Water pipes rattled above his head, welcoming him home with a groaning jangle of annoyance. In the thirteen years since he'd left Manchester, he'd had a flat in London, a bigger flat, and then an even bigger one that he shared with Harriet. He'd stayed in hotels for various business trips on both sides of the Atlantic, kipped at his parents-in-law's house, gone top-to-tail with one of his workmates on a stag do, and even fallen asleep in cinemas. Tens of thousands of hours of sleep, but there was still something about his child-hood bedroom that felt comforting . . . even if it didn't look like it had been decorated since he left. The walls were a browny yellow, with paper peeling back from the join with the ceiling, plus black and white speckled patches of damp in three of the four corners. The bedding was a scratchy white sheet and a scratchier tartan blanket that was almost certainly older than he was. Every time the wind blew, the single-pane windows rattled in the way they always had, like an aircraft taking off. The radiator blazed at full heat – it had only ever had one of two settings: off, or scalding. The inferno just about cancelled out the chill creeping through the glass.

Fighting the yawns was a losing battle, so Craig pulled himself out of bed and started hunting through his duffel bag. His clothes were clean but they all held their own memories. There were the jeans Harriet had bought him, the matching pair of tops he'd picked up because she'd said she liked them, the endless mounds of socks she got him every Christmas. Nothing was free from her or his life in London. If he'd had any financial security, he'd have ditched the lot and started again. As it was, he needed a job, though it was the worst time of the year for hunting. The only things going at Christmas were temp positions. In his hurry to get away from the capital, away from Harriet and his life down south, he'd barely planned what to do next. It could have been liberating, but, instead, Craig had been back in Manchester for less than a day and already his old way of life was starting to catch up with him. There was something about the area, the people he knew, perhaps even his parents, which meant disaster was rarely far away.

He put a pair of jeans and two long-sleeved T-shirts on the bed, before shifting the bag to one side. The gnarled corners of the carpet around the radiator pipes had sent memories flooding back. He crossed the floor and knelt, carefully peeling the carpet away from the floor while trying to avoid the burning metal. Underneath, there were wads of newspaper – cheap underlay – but Craig was searching for something else, turning back the layers of paper until he reached . . . bare floorboards. He continued edging along the room, scratching underneath the paper until concluding that his half-a-dozen porn magazines had definitely been discovered in the years since he'd left. He wondered if it had been his mum or dad who'd found them. Hopefully his dad. His father would have either found a hiding place of his own, or sold them down the boozer. Either of those were better options than his mum stumbling across them and knowing what he'd been up to.

The magazines held their own memories, not just filthy ones. He'd acted as the distraction when Mark had nicked them from the big newsagent in town. Mark had got away with six magazines, two dozen Dairy Milks, a box of football cards and a whole bunch of stationery, all while Craig had 'accidentally' stumbled into a book display and then helped the pair of assistants restack it. It had been Mark's idea, of course. It always was.

Craig poked at the mattress, wondering if the springs were more lethal at the bottom or top. As it was, they were equally stabby throughout, worse than the chair downstairs. It was probably the same one that he'd slept on as a child, in which case he hoped it had been cleaned.

Aside from the bed and his bag, the rest of the room was full of boxes. Craig thumbed open the top one, flipping through the stack of exercise books and marvelling at the state of his handwriting. Why had his mum kept everything? It was hardly the type of thing they could reminisce over – 'Oh, look, here's your French homework with a long line of red crosses on it'.

He continued searching through the top box, disregarding almost all of it until he found a photograph near the bottom. It was a class portrait taken when he was twelve or thirteen, some time around when he and Mark started skipping out of classes regularly. Everyone was standing tall in crisp dark trousers or skirts, with crimson sweatshirts or cardigans. Patrick Henderson was in the centre at the back, towering over the rest of the students as he always had. Craig wondered how tall he was now – he'd been six foot by the time they were thirteen, six three or four when they took their exams at sixteen. He'd barely said a word to Craig since that day on the football fields when Mark had left him bleeding on the ground. Everything about his personality altered, no longer the big bully, instead the introverted tall kid who didn't say much. The teachers saw the change but didn't know why it had happened. Only the boys present had seen the fury in Mark's fists.

Directly in front of Patrick was Mark, sporting a hint of a black eye, with a red graze peppered across his chin. He was smiling at the camera, head slightly tilted, top row of teeth showing. If he were to ball his fists, it'd be the classic pose Craig remembered so closely.

Craig was there too, on the end, directly behind Debbie Church. She had thick-rimmed dark glasses, freckles, and a chest he'd spent too many hours thinking about when he was that age. He'd called her Debbie the Dyke because he didn't know how else to talk to her, let alone admit he actually liked her. She wasn't the only girl he'd lusted after but not known how to tell. Being a teenage boy was filled with a clumsy awkwardness of not knowing how to talk to girls.

He slipped the photograph back into the box and then picked up his towel, heading along the hallway to the bathroom. He didn't need to try the door because his mum's warbling voice was echoing from the inside, belting out

Cliff Richard's 'Mistletoe and Wine' at the top of her voice. It sounded like a cat drowning.

Craig stared at the door for a few moments, wondering what he should do, before returning to the bedroom and putting down his towel. He couldn't remember the last time he'd queued for the bathroom. There were two at the flat he shared with Harriet and, before that, he'd lived by himself.

He padded his way downstairs, watching carefully for errant shards of glass, though the clean-up seemed to be complete. In the living room, his dad was watching BBC *Breakfast*, the volume turned up so loudly that it would drown out a pneumatic drill. Thirteen years on and things hadn't changed: his mum hogged the bathroom and his dad turned up the TV too far. Craig was thirty years old and this was what his life had come down to.

He returned to his room, getting dressed and figuring he'd find time to shower later. His mum had moved onto 'Saviour's Day', so was either rotating through Christmas number ones, or going through Cliff's back catalogue. Either way, Craig wanted none of it. He waved a goodbye to his dad, who didn't turn away from the TV, and then headed out into the cold Manchester morning.

Home sweet home.

Mark was sitting on a bench outside the Grey Goose pub, tapping away on his phone, breath spiralling into the air. There was a sorry-looking collection of Christmas decorations along the terrace of local shops as well as a tree that had slumped to the side in the wind. The sky was grey and murky, exactly as Craig remembered.

Craig sat next to him, hands in coat pockets, trying to stay warm. Mark slipped his phone into his pocket. 'Y'a'ight?'

'Parent stuff.'

'Are they rattled after last night?'

'That's just the thing – if anything, they've forgotten it already. It's not the first time they've owed money to someone dodgy. Mum's assuming it'll work itself out and Dad's pretending everything's fine, probably thinking he'll get a big win on the dogs and pay it off.'

Mark didn't say anything. He'd never known his own mother, and as for his dad . . . He stood, tugging a beanie hat down over his ears and shoving his hands into his pockets. 'I've been asking around since you called last night. It sounds like Rodge the Todge sold up a few months ago.'

Craig followed him along the High Street. 'Any idea why?'

'No one seemed to know much. A few lads round my way owed him money but not a lot. As soon as they found out he was selling, they paid it off.'

'Any idea about this Pung-You bloke? Neither of my parents seemed to know anything about him, least of all how to pronounce the name. All they said was that he'd taken over the outstanding debts.'

'No idea – I can ask a few more of the lads later if need be.'

Salford High Street was a few miles away from the chain and department stores of Manchester city centre. That was where the tourists and people with money went: this was where the locals shopped. There were three dozen stores along both sides of the paved street, with a pub at either end and a Wetherspoons in the middle. The crowds were nothing like those in the centre, but even early on a Thursday morning, there was still a collection of shoppers bundled up in coats, hats and scarves, hurrying from shop to shop, hoping for a bargain.

Tiger Pawn had been a High Street mainstay for years, legitimised by the actual trading in of items for a quick money fix, but underwritten by Rodge the Todge's off-the-books loan sharking. Craig had no idea how he'd avoided arrest, though it wouldn't surprise him if there were a handful of low-paid constables somewhere who'd borrowed a few hundred quid here and there and had turned a blind eye. It wasn't just how things worked in this area of the city, it was how people got by day to day, week to week. It was how they afforded Christmas and birthday presents, how they paid to have the car fixed.

The shop itself was an emporium of tat. There was a selection of glass-fronted cabinets in the area around the front windows, each crammed full of game consoles, old and new; mobile phones; tablets; radios and laptops. Each item had three prices, the all-in-one pay now, like any other shop, and then six-month and twelve-month options. Craig had once bought a Gameboy from Rodge, paying him a couple of pounds a week over six months until it was finally his. It was probably buried in one of the boxes littering his old bedroom.

There was a queue at the counter, so Craig and Mark joined the back, shuffling forward every couple of minutes as a steady stream of people entered and exited the shop.

With Christmas around the corner, this place offered what so many people in the area were searching for: either quick cash, or cheap goods.

Away from the electrical items, there were racks of games and movies close to the counter. A couple of thirteen- or fourteen-year-old lads were busy thumbing their way through the titles, plucking out anything that looked as if it might contain nudity, giggling, and then checking the price. Craig and Mark exchanged a knowing look. Been there, done that, though it wasn't so easy in their days of VHS tapes. Plus they rarely paid for items.

They soon reached the front of the queue, waiting behind an older woman who was trying to figure out which of two phones was better. In the old days, Rodge would have pointed to one, they'd have sorted out the money, and that would've been that. Now, there was a bored-looking young woman behind the counter, with long dark hair, glasses and a black spaghetti strap top that'd get her frostbite outside. Craig didn't go along with his parents' prejudice towards whoever they deemed 'foreigners', but she seemed Far Eastern, with brown eyes and slightly olive skin.

Once the older woman had chosen a phone, Craig moved to the counter and offered his parents' payment sheet. The girl took it through the security drawer and checked through it on the other side of the glass, then looked Craig up and down, her gum-chewing uninterrupted: 'You paying, or what?'

Regardless of her appearance, the accent was pure Manc: dragged-out vowels, slightly rolled Rs, and an undertone suggesting that you might get a brick in your face if you looked at her the wrong way.

'I was hoping to speak to someone about the amount owed.'

'What about it?'

'My parents were paying a hundred quid a month, now it's one-seventy.'

'So?'

'They can't afford it.'

She shrugged, pushing the payment sheet back through the slot and staring over his shoulder to the next customer. 'Come back on Monday.'

'Can't we sort something now? There must be someone I can talk to?'

She focused back on him, peering over the top of her glasses, jaw working ferociously. 'You deaf?'

Craig lowered his voice: 'I was told someone named Pung-You is dealing with things . . .' The girl looked from Craig to Mark and back again, a flicker of recognition drifting across her face, though she said nothing. 'There were men who came to my parents' house last night. I'd really like to get something sorted.'

'Sorry, mate. Monday.'

'That's four days away. What happens on Monday?'

'*Things* happen, now sod off unless you're buying something.'

'What about Rodger?'

'Who?'

'The guy who used to run this place.'

'No idea.' She glared through the glass, hand hovering

45

over a big red button that may as well have had the word '*trouble*' printed across it.

Craig pocketed the payment sheet, taking the hint and turning. He left the shop and waited outside for Mark to catch him up. His friend's hands were back in his pockets, the morning air biting compared to the heat of inside.

'How did she know you?' Craig asked.

Mark peered at the ground, lips pursed. For a moment Craig thought he was going to lie but the small shrug said it all, before he spelled it out: 'I kinda owe some money, too . . .'

6

TWELVE YEARS OLD

'Jacobs?' – 'Yes, miss.'

'Lumin?' – 'Yes, miss.'

'Macklin?' – 'Yeah, miss.'

There was a pause as Craig received a disapproving glare from Mrs Green for his minor act of insubordination. His teacher was as strict as she could be but fighting a constantly losing battle against a tide of students who knew – or thought they knew – all about their 'rights'.

She stood up slightly straighter behind her desk, looking away from the registration book towards Craig in the front row. 'Pardon, Mr Macklin?'

Craig smiled back sweetly. '*Yes*, miss.'

Mrs Green turned back to her book: 'Peters?'

'Yes, miss.'

The monotonous drone continued around the classroom as each student acknowledged they were there. Craig and Mark were seated together directly in front of Mrs Green's desk, not their choice, more a punishment because they 'didn't know how to behave' when they were at the back of the room. They had a daily competition to see if they could sneak a 'yep', 'yeah', 'yo', or, on one occasion, a 'yee-hah' past the teacher at daily registration. It was a game neither of them ever won.

When she finally reached the last name on the list, Mrs Green stood and crossed to the person standing uncomfortably close to the door, the person at whom everyone had been staring since she'd arrived. The teacher placed a friendly hand at the top of the girl's back and turned to the rest of the class.

'This is Kimberly King. She'll be joining our class for the rest of the year. I hope you'll make her feel welcome.' Her eyes shot towards Craig and Mark, then back to Kimberly, who she guided towards the desk at the front where nobody else wanted to sit – across a narrow aisle from Mark.

Kimberly smiled weakly towards her classmates, before ducking down and taking the seat. She was small and slim, with brown eyes and light hair that was almost blonde but slightly gingery. Her uniform was slightly too big for her and she kept tugging at the shoulder of the cardigan to get it to sit straight.

As she sat, she glanced sideways, catching Craig's eye behind Mark's back, her lips flicking up into what was almost a smile. Craig returned it, before focusing back on the desk, where Mark had his exercise book open at the back page. His biro was dancing across the empty page, forming the 'C' and 'H' that followed the 'BIT' he'd already etched. As Mrs Green turned towards the whiteboard and started to write, Mark angled the exercise book towards Kimberly, coughing to get her attention. Craig wanted to stop it but it was already too late. As she spotted the one-word insult, her face fell and she turned back to the board, arms crossed, eyelashes fluttering furiously.

Craig peered around the corner of the bike shed, checking to see if a stray dinner lady might be making her way out of the lunch hall. It never happened, but it was always worth watching out for, just in case.

The area at the back of the bike shed was traditionally for early student fumbles, but, at Craig and Mark's school, there was a different sort of action.

'See anything?' Mark asked.

Craig popped back behind the shelter. 'Nope.'

Mark crouched on the floor and unzipped his backpack, opening it wide for the crescent of assembled students to see. 'I've got twenty Benson and Hedges and fifteen Marlboros. It's 50p a fag – no credit.'

There was a mix of a dozen older and younger students, each delving into their respective pockets and emerging with change. Craig took the money and Mark handled the goods, dividing out the cigarettes in order of who had got there first. He was many things, but Mark did have his own code about what was fair. By the time everyone had paid up, they were left with just two Marlboros.

As the students pocketed their wares, Mark continued hunting towards the bottom of his bag. 'I've got two bottles of Smirnoff – five quid each.'

The tallest of the assembled throng stepped forward, thrusting a ten-pound note towards Craig before transferring the bottles into his own bag.

Mark continued searching as a couple of older lads

joined at the back. Craig wasn't sure, but he thought they were year tens, three years older than Mark and him. He knew what they'd come for.

Mark took a pair of magazines from his bag, holding one in each hand. The year sevens didn't seem too bothered, with one or two drifting away, but the older students were shuffling nervously on the spot. Mark grinned at Craig before turning back to the crowd. 'I've got *Juicy Jugs* and *Razzle*.' He dropped *Razzle* into his bag and flipped through the pages of *Juicy Jugs* for everyone to see. 'Who's bidding a fiver?'

The tallest year ten lad at the back flicked a finger towards Mark, though no one was making eye contact.

'Seven quid?'

One of the smaller year eights at the front nodded. He was a regular customer with a rich dad who knew how to keep his mouth shut. Part of the code of silence came from the fact that Craig and Mark had so much dirt on who'd bought what that no one ever told. The only problem they had with rich-boy was that he constantly wanted to pay with ten- or twenty-pound notes. As problems went, it wasn't a bad one.

'Tenner?'

The year ten and year eight students went back and forth, bidding and out-bidding one another until the tallest one shook his head at £25. The year eight lad paid up instantly, shoved the magazine into his bag, and then rushed away towards the playground. *Razzle* went for £15 to one of the other year tens and then the crowd started to disperse. As Mark repacked his bag, Craig counted the takings.

'How much did we make?' Mark asked.

'Sixty-two quid and fifty pence,' Craig replied.

'How about I get thirty and the leftover fags?'

'If you're happy with that.'

Craig handed over the notes, pocketing his own money – not a bad haul, though he could never quite shake off the niggling guilt about the various shop-owners from whom they stole their merchandise. Supermarkets were one thing, but some of the shops were small one-man operations. It was hard to say anything when Mark decided the place they were going to steal from next. Besides, the money *was* good.

Craig took a step forward but stopped as he realised who was in front of them. Kimberly was glancing between him and Mark, one hand on her hip. Mark almost walked into her, grunting and stepping backwards when he noticed she was there.

'What you looking at?' he sneered.

'Nothing.'

'Piss off, then.'

Kimberly didn't move.

'Go on.'

She prodded a finger towards Mark's chest. 'I can stand where I want.'

'Ooh, like that, is it? The Ginger Minger's got something to say.'

Kimberly turned to Craig, offering the same half-smile she had earlier, before moving to the side. Mark took a step to move past her but Kimberly was far too quick. Before he could react, she swung forward, clattering a fist into his nose. Mark reeled sideways, clutching the front of his face as he bumped into Craig. Blood was running between his fingers, dribbling across his lips.

Kimberly smiled at him, pointing a finger: 'Don't you dare call me a bitch again.'

As Mark lunged forward, Craig snatched at his arms, fearing his friend was going to hit her back. Instead, Mark used one hand to smooth his sweatshirt, the other to clasp his nose. Kimberly didn't flinch and it was Mark who eventually turned, grin partially masked by the smear of blood.

'You better watch yourself, girlie.'

7

Mark started to walk along the High Street slowly, Craig at his side. He was staring at his shoes, scuffing his feet as if they were teenagers again.

'*You* owe money?' Craig said.

'Not much, only about a hundred quid now. I'll have it paid off next week.'

'Why didn't you say something?'

'Dunno . . .'

For a moment, Craig thought that would be that. They'd never had the type of relationship where they spoke about feelings, let alone problems – and that was before they went so many years without seeing one another.

'. . . I got hooked on the roulette machines down the bookies,' Mark continued unexpectedly. 'I won a bit, then lost a bit, then lost loads. Rodge sorted me out and it's not a problem now. Well, it won't be after next month.'

They continued walking at a slow pace, heading back the way they'd come. 'What do you do for money?' Craig asked.

'This and that – the odd car-booter, plus I do house clearances and stick a few odds and ends on eBay. Buy low, sell high, y'know . . .'

It was the reply Craig expected, the only thing Mark had

ever done. No sort of real job. It didn't sound like it would produce a large income but that was Mark.

'Any idea what happened to Rodge?'

Mark nodded at the Grey Goose. 'That must be a good place to start.'

Despite it barely being ten in the morning, the pub was already lined with locals. The smell of bacon and eggs drifted from the kitchen as a coffee machine popped and whooshed behind the bar, a far cry from the dirty smoke-ridden boozer in which they'd managed to get served when they were sixteen . . . ish. Before the Wetherspoons arrived, locals had two choices: the Grey Goose or the Old Boot. Each would try to undercut the other by a few pence on the price of a pint, though the atmosphere was largely the same: smoky, stinky, and full of men. Now, the Goose had clean carpets, shiny tables, half-a-dozen TVs and signs pointing towards the toilets. Sacrilege.

Despite the changes, some things would always stay the same. Craig cowered under the terrifying gaze of the woman behind the bar. It took a certain type to manage a place such as this and the barmaid was a behemoth. She was wearing a grey vest top, showing off a collection of fearsome tattoos on her shoulders. One was a red rose, with barbed wire spiked through the centre and 'English Rose' under-neath; the other was the severed head of a panther. Her dark hair was piled on her head, scowl as permanently etched as the panther.

She sucked on her yellow teeth, in which there was something black wedged in the top row, then flicked her eyebrows in Craig's direction. 'Whatcha drinking?'

He was so intimidated that he almost forgot why he was there. 'Have you seen Rodge around?'

The barmaid jabbed a finger into her mouth, fishing around and emerging with whatever it was that had been stuck between her teeth. She eyed it suspiciously and then licked her finger clean.

'The Todge?'

'Yes.'

'Not seen 'im in ages.'

'Do you know where he might be?'

'No idea, love.' The 'love' sounded like more of a threat than anything affectionate. She nodded over their heads towards a bloke sitting in the window who was cradling a pint of cloudy ale as if it was his first-born. 'Ask Percy.'

Percy was wearing a tweed flat cap and jumped as Craig and Mark approached. He was comfortably into his seventies, missing at least half his teeth, and easily confused. It took almost ten minutes for them to get a reply. The last he knew, Rodger had been staying at a bed and breakfast a couple of miles away in the Cheetham Hill area of the city.

There was no other description for it: the Prince of Wales B&B was a dump. Grey paint was peeling from the front as if they lived in an area that had a particular problem with acid rain. The wooden beams above the porch were splintered and soaking. It looked like the type of place that even desolate war-torn refugees would shake their heads at.

The inside wasn't much better, the smell of wet dog infesting the porch; body odour reeked out the empty reception area. There was a filthy red carpet, a scratched wooden counter and paper peeling from the walls. Despite the lack of anything obviously valuable, a pair of CCTV cameras were fixed to the ceiling, pointing directly at them, red lights blinking underneath. Craig had been to enough dodgy places over the years to realise there was something not quite right.

He dinged the bell on the counter and a balding middle-aged man emerged from a side office. He had a combover so awful that it could be a criminal offence, threads of greasy black hair plastered to his flaky scalp and beady dark eyes that darted nervously between the two of them.

'Y'a'right, lads? Y'after a room?'

His voice was thick Mancunian but so high pitched that it sounded like he'd been guzzling helium.

'We're looking for someone named Rodger,' Craig replied.

Combover peered between them again. 'He owe you money or summit?'

'No—'

'I ain't getting in the way of no private disputes.'

'There is no dispute, we're just hoping to talk to him.'

'Aye, my arse are ya.' He jabbed a thumb towards the door. 'I know your sort, now git.'

Craig's gaze flickered up to the CCTV camera, wondering what was going on behind the scenes. From the way Combover's hand was hovering under the counter, there was every chance he had a weapon there. This wasn't the world in which Craig wanted to be involved.

He turned and headed back through the dog-stink into the winter air. It had barely got light, a murky greyness

56

hanging over the city. Mark was just behind him, smirking. 'What do you reckon's going on in there?' Mark asked.

'No idea.'

'He's probably dealing on the side.'

The path was crumbling, huge clumps of frost-glazed weeds growing across the concrete. As they neared the pavement, a man with a tatty dark beard almost bumped into them as he hurried towards the B&B, eyes fixed on the ground. He jumped back in alarm, apologising in a gruff Scottish accent, and spurting vicious whisky breath that could have knocked out small animals. They awkwardly do-si-doed their way past one another before Craig had a thought and turned back to the house.

'Hey, mate, we're looking for Rodger.'

The Scot turned, tugging on his beard. 'Oh, aye? He's not been here in weeks.'

'Do you know where he went?'

He nodded towards the building opposite. 'Number ten.'

If Lincoln House was named after the iconic US President, then it was the insult to end all insults. There was no statue, no crisp marble, no sweeping architecture. Instead, the glorified bomb shelter was two storeys of pure grey granite, caked with years of filth. The vertical guttering was clinging to the building by a single screw, with a consistent plop-plop-plop of water dripping from the roof into the leaf-smattered blocked rusty drain.

Craig and Mark walked along the line of ground-floor flats, though hardly any of them had numbers. By finding apartments three and twelve, they managed to discover number ten. It had a plain once-white door, drawn curtains blocking the windows, with a small yellow card pinned to the inside reading: *'No Free Papers Ever'*, followed by: *'I Mean It You Little Shite'*.

Charming.

It was now afternoon and the sun had given up on even bothering to make an appearance. The stinging wind was beginning to whip itself up, scratching at Craig's face. He could really do with getting inside.

He rapped on the door and took a step back, waiting for a few seconds and then knocking again. With no sign of movement, he hunched over, lifting up the letterbox flap and peering inside. There was a pair of steel toe-capped boots, a crusty welcome mat, and not much else. Craig continued staring, feeling watched.

'Hello?' His voice echoed through the hallway, unanswered. 'We just want to talk, Rodger. You know my parents.'

There was no movement and the door didn't open. Craig dropped the flap back into place, a metallic clang echoing loudly.

He turned to Mark. 'Shall we go?'

'Up to you.' He made it sound like, 'If you want to wimp out, you can'.

As Craig took a step along the path, there was a click and the door opened a sliver. In a flash, it was yanked open fully, revealing a squat man with olive skin, a hunched back, hooked nose and limp dark hair. Rodge the Todge had never had much in the way of looks but now he'd lost what little he had. Craig and Mark each raised their hands but Rodger wasn't having it. He lifted his sawn-off shotgun to chest height and pointed it at Craig, finger trembling against the trigger.

8

Rodger's gaze flicked from Craig to Mark and back again. 'Who are you?' he asked, voice quavering, though he was trying to sound assertive.

'Craig Macklin. I'm Carole and Dennis's son.'

Rodger nodded towards Mark, eyes narrowing as he shunted the shotgun between them. 'I know you.'

'Mark Griffin – I've borrowed money from you before.'

Rodger glanced sideways at the empty path and then nodded behind, lowering the gun slightly. Craig still had his hands raised and though he wasn't particularly keen on following the wild-eyed Rodger inside, he didn't have much of a choice given the shotgun. Rodger stepped backwards, not shifting his gaze from Craig and Mark as they entered the flat.

As soon as they were all in the hallway, Rodger ordered them to shut the door, then waggled the gun sideways, pointing them towards the living room. Craig started to lower his hands, thinking they'd been accepted, but quickly felt the barrel stabbing into his back.

'Whoa, whoa, sonny – you keep those hands up.'

Craig and Mark turned in unison until they were facing Rodger. His finger was still twitching over the trigger, one of his eyebrows jerking involuntarily. He looked terrified.

'We only want to talk,' Craig said.

Rodger shook his head. 'Get 'em off.'

'Get what off?'

'Your clothes.'

Craig glanced towards Mark, whose arms were wide, fingers stretched to show he wasn't concealing anything.

Rodger raised the weapon again, pointing it at Craig's chest, his voice growling and firm. 'Now.'

With little other option, they did as instructed, stripping until their clothes were in a mixed heap on the ground and they were wearing only socks and boxer shorts. Rodger made them turn around until he was convinced they weren't concealing anything and then allowed them to get dressed again.

Rodger eased himself into an armchair, resting the gun across his lap as Craig and Mark recovered their clothes. He looked far older than Craig remembered, which perhaps wasn't surprising. His skin was a perma-tanned leathery orange, with thick wrinkles lining his face. He couldn't sit still, elbow juddering into the arm of the chair, his eyebrow continuing to flick up and down. Every few seconds, his entire body would shiver.

The living room was like a walk-in flea market. The walls were covered with posters from rock and pop shows throughout the Sixties and Seventies. If they were authentic, then they were probably worth a bit. There was a huge advert for the Beatles playing Shea Stadium, and another for an Elvis show in Houston. Along the side wall were stacks of vinyl records, each neatly bagged in clear plastic sleeves. Sitting next to the door was a record player, connected to a pair of speakers. Craig was trying to keep an eye on the gun but it was hard not to be distracted by the colourful collection. Every corner of the room was covered by either boxes or music memorabilia.

When they were finally dressed, Craig and Mark remained standing as Rodger clasped the gun on his lap. 'Well?' he demanded.

'My parents owed you money,' Craig said.

Rodger nodded slowly. 'Your old man was into his dogs . . .'

'Right, but my mum said they needed the money for a new boiler.'

'Something like that.' He thumped a crinkled finger hard into the side of his head. 'The ol' thinker's not what it was.'

He could say that again. Rodger was out of breath, despite not moving, and his gaze kept dancing from Craig to Mark and then the door.

'I was told you'd sold up,' Craig said.

Rodger nodded quickly, before lurching into another full-body shiver. 'It was time to get out.'

'Why?'

'They told me – time to get out.'

'*Who* told you?'

Rodger's eyes were rolling from side to side like a pinball, the eye twitching becoming worse. 'The Chinese.'

It took Craig a second to remember the name: 'Pung-You?'

'Something like that.'

'Who's he?'

'No idea.'

Craig bit his bottom lip, confused. Rodger's overgrown

nails were tip-tapping on the wooden butt of the shotgun, his eyes darting all over the place. If they hung around too long, Craig had the sense someone was going to get shot. He wondered how long it had been since Rodger had had company.

Craig spoke slowly, not wanting any misunderstandings: 'You were told you had to sell up, but never met the person who was buying you out?'

'There were three or four kids,' Rodger replied, 'young men – nineteen, twenty-odd – Chinese. In suits. They came to my shop as I was closing and told me I was going out of business but that Pung-You and Haken would buy me out.'

'Haken?'

'I never met him either.'

'Did they give you an option?'

'They said they were offering forty thousand for whatever was on my books – the shop, the loans, everything. I had around thirty thousand out as loans, so it wasn't a great price. I asked who Pung-You and Haken were but they didn't say anything other than that's where the money was coming from. I thought they were all talk, so told 'em to do one. I've had all sorts trying it on over the years.'

The drumbeat of Rodger's fingers tapping on the gun was increasing in tempo. Craig could sense Mark's nervousness as he bobbed from one foot to the other, taking half a step towards the door. Craig didn't blame him but didn't think either of them should make any sudden movements.

'What happened?' Craig asked.

'Deaver.'

'What's that?'

Tap-tap-tap-tap.

'*He's* me ol' dog . . .' Rodger smiled for the first time but it was anything but comforting. A chill crept along Craig's back as the other man's finger settled on the gun trigger. 'He was a gorgeous little dachshund. I'd raised him since he was a puppy but he was getting on. He was blind in one eye and couldn't walk very far. He used to trot around my old back garden 'cos he couldn't go any further.'

The atmosphere was already tense but now it felt like the heating had been turned off and the door left open. Mark shuffled another few centimetres towards the door, making things worse as Rodger's grip tightened on the gun. They stared at each other for a moment before Mark froze.

Rodger continued to focus on Mark: 'They broke in one night. Didn't steal a thing, didn't even make a mess, but they hung Deaver from the washing line. I found him in the morning. Poor sod.' He gulped and sniffed loudly before his features hardened, gaze flickering back to Craig. 'Why are you here?'

'I . . . don't really know. My parents were struggling to pay and I couldn't get much sense from the shop. I thought you might be able to help, or at least let me know who I'm dealing with.'

'They're animals.' Rodger dropped the gun, jabbing a finger to emphasise this point. 'Animals!' His eyes were wide and wild, a mix of terror and fury. 'They came to the shop the next day and told me the offer was still there at thirty-five thousand. What could I do? Within a week, it was all sorted. I handed them the deeds to the shop and talked these Chinese girls through my books. It was simple enough but they didn't get it at first. They couldn't understand why my rates were so low.'

'The interest?'

'I wanted people to be able to pay. I'm getting on now and it's not worth the bother. You make a few hundred here and there and it all adds up. I knew there'd be hassle: they were crossing out my numbers, increasing everything. There was nothing I could do.' He nodded at Craig. 'You will tell your parents I'm sorry, won't you? I di'nt want none of this.'

Craig pointed towards the battered sofa. 'Can we sit?'

Rodger finally seemed to calm, moving the gun onto the arm of the chair, the barrel pointed towards the window behind him. He nodded, though still kept a hand on it. Mark didn't move at first, though eventually he followed Craig's lead and sat. For the first time since arriving, Craig felt as if they might be able to leave without anyone being hurt.

Rodger nodded towards Craig: 'Your dad used to come down Belle Vue to watch the dogs with me. He's a good bloke.'

'I'll tell him.'

'How much trouble are they in?'

'I'm not sure. Men came to the house last night and smashed a few things up because they're getting behind with the payments.'

Rodger shook his head. 'The violence is always a waste of time. If people don't have it, they don't have it. You're better off finding out what they can pay and taking that. Some will always try it on but you come to know the type.'

'Who are these Chinese?'

'No idea – they came out of nowhere but they also run the knocking shop over that tanning place on the High Street, plus the Grey Goose is one of theirs.'

'The pub?'

'Aye.'

Craig knew what it was but was surprised because there'd been no sign when he'd been inside. It took him a moment to realise that it was the perfect way to move into an area. If you kept the same people in charge, most locals wouldn't notice and would continue to give their business. Rodger was an exception because he owned everything. Paying him off instead of simply moving in was perhaps unusual, but Rodger's operation was slightly more entwined with the community than the other enterprises they'd apparently moved in on. If he told everyone he was selling up, rather than being forced out, then fewer people would pay off their debts early. It would keep people like Craig's parents owing money.

Rodger was beginning to become edgy again, fingers and arms twitching. 'How'd you find me?'

'We asked some bloke outside the Prince of Wales.'

'He must've seen me.'

'You said you had another house . . . ?'

A nod. 'They knew where that was. I didn't think they knew about this place.' He pointed at the records. 'I had to get a van for my stuff, couldn't leave it behind, but I didn't think they'd be watching.'

Craig raised his hands, again showing he wasn't hiding anything. 'Can I ask you one more thing?'

Rodger shrugged. 'We been talking, ain't we?'

'You're still holding the gun.'

The two men stared at one another, before Rodger lowered the weapon and placed it on the floor. 'What?'

'If they paid you off, why do you think you might still be in danger? If they wanted to hurt you, they could've done it before.'

Rodger was breathing heavily through his nose, fingers twitching towards the gun. 'You heard of Willy Porter?'

'No.'

'You got a phone or a computer?'

'Yes.'

'Look him up.'

9

Manchester Morning Herald, 14 October

POLICE SEIZE £500K IN FORGERY RAID

by Garry Ashford

Police last night hailed the success of an operation to clamp down on Manchester counterfeiters, as half a million pounds' worth of bogus goods were seized in the city.

In a joint operation with trading standards, UK Border Control and the National Crime Agency, Greater Manchester Police confiscated imitation clothes, shoes, bags and perfumes that were being sold to the public.

Nineteen people were arrested and remain in police custody.

Assistant Chief Constable Graham Pomeroy described the raids as 'a complete success'. He added: 'This has sent out a message to the criminal element in the city that this type of behaviour will not be tolerated. Selling fake goods might seem like a harmless crime but much of this money finds its way into the pockets of criminal gangs. This has struck a large blow against those who wish to circumvent the rule of law.'

The items were seized from market stalls, clothes

shops and rented garages across the city in an operation that had to be launched simultaneously in order to prevent 'spotters' from tipping off other premises. Police found copies from manufacturers including Gucci, Hugo Boss, Prada, Mulberry, Nike, and Ugg.

Barry Peters from North West Trading Standards said: 'The complexity of this operation is astonishing. We found hidden passages connecting shops, plus paper trails leading back to places like Pakistan and Taiwan. These fake clothes are made in sweatshops by children for either no wages, or slave wages, then smuggled into Britain. Shoppers buy these goods thinking they are getting the real thing but the quality of material is always lacking. We found perfumes with such high levels of bacteria that they pose a serious health risk.

'Make no mistake, this is a highly sophisticated, hard-to-detect level of criminality that is difficult for the general public to spot. As a rule, we would advise that if a price seems too good to be true, then it probably is. Anyone who is unsure can contact trading standards in complete confidence.'

Despite the amount of goods seized, Assistant Chief Constable Pomeroy, who said the seized clothes would eventually be donated to charity, added that the police were still trying to track down William Porter, forty-four, who he described as an 'individual of interest'. Mr Porter, who runs a market stall in Eccles, has not been seen since the day of the raids.

GRUESOME FIND AS MARKET STALL OWNER FOUND DEAD IN BIN
by Staff Reporter

Police last night appealed for witnesses after a mutilated Eccles market stall holder was found dead in a wheelie bin.

William Porter, forty-four, has been wanted by police since last month's raid on a number of premises suspected of selling forged clothes, bags, shoes and perfumes.

He was found dumped in a bin at the back of Piccadilly Station, with both arms and legs chopped off.

Police described the discovery as 'gruesome'. A statement read: 'We can confirm that a mutilated body was found in a bin close to Piccadilly Station. We would ask anyone with information to come forward.'

A police spokesman added that CCTV footage was being searched for clues.

Porter was suspected of importing and selling fake goods to be sold on his stall and police say they are looking into potential connections.

The statement added: 'Although assumptions should not be made, we are examining the possibility he may have crossed the wrong people.'

POLICE BAFFLED BY BODY IN BIN
by *Staff Reporter*

Police last night admitted they were stumped by the murder of an Eccles market stall holder.

The dismembered body of forty-four-year-old William Porter was discovered earlier this month in a wheelie bin at the back of Piccadilly Station. Police appealed for witnesses at the time but conceded they are struggling for leads.

Detective Superintendent William Aylesbury said: 'We would ask the public to think about any contact they may have had with Mr Porter. He ran a market stall in Eccles selling clothes and bags and would have been relatively well known to regular market-goers.'

Mr Porter, who lived by himself in Salford, was last seen running his stall on 13 October but disappeared hours before a police clampdown on counterfeit goods.

Police seized almost £50,000 worth of fake clothing from a storage locker rented by Mr Porter but have so far been reluctant to connect that to the murder, saying they are 'ruling nothing in or out'.

Craig finished reading aloud from his phone and leant back into the passenger seat of Mark's battered Ford Focus. It smelled strange, but he wasn't sure what the odour was. It reminded him of fire, of burning, but there was no evidence of scorch marks. As with many things with Mark, it wasn't worth asking. He'd probably dropped a cigarette at some point and it had singed the seat or carpet.

'What do you think of that?' Craig asked.

'That nutter with the shotgun did say the Chinese were animals . . .'

'It's no wonder Rodger's shut himself away in some bolt-hole with a weapon if he thinks they might be coming for him.'

'Why would they?'

'No idea.'

Mark turned the key and the engine rattled to life. The entire vehicle was shaking as he pulled away and it was only as Mark reached second gear that the tremors calmed. Craig reread the articles, skimming through the comments underneath from the usual bunch of ill-informed morons. It really did take a certain type to register for a newspaper's website and then start leaving comments. Did people really have nothing better to do with their lives? Despite the police statement linking the raids to organised crime, at least three-quarters of the comments said they didn't see what the problem was with fake goods, adding that it was only rich companies being ripped off. The matter of the perfume being toxic was apparently not an issue.

They drove in silence as Mark weaved his way across the city towards Salford. Gangs, murders, disappearances: this was the life that Craig had left the city to get away from. Well, the reason he'd spent so many years telling himself. There was the other thing, too.

As they passed the university, Mark stopped at a set of traffic lights. 'What do you want to do?' he asked.

'Get this over and done with,' Craig replied. 'I'm not certain who holds the debt – Pung-You, this Haken guy, or someone else. Nobody seems entirely sure. I can probably scrape together the money that Mum and Dad owe. I won't tell her exactly what's going on but I'll call Harriet in London when I get home. She won't be happy but should be able to transfer some money over. I'll go to the bank and take out the cash, then pay it all off in one go.'

Mark didn't reply at first, accelerating as the lights changed. As he switched gear, he glanced sideways. 'You coming round later? She really wants to say hello.'

Craig knew he could only offer one response but his stomach lurched as if he'd not eaten in days. There would be no avoiding it now, no excuses to hide behind. What was the real reason he'd stayed away from home for thirteen years? He'd know for sure in a few hours.

10

THIRTEEN YEARS OLD

The corridor was humming with the sound of school lunch-time. From one end, there were the dings, clinks and scrapes of children eating in the canteen; at the other was the clatter of shoes on tarmac, the thump of ball on brick, as other students raced around the playground. Craig, Mark and Kimberly had been waiting side by side on the row of chairs outside the headteacher's office for ten minutes. On the wall in front of them, a clock was tick-tick-ticking its way through the time they could have been messing around in the back field. Craig wasn't exactly scared of the principal but he was worried about his fate potentially being in the hands of the other two.

Kimberly was sitting in the centre, leaning forward, elbows on knees, constantly fidgeting. 'Someone must've grassed on us,' she said. 'I bet it was that little scuzzy kid with the mole from year ten. He's always looking at us weird.'

Mark was the most relaxed of the three, leaning back unconcerned, his legs stretched out in front. He spoke in a confident whisper: 'If they had anything on us, we wouldn't be here at lunchtime, we'd have been yanked out of classes and our parents would be here. Well, *your* parents. All that's happened is that someone's said something and it's got back to one of the teachers. They're going to call us in one at a time and see what we say. They'll try to catch us out and make out we have different stories. Just deny all knowledge. Say nothing about the bike sheds, ciggies and the like.'

Kimberly didn't sound convinced: 'That's easy for you to say.'

'It *is* easy. Just shrug and say you don't know what they're talking about. My bag's only got school stuff in it, so has yours. There's nothing they can do. No one's stupid enough to grass on us openly, so it's not even our word against theirs. When I was arrested last year, the police had me in this room with these bright lights. It was me and two of them. They were all in my face, shouting, "Why'd you do it?" They kept me up all night, trying to get me to confess to all sorts of stuff. I just kept telling 'em it weren't me. In the end they had to let me go.'

Mark winked at Craig behind Kimberly's back. The police thing was completely made up and, as usual, he was trying to impress her with tales of how tough he was. He certainly looked as if he'd been in *a* war – there was a thin slice across the bridge of his nose and his top lip was swollen. Neither of the injuries had been there the day before.

It was unclear whether she bought it but Kimberly pressed back in her chair, rubbing her face. 'My mum will go mental if she thinks I've been in trouble at school.'

'It'll be fine.'

There was a click and the door to the side of them opened. The fact that the school's headteacher knew each of their names said it all. Principals only remembered the names of students who were academically brilliant, or utter pains in the arse. Mark and Craig definitely didn't fall into the first category. Craig had no idea how old Mr Bates was, but he had grey hair, fierce black eyes and always wore a suit, features that were probably a given for most head-teachers.

Mr Bates peered towards the three of them, lips tight, brow wrinkled. He tutted and then nodded in Mark's direction. 'You first.'

Mark stood and smoothed down his uniform, before scooping up his bag from the floor. He sauntered past Mr Bates into the office as if he didn't have a care. In many ways, he didn't. If Mark was suspended or expelled, his dad probably wouldn't notice. Mark would brush it off as a badge of achievement but Craig often wondered if, deep down, all of this was because Mark wanted his dad to pay attention to him.

Mr Bates glared down at Craig and Kimberly. He told them not to talk to one another and then followed Mark into his office, shutting the door firmly. Craig sat in silence, arms by his side, until he felt a chill sensation on the back of his hand. When he looked down, he realised it was Kimberly brushing her fingers against his.

'Hey,' she whispered.

'Hey.'

'Do you think it's true? Say we don't know anything and it'll be fine?'

'Probably – if they knew we'd been . . .' Craig glanced around the empty corridor, lowering his voice even more, '*selling* stuff, then they'd have called our parents. They're guessing.'

Kimberly slipped her fingers in between his, squeezing so that they were fully holding hands. They said nothing for a moment but he suddenly felt calmed, as if it didn't matter if they were in trouble. Her fingers were slender and cool and she was skimming her thumb across the top of his.

'Did you see Mark's nose?'

'The scratch?'

'And his top lip. Did he say anything to you about being in a fight?'

'We walked home from school yesterday and then back in today. I think it happened at home.'

'His dad . . . ?'

Craig said nothing, not knowing for sure. Mark's scratches and scrapes made regular appearances and, if asked, he'd always laugh it off, saying some older kids had tried to mug him but that he'd fought them off. After a while, Craig had stopped asking and started assuming.

Kimberly wasn't as ready to let it go: 'Do you think we should tell someone?'

'Tell them what?'

'About Mark's dad.'

'Do you know for sure that his dad did it?'

'Who else?'

'I don't . . .' Craig stopped, uncertain of his own mind. 'I don't think he'd want us to tell anyone.'

Kimberly's thumb continued to dance delicately across the top of Craig's. He could feel her watching him, wanting him to turn. Eventually he did, sinking into her chestnut brown eyes. She'd allowed her hair to grow in the past few months. It was now past her shoulders, continuing to flit between blonde and a gentle red depending on the light. Craig wasn't sure what it was but he felt something every time he looked directly at her, alien sensations that made him both embarrassed yet deliriously happy. He quickly looked away, unable to hold her gaze for longer than a moment.

Her voice was even softer than before, but her fingers clasped his ever tighter. 'Do your mum or dad ever hit you?'

Craig focused on the ticking clock. 'Mum says she will but never does. She shouts a bit and then forgets. Dad's hardly ever home. What about you?'

'My mum shouts a lot if I'm in the way, so she'd go crazy if I was suspended because I'd be in the way all the time. She wouldn't say much if I was being quiet in my room, or if I was out.' Kimberly slipped her fingers out of Craig's and rubbed at a spot over her eye. 'She had the men over again last night. It was really late when they left.'

'What do they do when they come over?'

Kimberly shrugged, though Craig had the sense that she knew.

'What are your mum and dad like?' she asked.

'Dunno really: they don't talk much. Dad's either out or watching the racing; Mum drinks tea and reads her books. She goes to bingo every Friday night, which used to cause an argument. She'd tell Dad he had to stay in with me, he'd say he had something else on. Sometimes, one of the neighbours would come over to watch me but now they let me do whatever. It's kinda neat.'

Well, it was when he kept telling himself that.

Mr Bates's voice boomed through the walls for a moment, there and gone. They both turned towards the door and then sank back into their chairs when nobody exited. Kimberly had folded her arms and tucked her hands into her armpits. There was a draught blowing from somewhere, making the corridor colder than the classrooms.

'Why d'you reckon old people get married?'

Kimberly's question came from nowhere, sitting on the breeze and then fluttering away. Craig had never thought about it, although he often wondered why his parents bothered to live together. So many other students had mums and dads who lived apart but his were still together, even though they seemed to share nothing but arguments.

'I don't know.'

'Mark doesn't know his mum and I don't have a dad. Your parents don't talk to each other, so what's the point? Why not just hang around with your mates and have fun? You can do what you want, especially when you don't have to go to school.'

'Other kids have mums and dads who talk and do stuff. Didn't you hear Billie-Jo going on about Alton Towers? Her mum and dad took a whole bunch of kids for her birthday.'

Kimberly's hand glided back to Craig's, fingers interlinking with his once again. He fought back a shiver, unsure why her touch made him feel tingly. 'Would you talk to me if we were married?' she asked.

'Yes.'

'Maybe we'll get married one day when we're older? We'll go to Alton Towers and London Zoo and Chessington:

all those places. I once saw this thing about Edinburgh Castle in Scotland. We could go there.'

Before Craig could reply, there was a click and the door to Mr Bates's office was flung open. Their hands separated a fraction before Mark swaggered out, hands in pockets. He winked at the pair of them and then continued along the corridor. Mr Bates was in the doorway, peering towards Craig and Kimberly, looking as stern as ever. His gaze flickered between the two of them before ending up on Kimberly.

'Your turn, Miss King.'

11

Mark's home was the chaotic mess Craig expected. He lived a few streets away from Craig's parents, in the same Salford house as when his father had been alive. There was a certain sense of wastefulness that they'd spent thirty years growing up, only to end up exactly where they'd started. It wasn't uncommon for the area in which they lived. By the time they'd turned seventeen, at least a dozen girls from their school year were pregnant. There was a sixteen- or seventeen-year cycle of successive generations having children and then moving into a flat a street or two away from their mothers. If Craig were to sit outside his parents' house for a day, he'd almost certainly see a fair few people with whom he went to school, making their way to the shops, or taking their children to school. It was the type of estate from which many never escaped.

As Craig lounged on the sofa, he gazed around Mark's living room, not having to try hard to picture it as it had been. Despite everything else he did, Mark's father diligently read the *Manchester Morning Herald* cover to cover every morning. In the old days, there was a stack hundreds deep in the back corner next to the window. That had now gone, replaced by sealed cardboard boxes containing who knew what. Probably the 'this and that' which Mark sold at car-boot sales. In the other corner, there were three crates, each containing a dozen two-litre bottles of Coke still in the plastic wrap, cash-'n'-carry style. A half-hearted Christmas tree was wedged behind the armchair, the lights haphazardly wrapped around it but not turned on, with a menagerie of different coloured baubles. It wasn't much, but it was still more than Craig's parents had up.

There was football on the television, some lower-league match that neither Craig nor Mark were too bothered about. Mark was supping from a can of Carling, an empty one already at his feet on the carpet. Craig was taking it easy, wanting to keep alert.

'How were your mum and dad?' Mark asked, not turning away from the TV.

'Mum's still pottering around as if there's nothing wrong, Dad rustled up a bottle of Bell's from somewhere, so that'll keep him quiet for the night.'

'Did you sort the money?'

'I spoke to Harriet, who transferred it while I was on the phone. When we separated, she took the flat because we didn't know if we were going to sell it, or if she was going to stay and buy me out. She's still not sure but said she could spare a couple of thousand. She didn't even ask what it was for, she sighed and said "fine".'

Mark twisted in his seat, turning towards Craig on the sofa, can at his lips. 'What happened with the two of you?'

Craig peered towards the television, not wanting to answer but feeling the invisible spotlight upon him. They were supposed to be friends, or they had been at one point, he should be able to talk about it.

'I think we'd been together for too long,' Craig said. 'She wanted kids and to save for a house, I . . . didn't.'

It sounded plausible, close enough to the truth for there not to be many follow-ups, even if it only told half the story. Harriet wasn't the problem but she could never be who Craig wanted her to be.

Mark raised his can. 'Fair enough, pal. Plenty more fish an' all that. We should go out one night, just me and you.'

'Maybe.'

'What did your folks say when you told them you were paying off the money?'

'I've not told them,' Craig replied. 'It's not worth the hassle or arguing. I'm going to nip into Tiger Pawn tomorrow morning and get it sorted, then I'll tell them. If I let them know I have any amount of money, they'll suddenly find a list of things they need it for.'

Mark was back watching the football, though both sets of players seemed unclear about the colour of their own shirts as they kept passing to the other team. 'I can ask around if you're looking for a job . . . ?'

'We'll see . . .'

Craig wanted to say 'no', not particularly wanting a part of whatever Mark might be able to find. It'd be something on a market stall, or a driving job in a death trap of a van. A bit of money here, a bit there.

'I'm going to use these job websites but Mum and Dad don't have the Internet at their house,' Craig said. 'It's like the last thirty-odd years haven't happened.'

'Does that mean you're definitely staying around?'

'Maybe.'

They both turned as something banged in the hall behind. The front door bounced from the wall, then there was a jangle of keys before an echoing slam. Craig's chest suddenly felt tight, his heart beating so quickly that he was convinced he could see the material of his top throbbing in time. From the kitchen, the keys hit a work surface and there was a large sigh.

Suddenly, she appeared through the doorway, hair to her shoulders, more red than blonde. Her brown eyes were the same as they'd always been, bright and full of adventure. There were a couple of crinkles around her mouth but she looked more or less the same as she had on the day she'd punched Mark in the nose.

Kimberly swept a thread of hair behind her ear and broke into a beaming smile. She hadn't been big to begin with but she'd lost weight. Her teeth were a little crooked but she was still the person he remembered, still wonderful.

'Well, look who it is,' she smiled.

For a moment, Craig didn't think he'd be able to speak. The word croaked in his throat as he raised a hand, trying to be calm. 'Hey.'

Kimberly held up a large white carrier bag and turned to Mark. 'I didn't know what people wanted, so I did a tour. I got curry, pizza and chippy. You can have what you want.'

Mark was gleefully on his feet, skipping around the chair. He kissed her on the forehead, took the bag and then disappeared into the kitchen, saying he was going to find some plates, bowls and cutlery.

Kimberly stood still, looking at Craig, both arms out. 'It's been thirteen years. You can give me a hug, can't you?'

Craig stumbled to his feet. His knees felt weak, as if they wouldn't be able to take his weight. He somehow crossed the room, then his arms were across the back of her shoulders, hers around his waist. In a moment, he was thirteen again, aware of the changing feelings for the girl he'd spent a couple of years hanging around with and barely looked at twice. He closed his eyes, feeling her hair brushing across his nose and cheeks. She squeezed him, burying her face in the crook of his neck, before patting him gently and pulling away. Her eyes gazed into his in the same way they had outside Mr Bates's office.

'You look really good,' she said.

Craig suddenly felt self-conscious, running a hand through his hair before he realised he was doing it. As he peered closely at her, searching for a compliment that didn't sound cheesy or creepy, he couldn't help but notice the small changes. Her nose was slightly crooked and he was sure it didn't used to be like that. There were short, fair bristles that had formed a parting at the front of her hair where it looked like a clump had been tugged out at some point in the last month or two. There was also a smear of creamy powder around the top of her left eye, thicker than anywhere else on her face, the hint of a purple bruise underneath.

'You look good, too,' Craig replied.

It was all he could think of.

Kimberly picked up a carrier bag from the floor and placed it on the dining table at the back of the room. There was a box of paracetamol tablets, three tubs of decongestant pills and some batteries. She put them in the drawer of a cabinet and then tossed the bag into a bin.

She turned, taking Craig's arm and leading him to the sofa. 'You got a cold?' he asked.

Kimberly waggled her fingers in his face. 'Whoo, you scared of a few germs?' He laughed. 'Everyone's got a cold at this time of year,' she added. 'All the old dears stockpile for Christmas, so you've got to get in early. Anyway . . . let's talk about you. I couldn't believe it when Mark said you were coming back.'

'It was always going to happen sooner or later.'

'I thought you were doing well in London: decent job, wife, all that . . . ?'

Craig couldn't meet her eye: 'Harriet and I broke up.'

'Oh . . . so are you back for good?'

'No . . . well, maybe. I'm here for now.'

Mark appeared in the doorway, one plate topped with pizza slices, fresh can of Carling in the other. 'But there's no place like home, yeah?'

Craig nodded. 'Exactly. No place like home.'

Craig ate until he couldn't cram anything else into himself. He'd forgotten how good Manchester takeaways were. Kimberly had made a special journey to the curry mile and then picked up a couple of pizzas from the row of shops between their houses. It was the place from which Craig had been getting his tea since the age of eleven. That all came before they launched into the mound of chip shop chips drenched with thick, dribbling, oozing, wonderful beef gravy.

Southerners didn't know what they were missing.

He remembered the restaurants he and Harriet had visited in London; the business lunches and dinners shared abroad; that shortbread Diana had brought to the office one Christmas. They were all good, all up there, but nothing touched chippy chips with gravy.

For half an hour as they ate, it was like time had stopped. They were young, carefree and enjoying life. Even the incidents Craig was now embarrassed about seemed funny again. The people they'd teased, shopkeepers terrorised, teachers they'd run rings around. By himself, Craig was ashamed of the things they'd done, but with a giggling Kimberly and slightly drunk Mark, it felt like an important bond they shared. Some of it anyway. There was plenty they didn't speak of.

The pile of food had almost disappeared when Mark grabbed his can and stood, telling them both that he 'needed a shite' and disappearing through the house with a series of earth-quaking belches.

Kimberly leant back on the sofa, patting her stomach. 'I won't have to eat for a week.'

Craig put his plate on the floor and pressed backwards, stretching his legs and fighting a yawn. 'Me too.'

Kimberly started to run her fingers through her hair, tugging out a small series of knots. 'So, what happened?'

'With what?'

'With what's her name?'

'Not much. We grew apart, plus my company were looking to save costs. I figured it'd give me an out.'

A grin twinkled across Kimberly's face as she rested a hand on his leg. 'You're always welcome back here.'

She removed her hand almost as quickly as she'd put it there but Craig still failed to push back a shiver. 'How are you and Mark getting on?'

'Mark does his thing buying and selling. I do Mondays, Wednesdays and Fridays at a nail bar in town. We get by.'

Craig didn't know whether to congratulate or commiserate. There was nothing wrong with living that way, millions did, yet it wasn't what any of them thought they'd end up doing when they were teenagers with the world at their mercy. Of the three of them, Kimberly was the smart one, at least when it came to school.

'What 'bout you?' she asked.

'I was at this logistics place. It's more interesting than it sounds – I got to travel a bit and the money was okay.'

'But you still decided to leave?'

'It had run its course.'

'I suppose none of us are cut out for Monday to Friday, nine to five . . .' Kimberly rested her head on his shoulder, sighing. 'I wish you'd come to the wedding.'

'I was out of the country, I—'

'You don't have to tell me what you told him. I know . . .'

Craig gulped, feeling her chest rising and falling, wishing he knew what to say. All he could manage was a pathetic-sounding: 'Oh . . .'

Kimberly sat up straight at the sound of the toilet flushing, Mark's footsteps and accompanying belch. He entered the room grinning, Carling in one hand, vodka bottle with foreign-looking writing in the other.

'You ready to get messy?'

Craig stood, patting his stomach. 'I think I'm going to go. The tea was great, but I've got a few things to sort out . . .'

They all knew it was nonsense, the type of thing which nobody ever challenged. Mark shrugged, putting his drinks on the table and offering his hand. They shook and patted each other's backs before Kimberly led Craig to the front door. She was smiling weakly, the bruise above her eye more apparent than it had been before. He wanted to ask her about it but wasn't sure he'd like the answer. Kimberly leant forward and hugged him, a whisper flitting across Craig's ear. She stepped back and patted his shoulder. 'Sound okay?'

Craig peered past her towards the empty hallway and then made eye contact. 'Of course.'

12

It was twenty to five in the morning when Craig was woken by snoring from the room next door. It wasn't just one person's vibrating windpipe going for it, both of his parents were chuntering away like a pair of coked-up donkeys with breathing problems. There was no cohesion to the attack on Craig's ears. His father would exhale loudly enough to rattle the windows, then, as soon as he shut up, Craig's mum was trying to outdo him.

On his first night at home, Craig had felt a degree of comfort; now, between the rattling pipes, snoring parents and increasing sense that he didn't know where home was any longer, he was wide awake. It didn't help that the bed was so uncomfortable. When he couldn't sleep in his old flat, he'd browse the Internet and amuse himself but here, in the house that time forgot, there was no web connection and all the neighbours had WiFi passwords. He doubted his parents even knew what that meant. That left him using his phone's deathly slow connection and then searching through the boxes in his room. They contained so much junk that he lost interest part-way through the second.

At half six, he gave up and got dressed in the warmest clothes he had and headed outside. The air was cold, the dark streets quiet. The pavements had been gripped by a thick crusting of frost overnight. Across the road, the blocked drain had a layer of ice that had spread along the length of the kerb. Craig pulled up his coat collar, wrapped his scarf tighter and jammed his fingers deep into his gloves. He started walking, not knowing where he was headed but marvelling at how little had changed. The graffiti on the side of the Spar still promised the good time that 'Amy' could offer; there was still a rusting bike lock chained to the rank close to the bus stop, which itself was an empty shell because someone had set it on fire years' ago. The brown Datsun remained parked on Mrs Hearn's driveway, missing all four wheels; the church was asking for donations for its roof; and the tree at the back of the cemetery still had a long strip of lower branches missing from where Mark had started climbing and then fallen to the ground, bringing part of the tree down with him.

It was only as he reached the six-foot wall next to a car park that Craig realised he'd unknowingly been walking the route to his old primary school. The gates were locked across the front but he used them to haul himself up until he was sitting on top of the wall, peering down at the playground. An extension had been built onto the main building, the bricks a slightly different colour, but it looked largely the same. The windows at the front were decorated with tinsel and streamers and there was a large tree visible amid the darkness through the front door. Snakes and hopscotch squares were painted on the tarmac of the playground, with goals drawn onto the walls. When he was young, if anybody skidded over, there'd be scrapes, cuts and bruises. At least half of the playground was now covered with black padding.

Craig sat for a few minutes, taking everything in. It had seemed a huge area when he was a child, now it was tiny. School had never been for him, and if he hadn't ended up messing around with Mark and Kimberly, then it would have been someone else – or he would've stopped going. It seemed mad how much of a person's life was determined by what they did between the ages of six and sixteen, when, for the most part, they weren't mature enough to understand it.

He remembered where he was when the gate clanged. A car was halfway across the pavement, idling as a woman stared up at him.

'Can I help you?' she asked.

Craig jumped onto the pavement, embarrassed. She was almost certainly a teacher who thought he was casing the building. He shook his head. 'Sorry, I used to come here years ago. I was looking at the old place.'

The woman pushed the gate open and returned to her car, offering a half-hearted 'riiiight . . .' before pulling into the car park. Craig didn't wait for her to return, slipping along the pavement and weaving through the streets and his old web of cut-throughs in a long-winded way of reaching Tiger Pawn. From what he'd seen, the centre of Manchester was booming but the surrounding areas were dying. The days of butchers, bakers and candlestick makers were already over when he'd been young, but now the High Street was nothing but betting shops, hairdressers and pound stores. Was this really what people's lives consisted of? Or was he a snob, annoyed at how his life was turning out?

As if he wasn't unhappy enough, Craig was the first

person through the door at the Wetherspoons, ordering a coffee and full English, and finding a spot in the window that faced the pawn shop. It was due to open at nine and he had an hour to waste. The door dinged intermittently as men – always men – shuffled inside, heading to the bar and ordering the usual.

Craig fiddled with his keys and the attached army knife before sticking them back into his pocket. He'd had the knife for years, something he'd bought on a trip to Germany with Harriet. It was more sentimental than anything else. Not particularly sharp, more a utility device used to open bottles.

The High Street was busy, people rushing to work, kids slouching to school, almost ready to break up for the rest of the year. It was a Friday, so probably their final day. When he was young, before Kimberly, before the endless truancy, they'd bring board games to school on the last day of term. The teacher would either let them play, or put on a video for them to watch. Is that what they did now? Board games seemed a bit quaint.

The shutters across the front of Tiger Pawn eventually started to roll at a minute to nine. Craig finished the rest of his second coffee and then hurried across the street, first heading to the bank, and then back to the empty pawn shop. The same girl from the previous day was behind the counter, meeting him with a roll of the eyes and a sigh.

It might have been first thing, but she was already chewing her way through a stick of gum, not bothering to close her mouth. 'I told you yesterday to come back on Monday.'

Craig peered over his shoulder, making sure he was still

alone. He unzipped his coat so she could see the contents of his inner pocket. 'I've got the full amount that my parents owe. I was hoping to pay it off in one go.'

For a moment, the girl lost her composure, jaw closing temporarily until the chewing continued. 'I ain't authorised to take anything other than the weekly or monthly amount due.'

Craig re-zipped his coat. 'What am I supposed to do?'

'Come back on Monday.'

'I don't want to leave this hanging over the weekend. How hard is it to get this paid off?'

'I already told you – Monday.'

Her hand hovered close to the red button again. Craig wondered what it would bring, definitely not the police, so probably somebody big who could kick his arse.

'I don't want to carry this around for the weekend,' Craig said. 'How can I get in contact with Pung-You? Or Haken?'

He hoped for a reaction by using the names but got none: 'You don't.'

'Can I leave a message?'

The gum-chomping hesitated once more: 'Do I look like an answering machine?'

'I can write it down.'

The girl peered over his shoulder towards the still-empty shop, hoping for a customer so she could boot him out of the way.

'Just tell me,' she said.

Craig hadn't expected that. 'Right, er . . . I suppose tell them that my last name's Macklin and I was hoping to pay off my parents' debts.'

She rolled her eyes. 'That it?'

'I suppose.'

'Fine – someone will be in touch.' She flicked her head towards the door. 'Now piss off – and this time, don't come back.'

13

The High Street was buzzing as Craig exited the pawn shop, hands in pockets. The sun was just about up, although it probably shouldn't have bothered given how cloudy it was. Craig glanced both ways, wondering what to do with the rest of the day. He could go to the pub with his dad, stay at home with his mum, trail Mark around, or try to look for a job. As options went, they were all up there with slamming his unmentionables in a car door. His thoughts drifted back to the night before, saying goodbye to Kimberly at the front door and the whisper in his ear. For now, he had to wait.

Craig eyed the Wetherspoons, where a bloke with a flat cap had taken his spot in the window. He could spend a few hours there but . . . as spirals of depression went, it was a long way to sink so quickly.

He sat on a bench and started to scroll through his phone. The melting layer of frost seeped through his jeans, making him shiver as the breeze bit at his exposed hand. His contacts list was a who's who of people not contacted in years. There were former work colleagues, the blokes from the pool team of which he'd been a member in London, Harriet's friends and family.

Delete, delete, delete.

By the time Craig had finished culling the list of people he knew he'd never speak to again, there were barely a dozen names in his directory. Two of those were London takeaways that he couldn't bear to delete just in case. There was Harriet, with whom he'd have to speak through necessity; Mark's mobile; his parents' landline; his old work because they were currently still paying him; customer service numbers for his phone and bank, and a small handful of friends that he thought were marginally more likely to side with him than Harriet after the break-up. He was still owed the odd favour, too – a workmate he'd helped move apartments; another he'd given football tickets to one time. He didn't know when a bit of goodwill would come in handy.

He scrolled up and down, wondering if there was perhaps a hidden friend he'd forgotten but there wasn't. His life really was this pathetic. The only people with whom he was still in contact in Manchester were Mark and Kimberly.

He put his phone away, consoling himself with the thought that, *if* he got a job after Christmas, he could hopefully make some friends.

Craig put his gloves back on with little idea of what to do with his day. People were rushing past with shopping bags but who could he buy presents for? His dad would be happy with a bottle of booze – any bottle; his mother would declare anything to be 'wonderful', whether a pound-shop cushion cover, or a diamond ring worth tens of thousands. Either one would end up in the back of a drawer somewhere. She liked what she liked and that was that.

For the first time, Craig was beginning to realise why his father drank.

He heaved himself up and started the slow walk back home, following the main roads and hoping inspiration would come. There must be *something* to do in this city that didn't involve copious amounts of alcohol during the minuscule amount of daylight.

Craig was past his old school and heading towards the park when he heard the squeal of tyres. He spun, expecting there to have been a close call on the road behind, but there were three men in suits barrelling out of a dark people carrier towards him. They were all young, Far Eastern in appearance, with short dark hair. He took a step away, wanting to run, but they were already upon him. A sharp punch cracked into his kidneys making him cough, eyes bulging in pain. Before he could kick, shout, or fight, everything went dark as a hood was draped over his head. He was bundled sideways, picked up and launched into the vehicle as if he weighed nothing. Someone yanked at his wrists, pulling his arms back and strapping cable ties around them. The plastic was harsh and too tight, digging into his skin, but he couldn't complain because his breath was gone from the punch. Someone rocked him into a sitting position and then the engine growled and he lurched forward. The vehicle was moving but he had no seatbelt. Instead, he could feel the hands of his abductors pressing into his shoulders, at least one on either side.

Craig didn't bother fighting. Not only were his hands bound and eyes covered, he was hopelessly outnumbered. If there was one thing he'd learned from past escapades with Mark, it was to pick the battles. Some people were bigger, stronger and more important. This was definitely not his time.

The people carrier bumped up and down, making Craig acutely aware of how many potholes there were in the area. His head twice hit the roof and four times he was almost thrown out of the seat before being hauled back. His abductors either didn't speak English, or didn't speak it around him. He had no idea what language he could hear but they spoke quickly to one another, laughing and palling around as if out for a Sunday drive.

Eventually, the vehicle stopped and the door slid open. Craig was shoved out, landing on his knees and being yanked up. The ground was hard like a pavement and there was the grinding of something metallic, then Craig found himself being marched down a set of steps. Soon, he was shunted into a chair. It felt wooden and clammy as if it had been out in the rain for a while. Someone pushed him up until he was sitting straighter and then there was silence. Almost.

He'd heard that a person is more aware of their other senses if denied one. Considering he couldn't see a thing, Craig expected to have super-hearing, able to hear a mouse's sniffle from a hundred metres. It wasn't the case: those who claimed that were talking out of their collective arses. He squinted his eyes shut behind the hood, willing his ears to pick up the slack, but all he could hear was a faint dripping noise.

Useless.

'Mr Macklin . . .'

The man's voice whispered from the darkness, the accent difficult to place. Not Mancunian, not even northern. It was a mix of things, sort of English but with a twang as if there was a 'G' on the end of 'Macklin'.

'Hello?'

Silence.

Craig's breath was beginning to feel short underneath the hood and the material caught between his lips. He tried to spit it out, creating a salivary mess on the inside of the hood, before turning his head from side to side. He couldn't see a thing.

'Hello?'

'Can you behave, Mr Macklin?'

'Yes.'

There were hands scrabbling on the back of his head and then the hood was loose. It was whipped away in one, leaving Craig's eyes to burn in the dim light. He clamped them shut as his wrists were released from one another, the cable ties sliced apart. As far as Craig could tell with his eyes closed, he was free. He shifted his legs from side to side and brought his hands in front of himself, fingering the crease in his wrists from where the ties had sliced into him. He opened his eyes slowly, allowing crinkles of light to seep through, before realising that it was almost still dark. He was in some sort of basement, surrounded by dark brick walls, with only a dim yellow bulb above. The rest slowly began to come into focus. Standing directly in front of him was a man in a suit, who looked much like the three who'd abducted him, though he was smaller and slighter. His fingers were pressed together into a diamond, as if praying.

'I believe you wanted to speak to me, Mr Macklin?'

Craig tried to sit up straighter. The man wasn't tall,

which was probably why he was standing and Craig was sitting.

'Where am I?' Craig croaked, playing up his injuries a little. He felt fine but wanted time to acclimatise.

'I'm not sure that should be your first question.'

'What should be?'

'Perhaps you should ask who I am?'

'Okay . . . who are you?'

The man spread his arms wider, as if he was the messiah who had recently descended to claim the earth for his own. 'My name is Haken.'

He pronounced it 'Hay-Kin', slipping into a different accent momentarily. Craig didn't like to assume, but Manchester had Chinatown, though no designated area that he knew of for other East Asians. Haken's regular accent was definitely put on, the words over-pronounced as if he'd learned English from period dramas. If that were in any way true, Manchester must have been quite the shock.

'I gather you were asking after me?' Haken added, fingers back into the diamond shape.

'My parents owed money to Rodger. I was trying to find out who now owns that debt so I could pay it off.' He patted his jacket pocket, relieved the money was still there and hadn't been snatched during his abduction. Craig indicated towards the room. 'There's no need for any of this, I have your money.'

'How much do you have?'

'Two thousand, eight hundred – that's more than they borrowed in the first place.'

Haken nodded thoughtfully, his face half cast in shadow.

His age was hard to judge, though he looked somewhere around thirty, the same as Craig. He purred a reply: 'Two thousand, eight hundred?'

'I've got cash – you can take it now and we can go our separate ways.'

'You're assuming the debts of your parents?'

'I only want to pay it off.'

'Two thousand, eight hundred is not the correct amount, Mr Macklin. If you want to pay it off in one go, there's a fee. The amount for a lump sum is closer to six thousand.'

Haken's features barely moved as he spoke but Craig spluttered at the gall. Six grand?! His parents had only borrowed two and a half thousand in the first place and they'd been paying it off for months.

'I don't have that . . .'

'I thought not.'

'But surely I can pay it off month by month with this money?'

Haken shook his head. 'You could – but you're forgetting the penalties for non-payment. Your parents have been failing to make interest-only payments and now you've assumed their debt. The amount you owe me, if you were to pay monthly, Mr Macklin, is approximately eight thousand.'

'Eight grand?!'

Craig couldn't control himself; he sprang to his feet. As soon as he was upright, two men were on him, escaping from the shadows and grabbing his arms. He hadn't meant to do anything rash but now knew he was still outnumbered. The men pushed him back into the chair, glanced towards a nodding Haken, and then stepped away. The slight change of angle had made Craig spot something he'd missed before – as well as the pair who'd grabbed him, there was at least one more person in the room. Hidden by the shadows on the far side was an older man sitting on a chair. The white of his beard was so obvious that Craig wondered how he'd missed it in the first place.

'I don't have six thousand,' Craig repeated, trying to keep his voice calm. 'How much is it per month for the interest and everything else?'

Haken didn't hesitate: 'Four hundred and ninety-four pounds. For every month that amount is not met in full, the total will increase.'

Craig felt as if he'd been punched. This was how people were drawn in, by borrowing small amounts that turned out to be cripplingly high. His parents might have been a bit silly, but they thought they were borrowing from Rodger.

He rubbed at his head. 'I was told someone named Pung-You had taken over the debt . . .' He nodded towards the older man hidden by the shadows. 'Is that you?'

The older man didn't move. 'Your debt is with me, Mr Macklin.'

'So who's Pung-You?'

'Someone you need not worry yourself about.'

'But I am worried! You're telling me I have to pay five hundred quid a month.'

'Four hundred and ninety-four.'

Craig pressed his feet into the hard floor, balling his fists. 'I could go to the police.'

Haken's smile widened, though there was no amusement.

He was a small man but his gaze was ferocious, dark discs pinning Craig to the spot. 'You do that, Mr Macklin, if that's what you think is a good idea. Mr Porter thought that was a good idea. Have you heard of him?'

'Willy Porter?'

'Aah, so you have. When your police were tipped off about Mr Porter and his friends, he decided he was going to hand himself in and tell them everything he knew about me and *my* friends. Unfortunately, he didn't get as far as the police station. Such a shame.'

For a moment Craig wondered why Haken was telling him but the answer was obvious: why not? Craig had no way of proving it – he didn't know where he was and Haken might not even be the man's name. He wasn't being told about a murder, he was being threatened.

'Do you know me?' Craig asked.

'In a sense. What sort of business would we run, Mr Macklin, if we didn't know the details of our clients? Your father was very forthcoming when we asked what you did.'

'My *dad* told you about me?'

'Not me personally . . .'

Craig could believe it only too easily. Once he had a few drinks inside him, his father would spill secrets to anybody and everybody. Chances were, he wouldn't even remember doing it. Craig was beginning to feel a sinking sensation, as if he was a step behind everything that had happened. If his father had spoken about the nature of Craig's job, there was every chance he'd let slip that he was returning to Manchester, too. That was probably why Haken's men had attacked his parents' house on the night he'd arrived. They'd caused very little damage, just enough to pique Craig's interest.

'What do you want?' Craig asked.

'I'd like you to do a job for me. Logistics is your thing, yes? The translated word isn't so clear but I understand you arrange for things to be moved from one place to another.'

'Not any more – I left my job a week ago.'

The smile didn't move. 'I'm sure you still know people there, Mr Macklin.'

'Well, yes . . .'

'Then I'm sure you can find a way. I need you to find a shipment – any arrival coming into Manchester Airport from northern Africa. I want you to access the forms and add an extra container.'

'I can't do that.'

Haken wagged a finger. '"Can't" is an English word I don't like. Call a friend, pay someone off, I don't care. If you manage this, we're all clear. I want you to get that shipment to an address I'll give you.'

'I have to pick it up, too?'

'I'll be writing off a significant debt on your behalf. I want you to do a full and thorough job. We'll provide you with transport. You arrange for the shipment to arrive, you pick it up and take it where you're told. There'll be someone to meet you at the airport.'

There was no part of the plan that sounded good to Craig. 'What's being imported?'

'I think you're asking the wrong questions again, Mr Macklin.'

Craig sighed. He hadn't expected an answer but it was hardly going to be boxes of pineapples. He wanted to say no, though he knew there was more than money at stake. At a scrape, if he found a job, he probably could pay off the five hundred quid a month that Haken wanted – but then there'd be some sort of other hidden charge of which he hadn't been told. This was about him. Haken and his men had done their homework – thanks in no small part to Craig's father and his big mouth.

'When do you need it by?' Craig asked.

'As soon as possible.' Haken's hand darted into his suit pocket and he leant forward, passing a crisp white business card to Craig. There were no names or addresses, simply a mobile phone number printed in the centre. 'Call that number when you've identified a suitable shipment. I'll need to know when and where it's leaving. After that, it's up to you.' He paused for a moment and then added: 'You can leave now.'

Craig started to stand but the men stepped forward again from each side, pressing him down, one of them offering him the hood. He sighed, took a breath, and then put it over his head.

14

Saturday breezed past in a blur of anxiety. Craig's father had mumbled something that he might have chatted to a bloke in a pub about Craig's job but couldn't remember much else. It might even have been in the Grey Goose.

Typical.

After that argument, Craig left in a huff, slamming doors and scuffing feet, teenage-style, heading to the centre of Manchester where things were at least in the twenty-first century.

Relatively speaking.

Mark would have plenty of ideas about what to do, but Craig didn't want to let on how much trouble he'd landed himself in. Instead, he hunted around the Northern Quarter, finding an Internet cafe that was far too trendy for him. It was filled with backpackers, plus young people with tattoos and piercings. He felt like a dad hanging around the edge of an ice rink watching his children.

Considering the potential complexity of Haken's request/demand, Craig found the first part relatively easy to deal with. Because he was technically still an employee of the logistics company, he was able to use external access to log into the work system with his old details. The IT department would only be disabling his account when his contract expired. After searching through the logs, he found an inbound flight to Manchester from Morocco on Monday that would be carrying goods for the company. With a few clicks and a bit of typing, the details were altered to add an extra box to the list of incoming items. Nobody would bother to check, because why would they? The boxes would be counted on – including Haken's – and then counted back off. The numbers would match, with the only problem coming if anyone bothered to check the amounts against the initial invoice, which Craig knew would never happen. Even if it did, there were always the occasional mistakes on shipping paperwork.

When he was done, he phoned the number Haken had given him and passed on the details of the flight times. He was told to expect further instructions on Monday.

Craig spent the rest of Saturday mooching around the city centre, marvelling at how Christmassy it all was. It was, of course, nearly Christmas but there was now an industry in sticking up market stalls, ice rinks, enormous trees and elaborate decorations, all topped off by some prick from a talent show flicking a switch to turn them on. When Craig had left the area, it had been a string of fairy lights that would've stopped working before Christmas and the mayor hoping for the best as he jammed a plug into a socket during torrential rain.

The centre had been busy during the week but now it was so rammed with people that Craig found himself forced to shuffle at the same slow pace as everyone else. He eventually gave up, took a packed tram home, and spent the rest of the evening in his room.

By Sunday, Craig was full of nervous anticipation. He

hurried through the streets of Salford, head down, trying to warm his hands in his pockets. Every few minutes, he'd check the time on his phone, before either upping his pace, or slowing down. He wanted to be perfectly on time. Early would seem too keen; late would make him a fool.

It was one minute to midday when he reached the top of the path that sloped down to a railway bridge. One half now had bicycles painted on the surface, the other was still a pavement. Craig followed the track, heart thundering as he spotted her waiting for him underneath the bridge. This had been *their* spot when they were younger. When it was cold or wet outside but they didn't want to go home, Craig, Mark and Kimberly would come here, climb the sloping pillars and half-lie, half-sit over the path but under the bridge. They'd chat about everything and nothing; listen to Mark's tall stories and plans; gossip about their teachers and classmates; and occasionally talk about their parents.

Kimberly was already sitting high above on the wide concrete supports, bundled up in a thick coat, scarf and hat. She waved down at him as Craig started up the steep slope, using his hands to scramble against the smooth surface. By the time he was next to her, he was panting, embarrassed by his lack of fitness and agility. Kimberly giggled, poking him in the ribs and admitting that she too had found the ascent much easier in days gone by. Thin threads of blonde were poking out from her hat, wisping around her ears. She was wearing no make-up, exposing the fading black marks around the curve of her eye socket. She stroked his shoulder and then lay back, spreading her arms as if she were making a snow angel. Craig copied her, peering up at the bridge above.

'Can you see it?' she asked.

'What?'

Kimberly pointed directly above them: 'Look.'

Craig squinted into the darkness at the underside of the bridge: concrete and metal. There was nothing . . . but, as his eyes adjusted to the darkness, he saw the faint outline. Somehow it had survived the years of weathering and filth. The letters were scrappy and rough and the paint had run at the time, but he could see it clearly: *MG – CM – KK 4EVA*

'Do you remember when he did that?' Kimberly asked.

Craig stared at the curved metal girders hanging underneath the bridge. 'Mark almost killed himself. I thought he was going to fall. I'm still not sure how he climbed up those beams, let alone get down.'

Kimberly sat up, holding her arms behind for support. She gazed down into Craig's eyes. 'Thanks for coming.'

'Why wouldn't I?'

She shrugged. 'It's been a long time. Not your problem any more. You don't need to care.'

'Is that what you think? That I never cared?'

Kimberly breathed in through her nose and turned away. For a moment, she didn't reply, small gasps escaping into the cool air as steam. Considering how cold the day was, it was surprisingly warm underneath the bridge, the high supports providing shelter from the breeze. When it rained, the water would slalom down on either side, leaving a perfectly dry strip in the middle. It made it the perfect place to hang around if home wasn't an option.

When she eventually spoke, Kimberly's voice was a whisper: 'This is the first place I ever got properly drunk.'

'I didn't know that.'

'Remember that time we bunked off—'

'That happened a lot.'

She giggled: 'I know but we were about fourteen and Mark had nabbed that three-litre bottle of cider from Bargain Booze. He had to throw it up to us here because he couldn't climb and carry it at the same time.'

'I *do* remember – it took him about ten attempts. By the time we opened the bottle, it sprayed everywhere.'

'Right. He'd got away with a bunch of VKs too, so you two drank that and I had the cider. Before long, I was so pissed, I was singing and crying. Then I couldn't figure out how to get down the slope. I ended up slipping and landing on my elbow because Mark said he'd catch me and then didn't. It hurt so much that I was sick all over myself and the two of you carried me back to Mark's house. His dad was out and you dumped me in the bath with the shower spray.'

Craig sniggered at the memory. He'd forgotten but now it shone brightly. He could remember the weather, the time, the smell and what each of them was wearing. It felt like it had happened the previous day.

'Fancy a drink?' Craig asked.

'Of what?'

'Cider?'

Kimberly stretched out and slapped his arm, giggling as she did so. She lay on her back, wedging her head into his shoulder as they stared up at the set of initials.

'How does it feel being KG instead of KK?' Craig asked.

She didn't reply, twisting until she was fully cuddled into his side, hair resting on his chin. She rolled up her right sleeve and held out her bare arm for Craig to see. Her skin was naturally pale, except for her inner forearm, which was speckled by a rainbow of black, purple and yellow.

'I've always been good at bruises,' she whispered.

Craig didn't know how to reply. He already knew the answer: he'd seen it in the clump of hair missing from Kimberly's head, the crookedness of her nose and the concealed black eye.

A train clattered overhead, making the entire bridge shake violently. Craig continued to hold Kimberly throughout, pulling her into himself and closing his eyes.

'Mark?'

His eventual one-word question was utterly unnecessary yet unavoidable. He needed to hear her say it.

She hugged him tighter, voice faltering. 'I picked the wrong friend.'

15

THIRTEEN YEARS OLD

Craig, Mark and Kimberly sat in the gully between the tree and the hedge watching the front of Mark's house. They could peer through the overhanging branches, giving a complete view of the road, though passers-by could only spot them if they really looked. If it rained, they'd get soaked, but otherwise it was a perfect spot for avoiding their respective parents. Underneath the train bridge was better overall but also more exposed. During the day, they could be easily spotted, which wasn't the best when they were skiving off school.

Mark was curled up, eyes closed as if ready to sleep, head in Kimberly's lap. She was stroking his hair but bored. 'What time does he usually leave the house?' she asked.

Mark didn't open his eyes: 'Dunno. He always reads the paper first, then goes to the pub. It's a Friday, so there's a footy pullout in the *Herald*. He'll be reading that.'

Kimberly turned to Craig. 'What time is it?'

'Half ten.'

'I should be in an English lesson. You'd be doing music.'

'How are you in the top sets?'

She shrugged. 'Dunno, I remember stuff. It's not that hard.'

Mark twisted slightly, angling up though keeping his eyes closed. 'I like being in the bottom set,' he said. 'There's always some weird special needs kid you can blame stuff on.'

'You don't even go to classes,' Kimberly replied.

Mark shrugged. 'Fair enough.'

Craig shushed them, shrinking back behind the branches as Mark's father emerged from the house. Father and son looked identical, save for a small difference in height and the obvious additional wrinkles. They even walked the same way, slightly shuffling as if permanently a half-step behind. Mark flicked his legs out, yawned, and pulled himself into a sitting position.

'That's him gone for the day . . .'

Kimberly leant forward and squinted: 'It looks like he's arguing with himself.'

Even from a distance, Craig could see the man's lips twitching as he spoke to the empty space next to him. He turned in a half-circle as if there was someone behind and then spun back again before tripping over the kerb.

Mark's reply was dismissively scathing. 'He probably is.'

As soon as the man was out of sight, Mark, Craig and Kimberly edged out of their hiding place and dashed to the front door. Mark unlocked it and they piled inside. The hall-way reeked of cigarettes, the smell getting stronger as he led them upstairs and through the door directly ahead. His father's bedroom hummed of alcohol and fags. The ceiling was dark and sticky, the floor covered with empty bottles. Craig and Kimberly shared a 'can-you-believe-it?' glance but Mark was unworried, heading to the far side of the bed and lifting up the mattress, before thrusting a twenty-pound note into the air.

'I *knew* he had it in here,' Mark said, dropping the mattress back into place.

Craig started to back out of the room: 'Won't he know you've taken it?'

'It's mine in the first place – I'm the one who nicked those pornos that we sold, he stole it from me because he went through my bag. Besides, he might remember *taking* it, but I doubt he'll remember leaving it under the mattress. He's always losing stuff – I find all sorts under there that he brings home, then forgets.'

Craig didn't want to know.

He and Kimberly had a change of clothes in their bags, so the three of them got out of their school uniform and then left the house, heading towards the centre of Manchester. It was a little over three miles but they walked that most days when they bunked off, sticking to the ginnels and narrow passages that connected one housing estate to another, staying away from the main roads in case anyone bothered to ask how old they were. By the time they got to the centre, no one paid them any attention.

They were close to a main road near the city centre when Kimberly dug her fingers into Craig's shoulder and yanked him back behind a corner.

Mark slotted in behind them: 'What was that all about?'

'It's my mum!'

Craig peeped around the corner across the road towards a car park ringed by a chicken-wire fence, the presence of which made little sense as there was no gate at the front to stop people walking in. The attendant's booth was boarded up, too.

A woman with bright curly red hair clambered out of a black Vauxhall and then crouched to see her reflection in the car's window. Craig had met her once or twice, but only ever to say a quick hello/goodbye. Kimberly was never keen on either him or Mark meeting her mother, not that any of them went out of their way to mix friends and parents.

Mark stepped around the corner, only to be yanked back by Kimberly.

'What are you doing?' she hissed.

'We should go and say hello.'

She dug her fingers into his arm, squeezing until he yelped. 'Don't even joke. She already says you're bad influences on me. Now we're skipping school.'

Mark brushed her off, rubbing through his sleeve. '*We're* bad influences? I should go and introduce myself properly, let her know I'm not all bad.'

'*Don't.*' Kimberly wasn't joking, baring her top set of teeth, vampire-style.

Mark held his hands up. 'All right, all right. I'm only messing.'

Craig continued peeping around the corner as Kimberly's mum took a bag from the passenger seat and then headed out of the car park, disappearing through an alley between two buildings.

Kimberly breathed a sigh of relief and then stepped onto the pavement. She nodded towards the building opposite. 'That's my mum's work. She's at some job agency. I didn't recognise it because I've never been round the back.'

Mark was leaning against the fence, a sparkle of something Craig didn't like in his eye. He was in the mood for trouble. 'Sounds like a boring job,' he said.

Kimberly shrugged. 'I dunno. She hates her boss, calls her the Queen Bitch. Every time she gets home late, it's because her boss keeps her late to catch up with stuff. She doesn't even get paid extra.'

Mark sprang away from the wall, rubbing his hands together. 'How about we teach the Queen Bitch a lesson?'

Before either of them could stop him, Mark had raced across the road into the car park. They caught him as he was peering towards the signs high on the brickwork lining the wall above the parking spaces.

'What's the name of your mum's company?' he asked.

'Something-or-other recruitment.'

A shiny black BMW sported a number plate from the previous year. Mark nodded up to the sign above:

Madeleine Bright Recruitment: MANAGER ONLY

'Is that it?' he asked.

'I think so.'

He glanced between the two of them. 'What do you reckon?'

Craig knew there was no point in arguing, his friend's mind was already made up. Kimberly bounced from one foot to the other, hesitating. 'I don't know . . .'

Mark didn't bother waiting, dropping to one knee and removing the penknife from his pocket. He dug the blade deep into the door and started to carve a 'B', giggling to himself. Craig didn't exactly approve but there wasn't much he could say and it was too late anyway. As Kimberly watched the windows for anyone who might spot them, Craig kept an eye on the road. By the time Mark had finished, 'BITCH' had been etched into one door, 'WHORE' into the other and 'FAT SLAG' across the bonnet. Mark was as giddy as a toddler with an ice lolly, pocketing the knife and standing back to admire his handiwork.

'C'mon, let's get out of here,' he said, walking backwards, grin fixed.

Craig and Kimberly followed his lead but Mark was so high on adrenaline that he raced away from them, not bothering to look over his shoulder. He tore out of the car park and headed towards the city centre. Craig slowed for Kimberly, holding out his hand and feeling that wondrous sense of happiness as she linked her fingers into his. She beamed as they stretched their arms out across the pavement, jogging side by side, not a care in the world.

16

Craig spent the whole of Monday daytime walking. He headed to Manchester city centre, touring the Arndale shopping complex and weaving through the markets, before crossing back over the River Irwell into Salford. He continued in a huge loop, taking in the university and MediaCity, before finding his way back to the railway bridge. He lay in the same spot as the previous day, this time by himself, realising that he'd always known this would be what happened between Mark and Kimberly. It was especially true after what had happened to Mark's dad, yet seeing her bruises made it all too real. As well as the black eye and marked forearm, there were fist-shaped scars around her lower ribs and back that she'd shown him, saying there were others on her thighs. He'd not known what to say, let alone what to do, in the end offering the one thing it felt like she wanted: comfort.

It had taken five days of being back in the city for everything to fall apart.

It felt as if the sun had barely come up before it was dipping again. The mass of cloud and gloom masked anything approaching a sunset, until the streetlights pinged on to cast their own orangey haze.

Haken's van was waiting for Craig outside the Londis close to Buile Hill Park in Salford. Craig had only been given the registration when he called the number on the card but the van turned out to be a dark blue Transit-type vehicle, with the keys hidden under the rear right mud flap. Craig climbed into the driver's seat and turned the key. He'd expected some sort of rusty death trap, but the drive was pleasantly smooth, the engine quiet, and the pedals responsive. He followed the directions he'd been given on the phone, taking the motorway ringroad out of the city and heading towards the airport. Traffic was backing up from the Trafford Centre, late-night shoppers desperate to throw their cash at department stores in time for Christmas, but the rest of his journey was effortless. He followed the signs for terminal one, pulling into a hotel car park in sight of the airport and switching the engine off.

It was a little after nine and the surface was beginning to frost. Steam was building on the inside of the van's windows and it felt even colder than it had the previous few nights. A plane boomed overhead, soaring into the night sky, LEDs blinking furiously underneath. Every room in the hotel seemed to be occupied, light beaming towards the car park. Craig was surrounded by people, overwhelmed by the noise, yet felt as lonely as he ever had. He scrolled through his list of phone contacts again, hovering over the takeaway that had been closest to his London flat. For a moment, he wondered if he could call. It was Monday night and Leo would be answering the phones. They weren't friends as such, but they knew one another to say hello to and had once gone on a joint bender when they'd met by chance in a local pub. They'd ended up singing Oasis songs on the karaoke machine on the top floor of some pub-cum-club, where Leo had pulled a raven-haired barmaid. After that, Craig got free garlic breads every time he phoned in an order on a Monday. He could press the button, wait for Leo and then say, 'hi mate'. They probably *could* chat for a few minutes, but what then? At some point Leo would ask what he wanted to eat, then Craig would have to admit he didn't even live in the area any longer.

Before he could do anything even more stupid, Craig's phone started to vibrate. 'UNKNOWN' appeared on the screen as he swiped to answer.

'Hello?' Craig said.

'Where are you?' He didn't recognise the male voice, though it was probably Haken.

'At the airport, like you said.'

'Do you know the freight area?'

'No.'

'What about the Premier Inn?'

Craig turned to look over his shoulder. 'I think I saw it from the roundabout.'

'Go there, drive past and follow the road. You'll end up on what looks like an industrial estate. Keep going past all the signs until you reach a dead end.'

'But—'

The line was dead.

Craig did as he was told, retracing his steps back to the roundabout and then heading past the Premier Inn into an unlit area. Wheelie bins and crates lined the narrow road, with tall barbed-wire-topped chain-link fences on either side. He waited with the engine off, staring into the gloomy distance, wondering what he was helping to smuggle into the country.

It took a few minutes for his eyes to adjust to the darkness, allowing him to see the large block-shaped warehouses on either side of the fences. In front there was a long strip of tarmac, lit only by the dim grey of the moon trying to peep through the clouds. After five minutes, Craig was so cold that he twisted the key and started the heaters. He held his gloved hands in front of the vents and breathed in the warm air, hoping the battery would last.

Craig jumped as his phone started to vibrate. It leapt off his lap, landing in the footwell and juddering its way under the seat until he finally managed to grab it and answer.

The man's voice was as calm as before: 'You there?'

'Yes, I—'

The call ended once again, leaving Craig in darkness. He peered around nervously, unable to see anything other than the warehouses beyond the fence and clutter in front of it. After pulling his hat down lower over his ears, Craig climbed out of the van, plopping onto the grit and only just managing to keep his footing on the slippery surface. He rested against the chilled metal door and listened. A plane was roaring in the distance and there was the usual hum from the motorway, yet it felt eerily quiet. He turned in a circle but there was no one around.

As he settled back facing the fence at the end of the path, pinpricks of white appeared in the distance. The blobs started to grow, expanding rapidly in the darkness until they were a pair of distinct glowing discs. Craig approached the fence, pressing his gloved fingers through the wire and peering into the gloom. He could hear the soft buzz of an engine getting louder until the shape became apparent. A forklift truck was racing towards him, completely by itself on the wide, open stretch of tarmac. It skidded to a stop metres from the fence and the lights went out, leaving them in darkness again. The shape of a man in a huge pumped-up puffer jacket stepped out and hurried towards Craig. With the hood up, his features were impossible to make out in the dark, other than a thick bristle across his chin and cheeks. When he reached the wire, he fumbled into his pocket and unclicked the padlocks, pulling the chains through with a noisy clink, before wheeling the gate open.

He stood and stared at Craig. 'You thick, mate?'

'What?' Craig replied.

'You've gotta reverse the bloody thing.'

'Oh, right . . . er . . .'

'Get on with it then.'

Craig tried to do as he was told but a mix of the cold and nervousness meant he was struggling with the basics of driving. First, he stalled the van while trying to edge forward, then his three-point turn ended up with seven points as he struggled to judge the distances without headlights. Eventually, he turned the van around and reversed back slowly towards the gate, stopping when the man thumped a fist onto the side. Craig opened the back doors and waited as the stranger got back into the forklift, leaving the lights off and squeaking forward until he was in line with the van. Sitting on the prongs was a wooden crate a metre or so wide. There were no markings that Craig could see, only the sand-coloured wood. The forklift driver expertly crept forward in the gloom until the crate was in the back of the van. He lowered the fork, dropping the container, and then sped backwards into the yard. Without a word, he got back out and approached the wire, picking up the chains from the ground and starting to re-lock the gate.

'Is that it?' Craig asked.

'I've done my bit.'

Craig nodded at the van. 'What's inside?'

'Beats me, mate.' He glanced up, the fragile glimmer of moonlight catching his eyes. 'Now do us both a favour and piss off.'

Craig clicked the rear doors closed and climbed back into the cabin. He knew more or less where he had to leave the van in Salford, but would double-check the exact address when he was away from the airport and off the motorway. He pulled away, edging slowly along the path with the headlights off, avoiding the scatter of junk on either side. The last thing he wanted was to impale the van on a tipped-over wheelie bin by accident.

As he passed the Premier Inn, Craig flicked the lights back on, following the signs for the motorway and then accelerating down the ramp and joining the carriageway. This should be the easy bit: fifteen minutes around the motorway and that was that. Haken would have his goods, his parents' debt would be clear, and he could finally get on with working out what he wanted to do with his life.

A car barrelled past him in the centre lane doing at least ninety, stereo thumping, exhaust howling. Craig wasn't a regular driver, he hadn't needed to be living in London, but he felt a stab of annoyance. The last thing he wanted was for the police to be keeping a close eye on the roads because of some idiot intent on killing himself.

His foot was solid on the accelerator, keeping the van at a steady sixty-five, with no thoughts of leaving the inside lane. There was a smattering of vehicles on either side of the carriageway, though the matrix signs were clear, meaning the late-night shoppers had presumably gone home with significantly lighter wallets.

Craig continued driving as carefully as he could, though his heart jumped as a police car zipped past, heading in the opposite direction. Its lights weren't spinning and there was nothing untoward but Craig kept an eye on his mirrors, fearful that it might get off at the next junction, turn around, and re-enter the motorway behind him.

Realising he was becoming unnecessarily apprehensive, Craig reached down and fumbled with the radio. It took him a moment to find the right button but, moments later, an upbeat rock track was bouncing from the speakers. Craig started nodding his head in rhythm, drumming his fingers on the steering wheel. It was only when the chorus kicked in that he realised it was Christian rock. The female singer had a pair of pipes on her, belting out the anguished pay-off line:

'Jesus, oh Jesus, you move me like psychokinesis . . .'

It was catchy in a crazy sort of way. That was the problem with having a saviour whose name didn't rhyme with very much: everything was fine until people started to write rock songs.

Craig was trying to think of any other words that might

rhyme when a set of bright white headlights blazed in his rear-view mirror. There was a car close behind, matching his speed, not trying to overtake. The lights were too bright for him to be able to make out the shape until they reached a bend. The car behind backed off slightly, allowing Craig to see the glimmer of fluorescent strips along the side . . .

Suddenly the cabin felt arctic. Craig could see his breath spiralling towards the windscreen, wondering if that had been happening the entire time.

Had the police car really done a loop at the previous junction in order to follow him, or was it a different one? It probably didn't matter – either way, he was being trailed by a patrol car. There was a row of blue and white lights across the top, bright strips along the side. The vehicle was making no effort to pull him over or to overtake, it was simply following.

Craig had three more junctions before he had to get off but figured it couldn't be too hard to find his way back to Salford away from the motorway. As the sign with three diagonal lines appeared at the side of the carriageway, Craig indicated left and started to slow. He continued watching his mirror, relieved to see the police car wasn't following his lead. It was slowing but not indicating. He took the exit, continuing to slow and expecting the police car to continue past him on the motorway.

It took the exit.

Uh-oh.

Even though the officer hadn't indicated, the car continued to follow, slotting in behind as Craig stopped at the traffic lights. His heart was thump-thump-*thumping* so strongly that, for a moment, Craig wondered if he might be having a heart attack. What were the signs? Something about tingles in the arm? Shortness of breath? He had both of those – although it was bloody cold. This was really bad.

The traffic light flicked to amber and Craig pulled away steadily, not wanting to do anything stupid. He followed the roundabout and then made a late decision, indicating and joining the slip road to get back onto the motorway, accelerating hard so that he was already at seventy by the time he reached the carriageway.

The police car slipped in behind, leaving Craig in no doubt that he was being followed. Should he call the number Haken had given him? Being on his phone while driving would only give the police an official reason to pull him over. The device felt weighty in his pocket, willing him to call, but Craig focused on the song lyrics, wanting to concentrate on anything except the nightmare unfolding around him.

'Jesus, oh Jesus, you're a part of me, like prosthesis . . .'

Craig continued driving around the ringroad, remaining in the inside lane doing sixty-five. He exited where he had originally planned, following the ramp until dropping onto the East Lancs Road, police car directly behind. He needed to stop to check the exact address, plus he wanted to see if he'd still be trailed, so Craig pulled off the main road onto a side street next to a pub, slowing as he weaved his way around parked cars towards a housing estate. As soon as he rounded a corner onto a street with a dim row of orange lights, the area was illuminated by a dazzling, spinning row of blue lights.

The police officer behind had finally made his move.

Craig had two choices: stop or run. Mark had always been the runner, Craig the stopper. Years later, he was no different, indicating and pulling over to the left side of the road. The car halted behind, blue lights now off as the door opened and a man emerged. He pressed a police cap onto his head, before turning and beginning the slow walk towards Craig's van.

17

Craig switched off the engine, silencing the radio as he continued to watch the mirror, wondering if the officer was walking slowly, or if it simply felt like it. His heart wasn't slackening, continuing to hammer away like a child with a xylophone. He touched his upper left arm, wondering if it was actually tingling. A heart attack could be a relief right now.

As the officer neared, Craig pinged the window down, forcing a smile. Because of the van's height, he was a few centimetres taller than the officer, though there wasn't much in it. The policeman was in a dark uniform, cap peaked so that it shielded the top half of his eyes. His features were hard to make out beyond that he was white, thin and athletic with dark hair. Craig doubted he could identify him in daylight.

'Hi,' Craig said.

'Who are you?' the officer asked.

'Craig Macklin, er, sir . . .'

'Licence.'

Craig fumbled into his wallet and took out his card before passing it through the window. The officer took it, holding it up to the light, before giving it back. Craig had never been stopped by the police before and didn't know what was normal but he did think the police usually asked for the vehicle documents too, possibly even insurance. He'd not even checked the licence details.

The officer was glaring at him. 'What's with the London address?'

Craig tried to make eye contact, wanting to seem like a normal guy, but it felt as if the guilt was etched across his face. He ended up peering just over the officer's shoulder towards the road beyond. 'London's where I was living until recently but I'm a Manc lad.'

'What are you doing up here?'

'Not much . . . visiting my parents.'

The officer's eyes ran along the length of the vehicle. 'What's with the van?'

'Nothing, I'm borrowing it.'

'Anything in the back?'

'I don't . . . I'm not sure.'

The officer nodded slowly, before rapping the metal with his fist. 'Let's have a look, shall we?'

If Craig's heart was going to pack it in, then now would be a *really* good time. Unfortunately, he was blessed/cursed by being generally healthy, so he clambered out of the cabin and followed the officer to the back of the van. He opened the doors and stepped back as the officer pointed towards the wooden crate.

'What's in there?'

'Just sort of . . . stuff.'

Appalling.

The officer was rightly unimpressed. *'Stuff?'*

'Yes . . .'

'Let's have a look.'

Craig heaved himself up the steps into the van and started to feel around the top of the crate. The lid was attached by a series of metal clasps around the edges, which he popped one at a time until the cover lifted upwards. Light filled the compartment as the officer shone his torch inside, flitting the beam towards the back corners, momentarily dazzling Craig, before settling it somewhere around his chest.

'That it?' the officer asked.

'Yes.'

The other man climbed inside and then flicked the crate's lid away, peering inside. Craig could see the pepper spray and truncheon on his belt, plus the radio clipped to his shoulder. If he was really quick, he might be able to grab the spray, shoot it into the officer's face and run for it . . . except that the man already knew his name – plus Craig didn't know how the pepper spray might work. Was there a trigger? Some sort of safety catch?

The officer placed the torch on the ground and leant into the crate, pulling out a handful of straw-thin paper strands. He dropped them on the floor and then delved deeper, emerging with . . . a soft doll. It had woollen dark hair and big shiny eyes, the type of thing young children would love to pull apart.

The officer reached back in, removing a second doll: 'All toys in here, is it?'

'I guess.'

Craig knew there was no way Haken would go to such trouble to import toys from Africa. The dolls were likely filled with more than soft fluff. He watched the officer pressing the middle of the doll, praying nothing squeezed out from the seams. Would it be jewels? Drugs?

Except it was worse.

The officer delved deeper into the crate, reaching to the bottom and rooting, before standing up straighter, eyes lighting up like an arcade machine.

'Well, well, well,' he said, giving it the full cliché. 'What do we have here?'

He peered up at Craig, one hand hovering over his pepper spray, the other holding his treasured find. The metal was heavy, dark and terrifying. Craig had never seen one anywhere other than on television but knew exactly what it was: a semi-automatic sub-machine gun.

18

The officer switched his grip so that he was holding the weapon in both hands. He peered along the sights, aiming it towards a frozen Craig and then dropping it back to his side. He nodded towards where the back compartment of the van met the front seats. 'Go and kneel over there.'

Craig glanced towards the gun, the pepper spray and the open doors, wondering if he could run for it. The officer was already ahead of him, stepping to the side and blocking the way. He was taller and almost certainly stronger than Craig, though assaulting an officer would only be a speck on a criminal record compared to transporting machine guns.

The officer seemed unafraid, squaring himself up, ready for a battle. '*Move.*'

Craig weighed him up once more, before retreating until his back was against the driver's seat. He slipped into a kneeling position, wondering if he could get the van keys out of his pocket, slide between the gap in the seats, and roar away all before the officer managed to stop him. It was unlikely.

The officer placed the machine gun on top of the crate and then reached in, pulling out two more weapons, lining them up on the metal floor of the van. He peered up at Craig: 'Hands behind your head.'

Craig did as he was told, wondering if he'd been set up.

Had Haken really been so offended by him wanting to pay off a debt that he'd arranged this? It seemed implausible. It would ruin Craig's life but what did Haken get from that? He wouldn't even get his money.

'Turn around.'

Craig shuffled until his back was to the officer. He felt the man creeping closer and then handcuffs snapped around both of his wrists. The cold metal made him shiver, as the officer twisted him around until they were face to face. It was all over now.

'How many more weapons do you have?' The officer was somewhere in his forties, grey flecks creeping into the edges of his otherwise dark hair. He sounded local but Craig was so stunned that it was hard to pay attention to much of what was occurring.

'I don't know.'

The officer stepped backwards, returning to the crate. He pulled out handfuls of dolls, before digging deeper and removing weapon after weapon, laying them out one by one in front of Craig. His knees were sore against the hard metal of the van, his back aching from continuing to kneel. The handcuffs weren't tight and he could rotate his wrists, though there was nowhere near enough room to slip his hands through.

When the officer reached the bottom of the crate, he picked up his torch and shone the light into Craig's eyes, dazzling him, before then flicking it away with a smile that Craig only caught the end of through a haze of pink and green stars.

The officer's voice sounded triumphant as he stooped to

peer down at Craig: 'I count eight sub-machine guns – Bulgarian Shipkas, unless I'm very much mistaken. Then there are twenty-three pistols and thirteen silencers.' He turned to point at the haul. 'Where are you taking everything?'

Craig thought of the Post-it note screwed into the bottom of his wallet. The man on the phone had told him to memorise it, not write it down, but his recall wasn't that great, plus he didn't know the area as well as he once had, especially by road.

He shook his head, knowing it was a silly place to start talking. *If* the time ever came to spill his guts, it would be on tape with a lawyer present.

'Not talking?' the officer added.

Craig remained silent.

'Where did they come from?'

Nothing.

'Whose van is this?'

Silence.

'Are the guns yours?'

Nope.

'Who do they belong to?'

Craig stared back at him, suddenly realising what he'd missed. 'Aren't you supposed to read me my rights?'

The officer glared back, before standing taller and returning to the crate. One by one, he returned the guns and then he placed the dolls and straw on top, followed by the lid.

He stepped back to Craig: 'Turn around.'

'Why?'

'Do it.'

They stared at one another for a few moments before

Craig shuffled around, knees grazing across the tough metal. He felt the officer move towards him and then a click before his wrists were freed. He rubbed at the skin underneath, not because it hurt but because it felt like he should. Everyone did it.

'What's going on?' Craig asked.

The officer was backing out of the van. 'Drive safely, Mr Macklin.'

'That's it?'

'I believe you have a meeting place to get to. Chop, chop. Best not be late.'

19

Craig closed the van doors and got back into the driver's seat, watching as the police car did a three-point turn and eased away. Haken's reach was beginning to become apparent: it had been a test to see how easily he caved. What would have happened if Craig had given Haken's name? Or revealed from where he'd picked up the weapons? Or where he was taking the crate? Plus, he was transporting guns. Guns! He'd gone from a dull but relatively well-paid job to trafficking weapons.

He tried to start the engine but Craig's hand was shaking so badly that he couldn't fit the key into the ignition. He stopped scratching and leant back, closing his eyes and taking a breath, wondering how much of this Haken had pre-planned. Probably everything – all because of his dad with his stupid big mouth.

The van finally grumbled to life and Craig rechecked the address of where he was supposed to deliver the crate. There was no sign of any traffic, let alone the police car, as he crept back onto the East Lancs Road and headed towards Salford. He turned right at a ramshackle pub, passed a small row of shops, and then took the third left into a courtyard flanked by a square of garages overlooked by the back of a terrace of houses. He switched off the headlights, leaving the engine ticking as he took out his phone, ready to call

Haken's number. Before he could press a button, there was the sound of grinding metal. Off to the side, one of the garage doors was creaking its way open, two men standing underneath. One of them waved a hand towards the van and this time Craig didn't make the mistake of going front-first, instead reversing towards the garage and then getting out. By the time he reached the back of the van, the men already had the back doors open, two of them climbing inside. Craig counted six shadows in total, each in black, not tall, but not short. Between them, they slid and then hefted the crate onto their shoulders pall-bearer style, an impressive feat of strength that left Craig wincing in awe.

In just a few minutes, the crate was inside the garage, thousands of pounds' worth of guns ready to terrorise the locals. Craig lived barely a mile away and this was his fault.

As the door started to close, one of the men stepped outside, holding out his hand.

'What?' Craig asked.

'Keys.'

'Oh . . .'

Craig delved into his pocket and handed over the fob for the van. He expected the man to say something else but he simply turned and ducked into the garage, leaving Craig alone in the courtyard. He peered up at the cloudy sky and delved his hands deep into his pockets, trying not to shiver, wondering if it was going to rain or snow. As days went, he'd had better.

Craig barely slept, the creaky pipes and ungodly snoring creeping into his restless dreams, leaving him disorientated.

The dodgy mattress was doing little for his back, either. As he shifted into a sitting position, he felt a stabbing pop just above his arse from where a spring had been jabbing him. For a while, he sat, staring into the darkness of the room, listening to the surrounding cacophony. A succession of yawns sent tears dribbling along his cheeks and his chin was rough from not having shaved in a couple of days.

People were going to be killed because of him and there was little he could do. Even the police were no longer an option, as he had no idea who he'd end up talking to. Haken might only have that one officer looking out for him, but that was enough. The fear of others being involved would stop Craig reporting anything. Who could he trust? His oldest friend, Mark – the wife-beater? His father, the drunk? His mother, who lived in her own reality?

He cared for his parents – they had brought him up, after all – but he knew he couldn't rely on them.

Then there was him, the weapons-trafficker.

Craig lay back on his bed, wriggling onto his side and wedging himself between two errant springs. He tugged the scratchy covers over his shoulders and closed his eyes, counting pipe-clangs instead of sheep.

It wasn't snoring that woke Craig the next time, it was something far, far worse. His mother was in the bathroom, singing at the top of her voice. She'd moved on from the Cliff Christmas medley and was belting out 'Last Christmas' by Wham!. Basic elements such as pitch and tune were utterly lost on her, not to mention the words. Somehow, she'd created a 'Last Christmas'/'Away in a Manger' mash-up, the lyrics to which were certainly inventive, albeit completely nonsens-ical. At least she wasn't trying to rhyme 'Jesus' with 'sneezes'.

Craig rolled out of bed, catching a spring in the side for good measure and then checking for damage. There was a series of small slices just under his ribs from almost a week of tossing and turning in this death trap of a bed.

He got dressed as quickly as he could, trying to ignore the off-key warbling, and then headed downstairs to the empty kitchen. Unsurprisingly, there was no sign of his father. There might have been a lock-in at the Legion and he'd not come home, or he'd got up early to head out for an early drink somewhere. Either that, or there was an early dog race card to be watched. It wasn't worth worrying about.

Craig looked through the contents of the fridge – an out-of-date yoghurt, a smidgeon of milk, margarine, some tomatoes, mouldy cheese, eggs, and not much else. The bread in the bin was some nutty-oaty-healthy stuff that was so hard Craig could have banged in nails with it. With few other options, he put three slices in the microwave, zapped it for twenty seconds, then stuck it in the toaster. As break-fasts went, it was up there with industrial-strength gruel.

Craig sat at the table to eat, using his phone to browse the Internet at a frustratingly slow speed. He'd barely been able to check the football fixtures when he heard his mum coming down the stairs. She'd moved on to Shakin' Stevens's 'Merry Christmas Everyone', except, in her version, there were a lot more 'la-la-la's. She breezed into the living room wearing a bright pink dressing gown that hadn't been tightened enough around the waist. Craig's gaze shot back to the plate, wishing he could un-see what he'd just witnessed.

'Morning, love . . . I didn't know if you'd be up.'

She slotted into the seat across the table from him, thankfully tying the gown tighter.

'I spoke to the people we owe money to,' Craig said.

'Oh . . .'

'The debt should be all sorted. No more men will come round.'

She nodded slowly and he wasn't sure she understood. 'Right . . .'

'Next time, please talk to me before you borrow anything.'

'Um . . .'

Craig realised he was talking to her like *she* was the child. He stretched his hand across and squeezed hers, managing a small smile. 'Okay?'

She nodded. 'Of course . . . I'll tell your father when he gets home . . . thank you.'

Craig started his final slice of toast, reluctant to admit that the bread wasn't so bad after all.

'Are you staying in today, love?'

Craig shook his head. 'I've got someone to see.'

Craig lay back, peering up at the initials underneath the railway bridge: *MG – CM – KK 4EVA*.

It had been barely two years after Mark had swung himself through the rafters like an orang-utan that Craig had left the city, making the 'forever' part of the message

141

irrelevant. Craig had left, Kimberly was now KG, a beaten one at that, and it was only 'MG' who was still going strong.

Craig checked his watch: five past two. Kimberly was late. She had told him that she'd try to meet him on her day off from the nail bar but that she couldn't make any promises. Craig didn't want to push and didn't want to call her out of the blue. If Mark was happy enough to lay his hands on her, he was almost certain to keep a close eye on who she called and texted.

Ten past two. She probably wasn't coming. Perhaps Mark was at home and she couldn't get away? Maybe he'd hurt her so badly that she couldn't leave the house? With his parents' debt gone, Craig wanted to leave the city once more. He could return to London, find a different area and start anew. He'd done it before and it was a big enough place that he'd likely never run into the people he once knew. If not that, somewhere else. Liverpool? Leeds? Or somewhere in the south west? Bristol? Anywhere but here. Moving would be easy enough – he'd grab his bag and do it that evening if it wasn't for one thing. One person.

Kimberly.

How could he leave her now, knowing what he did about Mark? He'd never be able to live with it if the call came one day to say that she'd had a tumble down the stairs, or endured any number of other horrors that Mark might inflict on her.

Quarter past two. Still no sign. She could be in intensive care at this very moment, beaten black and blue by Mark because she'd said the wrong thing, or looked at him the wrong way.

Craig steadily slipped his way down the slanted columns until he was on the cycle path underneath the railway bridge. He moved onto the pedestrian side and headed up the slope towards the housing estate that would lead back to his house. What should he do?

Before he knew it, Craig was at the main road. It was barely three o'clock but the light was already dimming. Had the days always been this short in the middle of winter? He couldn't remember. Most of the cars already had their headlights dipped, with a handful of streetlights starting to blink as they thought about turning themselves on. Craig started to walk, reasoning that, if nothing else, the endless traipsing was keeping him fit. Cold and frostbitten, too, but fit.

He was within sight of his parents' house when he spotted the dark people carrier parked across the road with its lights out, almost swallowed by the creeping shadow from a swaying tree. Craig stopped, turning in a circle, wondering what he should do. It didn't seem like he'd been followed, more that they were waiting for him. He could turn and walk away, perhaps even run onto a train or bus and not come back, but what then?

With a sigh, he crossed the road, walking until he was alongside the vehicle and tapping gently on the side. The driver's window hummed down, revealing a man in a suit, probably the person who'd snatched him days previously.

Nobody said anything but the rear door slid open, revealing a second man and an empty seat.

Craig peered between them: 'No hood?'

The window hummed into place, no reply forthcoming

as Craig stepped into the back of the carrier and sat. Given the lack of a blindfold and the fact he got a seatbelt, it was practically a warm welcome.

20

The driver and the other man in the people carrier spoke sparingly to one another in a language Craig didn't understand. For the most part, the journey to the centre of Manchester was direct, following the main roads and looping around Mancunian Way to the south, then cutting through the university area until they passed the Palace Hotel, before Craig lost where they were. The vehicle pulled up half on the pavement, engine idling as the man in the back with Craig slid open the door and climbed out. Craig followed and the vehicle quickly skimmed away towards the traffic lights. The icy breeze cut at Craig's exposed skin, a sharp contrast to the warmth of the people carrier. He turned, trying to get his bearings but the other man wasn't waiting, scuttling quickly towards an alleyway doused in darkness. Craig rushed to catch him, feeling suddenly nervous as the shadows ebbed across him. Behind and ahead were the lights of the city, plus shoppers and tourists, but for a few metres, he was hidden.

His unease was apparently misplaced, if only temporarily, as they emerged into a rash of bright neon lights. Manchester's Chinatown was in full party mode, perhaps not ready to celebrate Christmas itself but definitely looking to entice the seasonal crowds. In front of him and above, there was a large, bright Chinese arch, illuminated from below with green and red lights, with intricate golden letters painted across the top. The supporting red columns were immersed in thick white concrete, with impressive spiky carvings along the top. Off to the side was a small park, with a red-pillared pavilion in the centre. There were blinking lights everywhere: the takeaways, dry cleaning places and launderettes he expected, but there was even a bank and betting shop, each with Chinese letters underneath the regular signs.

The area was packed, with rows of street sellers lining up in front of the shops, selling steaming food and small crafts. Because of the crowds, the heat from the restaurants and the market stalls, it was significantly warmer than the main thoroughfares. Craig felt himself sweating underneath his hat and even thought about removing his gloves. There was also an excited low hum that only came when people knew they were *almost* set for a week off work, all topped off by a blend of meaty food smells mixed with what Craig thought was roasting chestnuts. If it wasn't for the fact he'd been brought here under questionable circumstances, he might even be enjoying himself.

There were so many people that the suited man couldn't hurry away. He edged in between the crowds, not bothering to check to see if Craig was behind. Craig followed, though slowed his pace enough that he could take everything in. If this was where Haken was based, the place where he'd been brought in a hood via a different entrance, then he wanted to remember the details. It might be useful one day.

The suited man eventually stopped outside a launderette, turning and waiting until Craig joined him. For a moment, he thought it was an elaborate way of picking up some newly clean washing but the man spun on his heels and headed into a narrow shop wedged between a pair of buffet restaurants. The only English word on the sign was 'apothecary' and, if it wasn't for the rack of dreamcatchers hanging above the door, the shop would have been completely missable among the neon.

The inside smelled of some sort of incense, the odour bitter and catching in the back of Craig's throat as he ducked under the low beam at the top of the door. There was a handful of spotlights but nothing bright enough to actually illuminate the shop properly. What he could see were walls covered with a wide variety of imported tat. There were more dreamcatchers, Chinese lanterns, dolls, dragons, brightly coloured rabbits, racks and racks of dangling lampshades, hats: all sorts of touristy tat that would no doubt be lapped up and then spend the rest of its life at the bottom of a landfill somewhere.

A girl much like the one from the pawn shop was behind the counter, headphone cables vanishing into her top. She glanced sideways at the man in the suit but said nothing as he passed around the side of the counter and headed through the door beyond. Craig followed, treading down a set of darkened steps into a basement corridor that stretched both in front and behind. There were no home comforts, just brick walls.

He wanted a few moments to gaze around, to try to figure out if the warren stretched underneath the street to the shops beyond. It looked like it but the suited man grabbed his sleeve and pulled him towards a door before he could pay too much attention. After a second quick glance, he was shunted into a dark room, the door slamming behind. Craig squeezed his eyes closed, opening them slowly and hoping to readjust. If the passageway was as long as he thought, it meant there must be at least one more entrance, perhaps even underneath the launderette. With the number of doors, it could be even larger, a second town within the town.

Craig gradually began to take in his surroundings. He was in some sort of basement, with low ceilings and four walls of ancient-looking brickwork. The floor was covered with a thin crimson carpet and there was a single lightbulb hanging by a grubby cord, held in place by a hook. At least half of the room was filled with large boxes, clothes spilling from the top. Craig was by himself but uttered an echoing 'hello' just in case.

No one answered.

He approached the first box and took out a red sweat top, designer label stitched into the collar. There were plenty more underneath, different sizes and colours, but with the same name on the label. The adjacent box was filled with bright white men's trainers all in boxes adorned with a different brand. Craig wasn't overly familiar with designers but it didn't take a genius to work out that it was most likely all fake. These were no doubt the type of goods that the police had raided from Willy Porter and his friends, tipped off by Haken in order to eliminate the competition.

Craig was holding onto a pair of size tens when the door clicked behind him. He turned to see Haken smiling, arms behind his back. 'You like, Mr Macklin?'

'I was only looking.'

'You can take what you want. There's plenty to go around.'

Craig put the shoes back into their box, closed the lid, and placed it carefully back into the larger box. 'I'm okay.'

'Suit yourself.'

'I don't understand why I'm here. You said the debt would be clear . . . ?'

Haken's smile remained in place but Craig knew he was screwed, one step behind again. The other man nodded towards the door, offering a brief 'come', before leading Craig into an adjacent room that was more like a cupboard. At one end, a laptop was connected to a pair of monitors, one of which was blank, the other showing the inside of the apothecary's shop above. A customer was browsing through the lanterns, taking one off the rack and asking a question to the girl behind the counter. With Craig and Haken inside, the room was a cosy fit. Haken had one hand on Craig's lower back, the other on the top of a leather office chair that looked completely out of place among the exposed bricks.

'Sit,' Haken said. Craig did as he was told, spinning to face the man, who continued, 'Debts are such complicated things, don't you think . . . ?'

'Not really, you owe something, you pay it off, then it's finished.'

The lightbulb above was dimmer than the one from the previous room, the orange flickering intermittently like a candle. Haken seemed to smile permanently without ever exuding anything close to humour. 'You might be correct but in paying off one debt, you are always in danger of accruing another.'

'I didn't borrow any money – I did as you asked.'

Haken nodded towards the laptop. 'Press the space-bar.'

Craig tapped it hard, watching as the second monitor came to life. It was the van he'd driven the previous night pulling into the square with the garages. Somehow, despite the darkness, the camera had captured a perfect image of him in the driver's seat. The footage lasted only a few seconds, with the van heading towards the camera and then twisting out of sight.

'What are you showing me?' Craig asked.

'That van was reported stolen in the early hours of the morning. I've had to pull some strings in order to keep this footage away from the authorities.'

'You gave me the van!'

'That may be the case but it nevertheless means you remain indebted.' Haken's fingers were pressed into a prism again, piercing eyes staring through Craig.

Craig pinched at the bridge of his nose, suddenly feeling tired. 'I did what you asked.'

'That you did.'

'Are you the person in charge? Who's that older man from the other room? Is he Pung-You?'

Haken's features were focused and still. 'You only need to know me.'

'What do you want?'

'I need someone of a certain expertise.'

Craig couldn't stop himself from sounding angry – he

was. He leant forward in the seat and jabbed a finger. 'To do what? I'm not some hard man who can go around intimidating people. I'm not a getaway driver, or someone else you might need. I'm just a normal bloke. I'm not your man.'

Haken didn't flinch, which was more worrying than his perma-smile. Most normal people would at least take a step backwards. He had the fearlessness of a person who knew he couldn't be touched. What if Craig really did attack him? What then? Race up the stairs, out through the shop into the streets of Chinatown? There would almost certainly be people waiting and, even if there weren't, they'd catch up with him sooner or later.

'I told you last week that we do our research,' Haken said.

'So what? There's nothing there. I've not lived here for thirteen years.'

'But you had a . . . colourful youth.'

'There's no way my dad told you that much.'

'Not this time; your transgressions are a matter of record if a person knows where to look.'

The penny was dropping: the police officer from the previous night would likely have access to all sorts. It was so many years back, half a lifetime ago. Could he *really* know about what had happened when he was seventeen, or was he talking about something else?

'I'm not your man,' Craig repeated.

'I've heard you're well acquainted with robberies.'

Craig almost breathed out with relief – Haken was talking

about the *other* thing. 'I was young, I'm not that kid any more.'

Haken's smile widened. 'I have a saying, you might have it too. Once a thief, always a thief.'

21

Mark led Craig and Kimberly along the back of the pizza shop and waited next to the overflowing metal bin. Cardboard containers littered the floor, with pieces of pizza crust and smears of red that were probably tomato sauce, though, given the area, could be blood too.

'I'm not sure about this,' Craig said, nudging Kimberly with his elbow and hoping for support. If she agreed with him, then she said nothing, not that Mark was listening anyway.

It felt like he'd been building up to this for weeks, like a pressure cooker simmering and shaking until it was ready to pop. They'd been keeping their heads down for a while, generally going to school when they were supposed to and cutting back on the illicit merchandise they sold. Some of it was down to Kimberly: her grades were so consistently good that she was reluctant to skip school because the absences would go against her, regardless of her actual work. Craig could feel the shift in himself, too. It wasn't that he enjoyed lessons any more than he had before, but people kept banging on about what they were going to do after school.

They were still children but at least once a week they were being told they had to decide on a career in order to

153

pick the correct path after their exams. For the first time, it was beginning to dawn on Craig that he'd need something – some*one* – other than Mark. It was far too late for his grades to be salvaged but he could at least turn up and do the bare minimum. If he was *really* lucky, he might actually learn something useful.

With Craig and Kimberly now less keen to skip school, Mark's conduct had become more and more erratic. He'd been suspended for five days after punching a lad two years older and nearly a foot taller than he was, almost as if he wanted a battering just to show how much he could take. As the bruises, scrapes and scratches around his arms and face became worse, so did his behaviour. During those five days, Kimberly and Craig had continued to attend school, which drove Mark wild. He waited outside each day for them to get out, a furious ball of energy, full of tall tales about what he'd got up to during the day. Every story was largely the same: a group of adults or older kids had picked on him and he'd kicked their arses. Either that, or he'd terrorised a shop-owner somewhere and then run for it before the police arrived. Craig believed none of it, suspecting that Mark spent every day either trawling the streets, or lying on the column underneath the railway bridge.

The isolation of those five days was what had spiked his descent. After the suspension, Mark continued to miss school, and was now full of ideas for what to do in the evenings. Much of it was fantasy – car-jacking someone at a set of traffic lights; burning something down, invariably the school; attacking one of the vans that delivered cash to ATMs. None of these would ever happen, they were an extension of Mark's tall tales, but with every idea that Craig and Kimberly shot down, he became more and more worked up.

And still he continued to show up with more marks on his face.

The fact they were at the back of the shop now was more to appease Mark than anything else, a concession to them still being friends. It was dark, after ten, and Craig's parents, well his mum, would be wondering where he was.

Mark continued past the doorway at the back of the pizza shop and kept going until he was in front of a grubby double-glazed door. He looked at them excitedly, voice lowered but wavering with anticipation.

'Well?' he said.

Craig shrugged 'Well what?'

Mark pulled down his cap, then raised the hood of his top and tightened it under his chin. 'It's old man Hannon's shop on the other side of there. He caught me nicking Twixes the other week and said he'd call the police. I'll show him.'

'What are you going to do?'

Mark's eyes rippled with danger. 'What d'you think?'

Craig wanted to argue but didn't have time. Before he knew it, Mark was shimmying up the drainpipe, legs clamped tightly in a way that made Craig think he'd tried this by himself in the past.

High above the door was a narrow window, opened just a fraction. Mark moved with the fluidity of a gymnast, clinging onto the pipe with his legs and stretching through the gap in the frame. With a low grunt, he swung across the wall, clinging onto the window ledge and even finding time to grin down at them.

'Be careful,' Kimberly whispered loudly.

Mark's smile said it all: he was having the time of his life. With one hand clinging onto the windowsill, he showed ridiculous strength to support his weight, reaching through to unlatch the window with his free hand. After another grunt and heave, he pulled himself up, squeezing through the window headfirst and then disappearing.

Kimberly gripped Craig's hand and squeezed. 'I don't think I could've managed that.'

'What are we doing here?'

She shrugged. 'Having fun.'

Craig stared at her. 'It's only fun if we don't get caught.'

'So don't get caught.'

She wouldn't meet his gaze, staring at the door, and leaving him to wonder what she was thinking. She'd been doing well at school, but did she have the same reckless streak as Mark?

As he got older, Craig was beginning to think that he no longer did, if he ever had. He was starting to see the consequences of their actions, the people they hurt, the things they couldn't take back. He knew that he was here through fear of loneliness – without Mark and Kimberly, he had nobody.

There was a click and the door popped open, revealing a grinning Mark, arms wide. 'Ta-da!' He waved the pair of them inside and closed the door behind, removing two torches from his combat trouser pockets and handing one to Craig, clicking on the other himself.

'We don't want to turn the lights on,' he said, stating the obvious.

They were in some sort of store room, their beams of light dancing across the surface of various boxes, mainly containing crisps and chocolate. There were stacks of bundled-up newspapers and magazines, plus crammed black bin bags tied at the top. Mark had definitely been here before, weaving through the items without bothering to peer around, heading through a door into a short corridor and then what turned out to be the main area of the shop. Kimberly followed, with Craig at the back, wondering how much of this Mark had planned. If he had been here by himself on a previous evening and plotted it out, then he was smarter than Craig had ever given him credit for.

There were shutters at the front of the shop, the bluey-white light from the street seeping through the minuscule gaps in the metal, casting an eerie dotted grid of light across the floor. The store was a combination of an old-fashioned sweetshop and a newsagent. Behind the counter were racks of plastic tubs full of goodies, with rows of chocolate bars on the other side of the till. On the other wall were stacks of magazines, with an empty space across the bottom for the following day's newspapers.

Over the years, Craig and Mark had stolen all sorts of things but they'd usually been from larger stores, rarely from somewhere this small and definitely not by breaking and entering. It was mainly pocketing the odd item, or creating a diversion. This was a huge step up from that. Craig had been battling his conscience more and more recently and he knew he should leave and persuade Kimberly to come with him, if not Mark too. Already it was too late.

At the sound of an enormous crash, Craig spun, catching his knee on the corner of the counter and wincing with pain. Mark had taken the till from the desk and hurled it to the floor. It made a large metallic clang but didn't open. Mark picked it up, disappointed and unaware Craig had hurt himself. Before anyone could protest, Mark reeled back and threw the till into the wall of sweet tubs, sending a cascade of containers tumbling down on top of him. Mark emerged from underneath, hood now down, beaming and rubbing his head.

'Glancing blow.' He winked.

'Someone's going to hear,' Craig said.

Mark ignored him, bending over and picking up the till again. This time, it was open. He wrenched open the drawer but came out empty-handed.

'Anything?' Kimberly asked.

'Nothing. They must've cleared out the money before shutting up. I didn't think of that.'

Craig pointed a thumb towards the corridor. 'Shall we go?'

Kimberly took a step towards the exit but Mark still wasn't listening, leaning over the counter and thrusting handfuls of chocolate bars into his pockets. He pointed towards the magazine rack. 'Grab what you can.'

Mark pulled out a carrier bag from his back pocket and began emptying the rack of chocolate into it, as Kimberly shoved a dozen magazines into her waistband. Mark was shrieking and skipping, jumping up and down on the spot, as if possessed. When his bag was full, he started pulling over the spinning racks of crossword books and then elbowed a glass display case – anything to make a mess.

Craig grabbed a handful of magazines, desperately wanting to get away. He hissed Mark's name but got no response, so ended up tugging back his friend by the shoulder. Mark spun, teeth bared. 'What?'

'We've gotta go, you're making loads of noise.'

'Good.'

Craig and Kimberly exchanged a worried look as they waited by the door to the corridor but Mark couldn't be persuaded, kicking the glass at the front of the case until it shattered, then reaching in to sweep boxes of football cards and stickers into his bag.

'Mark!' This time it was Kimberly whispering his name.

'What?'

'Let's go.'

'Just a minute.'

Mark aimed a swipe at a postcard display and then hurled a sandwich board at the back wall, sending the shelving toppling to the floor with a loud echoing crash.

'Hee hee!'

Mark was giggling as he tore past them, heading to the back door, hefting his carrier bag with both hands. The alley at the back of the shops was mercifully empty and quiet as they emerged. Mark stopped just outside the door, Kimberly sandwiched between him and Craig, who was still inside. Mark peered both ways and then dropped his bag, patting at his head.

'What?' Kimberly said.

'My hat.' He checked his pockets, then the top of the carrier bag, before turning back to Craig. 'Go back and get it – we'll meet you by the bridge.'

Craig had no chance to argue because Mark grabbed the bag and set off, hurtling in the opposite direction from which they'd entered. Kimberly had time to offer a quick shrug before she followed, scampering along the path in pursuit. Craig's knee was still throbbing from where he'd hit it on the counter. He wanted to run too – this hadn't even been his idea – but he never said no to Mark.

He turned and headed back into the carnage of the shop's main area. Sweets crunched under his feet, splintering among the glass from where Mark had kicked the cabinet. Craig hunted through the plastic containers, finally finding Mark's cap at the bottom of a pile when he froze. Blue spinning lights rampaged through the gaps in the shutters, which meant only one thing.

Craig jammed the cap on his head and ran for the corridor. He'd managed a few steps when he skidded on something underfoot, succeeding only in crashing into the doorframe headfirst. He groaned, rubbing his temples and trying to clear the stars. Shite, shite, shite. He had to go. Craig hobbled to the back door, knee struggling to support his weight as he hurdled a toppled box of Quavers. He slid into the alley just in time to see the shadow of a police officer at one end.

'Oi! Stop!'

Craig did anything but, dashing in the opposite direction and trying to ignore the pain in his knee, running for all he was worth. If he could get to the main road, it was a short distance to the cut-through that would take him onto the maze of the housing estate. They'd never catch him there. All he needed was a bit of luck.

Luck that never came.

Craig slipped around the corner only to bound straight into the waiting arms of two more police officers. Before he knew what was happening, he was face down on the concrete, a knee in his back as a police officer shouted 'got you' into his ear.

22

NOW

Haken said they could arrange to drive him home but Craig had seen enough of the inside of the people carrier for one day. Besides, he was still trying to kid himself that this was going to be the final job he did for him; that he wasn't Haken's plaything in the same way he had once been Mark's. Haken assured him there was only one more task but there would surely be one more after that, and then another. He could be doing 'one more job' for years.

Craig emerged onto the streets of Chinatown where, if anything, there were even more people. It was four o'clock on a weekday but the street was so packed that the crowds were barely moving, just about managing to shuffle in unison. Craig headed down the steps from the apothecary's shop and joined the sea of people, lumbering with the masses until he was spat out at a crossroads where the crowd split and headed in different directions. Craig wasn't entirely sure where he was, but walked towards the area that looked the emptiest, cutting across the small Chinese garden and around the pagoda until he emerged into a car park.

A few hours previously, he'd been contemplating leaving Kimberly behind and finding somewhere else to make a new life; now he couldn't even do that because at least one police officer was in Haken's pocket. Someone who'd be able to follow trails of phone bills and cash machine withdrawals. Like it or not, at least for now, he was stuck doing whatever it was Haken wanted him to.

Once again, Craig started to walk, soon finding himself away from the city centre and on his way back to Salford. It was around three miles to his house but, after he crossed the River Irwell, Craig began to zigzag through streets he didn't know, desperate to find something, anything . . . a way out. Before he knew it, he was on the High Street close to his house, walking past the Wetherspoons where he'd spent the morning waiting for the pawn shop to open. It was almost five o'clock and already freezing, the Christmas decorations looking sorrier by the day. The tree had slumped so far to the side that it looked like a drunken fat bloke who'd lost a fight with a glitter machine, leaning against a wall trying to catch his breath. Craig continued up the street, thinking about popping into the Grey Goose for a pint or two that would help him build up some courage before doing what Haken wanted. That was until he remembered that Rodger told him the Chinese were running the pub. That meant Haken and co. It was one thing to be in the man's debt, another entirely to throw even more money at him.

Craig spun on his heels and headed in the opposite direction. The Old Boot was the pub he and Mark used to go to if the staff behind the bar in the Goose were asking for ID. It was at the opposite end of the High Street, but had completely changed from his day. It was now called the Rampaging Frog, with poster after poster advertising 'live music', which almost certainly consisted of some god-awful band doing covers of Oasis and Stone Roses songs. Craig's suspicion was confirmed by the sandwich board outside proclaiming that night's act: 'The Happy Sundays'.

His first thought was 'sod that', but given the choice of this, the soulless Wetherspoons, or Haken's Grey Goose, it seemed the lesser of three evils. Craig was about to head inside when he was passed by a gaggle of marauding women either on a hen night or Christmas party. They were all dressed as Santa, bellies and terrifyingly large breasts pouring out of the material that he *really* hoped hadn't been stitched by the same people who made those fake designer clothes. There were some sights he didn't need to see.

The group were holding hands, murdering 'Jingle Bell Rock', only they were singing about something that rhymed with 'rock'. The combined gust of perfume took his breath away, while the shouted cry of 'Jägerbombs!' from the front didn't fill Craig with any sense that he might be able to get down a quiet pint. If that wasn't enough, the woman at the back broke free from her friends to grab his arse and ask if he had a 'Santa sack that needed emptying'.

Delightful.

He mumbled something that was probably, 'I'm all right', even though he meant, 'There's not enough alcohol in the world'.

She waggled her little finger at him, uttered 'fair enough', and then disappeared inside, jiggling her ample arse in his direction. For the merest fraction of a second it crossed Craig's mind that he was on something of a dry spell. As quickly as the thought had arrived, he sent it packing with a metaphorical boot up the arse.

Turning once again, he headed back up the High Street. He was about to pass an alleyway that ran between two shops when he heard a low moan flitting from underneath an arch shrouded by darkness. He knew he should keep walking but there was something so guttural in the sound that Craig was unable to ignore it. He ducked his head inside, barely able to see anything. The only streetlights were further up the path.

'Hello?' he called.

'Ugh.'

'You all right, mate?'

The shape of a man was curled into the corner, using the roof of the arch for cover from the elements, though exposed to the cold because of his lack of a proper coat. He was withered, a bundle of bones wrapped in thin, patchy clothing. He was illuminated by the glow of twinkling red and green bulbs from the tree on the High Street, looking the least festive as it was possible to be.

'Got any change?' the man mumbled.

Craig patted his pockets, knowing there were notes in there, though he didn't have to lie. 'Sorry, mate.'

'Anyfing else?'

'Like what?'

'Y'know . . . ice. I'll pay you back.'

Craig backed away, momentarily confused. He wasn't up with street slang, let alone drug terms.

'Sorry, pal.'

Craig didn't hesitate this time as he headed into the

Wetherspoons. Moments later, he was back in his window seat, frothy pint of ale in front of him, not even two pounds lighter, wondering why he hadn't come here in the first place.

He drank deeply, wondering what the sweet spot would be for staying sober enough for the evening's activities, while giving himself enough oomph to actually get on with it. Within seconds, he'd downed half a pint, feeling an instant rush.

Good.

Shutters were beginning to close as the street gradually emptied of shoppers. Craig was watching a woman lock up the coffee shop next to Tiger Pawn when he noticed a familiar shape heading past. Mark had his hands in his pockets, head down, but he was shuffling in the way only he did. Craig moved closer to the window, observing Mark hurry past the coffee place, the pawn shop and a bookie's, before heading through a door and disappearing. Craig held a hand over his eyes, pressing against the glass and squinting to see if there was a sign. As far as he could tell, it was unmarked, an anonymous door between a betting shop and CosmopoliTan. He supped another mouthful, thinking, trying to move the murky cloud from his mind. It came to him in a flash.

'. . . *they came out of nowhere but they also run the knocking shop over that tanning place on the High Street . . .*'

Rodger had listed the places he knew of that were run by the Chinese.

Craig downed the rest of the pint in one, checking his watch and then continuing to keep an eye on the door between the two shops. A couple of moments later, someone emerged, bursting through the door and not looking back as he disappeared up the street towards the Grey Goose. It wasn't Mark – but it was a man by himself.

He gave it five more minutes before curiosity got the better of him. Craig left the pub and crossed the street, pushing through the unmarked door and finding himself in a clammy dark hallway with a set of steps at the end. The walls were bare of paint or paper, with yellowy plaster chipped onto the floor. Somebody had felt-tipped a very naughty word onto one wall, with the other sporting what could only be described as a biologically detailed drawing of male and female genitalia meeting in a way that could only happen with the aid of a zero-gravity machine. He stared at it for a moment, wondering if he was looking at it upside down, before remembering what he was supposed to be doing.

Craig headed up the stairs, struggling slightly because of the lack of banister. At the top was another unmarked door, with spiky scratches carved into the dirty white panels. He checked behind him, took a breath and then pushed his way inside.

The first thing he saw was red. Lots of red. The walls were washed with dark crimson, with a ruby carpet underfoot. An empty claret velvet bench ran along the right-hand wall, with a cherry-wood desk behind the door. A woman was behind the counter, wearing a skimpy bikini top, long blonde hair curving around her shoulders.

Knocking shop, indeed.

'How can I help you, sweetie?'

She was far more attractive than Craig would have expected, somewhere in her twenties, slim yet curvy. He suddenly felt very self-conscious, shuffling awkwardly on the spot, keeping one hand on the door.

'I was just . . .'

'We have showers if you'd like to freshen up . . . ?'

Craig couldn't look her in the eye, mumbling something about being in the wrong place and rushing back to the stairs again. He was in such a hurry that he nearly crashed into someone on the steps. He caught an elbow in the side for his trouble as a lad in a black cap raced past, head down. A splash-speckled BMX had been abandoned in the hallway, which seemed a curious way for a client to visit a brothel.

Each to their own . . .

Behind him, Craig heard the bikini-clad woman snapping a stern, 'you're late', but didn't fancy hanging around to see what the bike rider had been tardy over.

Back on the street, a different set of party-goers were waltzing along the centre. This group was at least mixed in terms of gender, though they were far more smashed. A man was triumphantly waving a traffic cone in the air, while one of the women had broken off to empty her stomach into the already overflowing bin outside the pound shop.

Craig walked in a large circle to avoid them before re-entering the Wetherspoons. He didn't bother going to the bar, instead retaking his still-empty seat in the window and watching across the street. The first person to emerge from the brothel wasn't Mark, it was the lad with the black cap.

As Craig squinted, he realised it was a Far Eastern-looking teenager, perhaps sixteen or seventeen.

One of Haken's men?

He fiddled with a dark backpack, fixing it onto his shoulders, and then wheeled his bike along a few stores. The Tiger Pawn shutters were half-closed but the teenager crouched underneath, squeezing his bike through the door and disappearing inside. Nothing happened for a minute or two before he reappeared with his bike, once again zipping his backpack closed. He tightened it on his shoulders, clambered onto the BMX and then took out a mobile phone, riding up the street towards the Grey Goose, using one hand to talk on the phone, the other to steer.

No sooner had he disappeared than Mark emerged from the brothel's doorway. He checked both ways, shoved his hands in his pockets and then walked quickly in the direction of the Rampaging Frog.

Not only did he beat up his wife, he shagged prostitutes behind her back. What a lovely friend he was.

23

Less than twenty-four hours had passed and Craig was back at the garages where he'd dropped off the weapons the previous night. A different van was parked in front, this one plain white and recently cleaned. Three men were waiting at the back, whispering in a foreign language until going silent when Craig arrived. Without another word, one of them opened the garage and they headed inside, Craig following.

There was no sign of the weapons crate, though the inside walls were lined with boxes similar to the ones Craig had seen underneath the apothecary's shop. The door creaked back into place, leaving only a flickering dim bulb above to provide light. One of the men eyed Craig top to bottom and then delved into a box, thrusting a set of clothes towards him. Craig took them, standing still as the man continued to eye him.

'You want me to put these on?' he asked.

The man said nothing, steady gaze unmoving. He was the person who'd been driving the people carrier earlier in the day, most likely one of the men who'd abducted him from the street. In fact, these were probably all three of the men. After spending the day being stood up by Kimberly, picked up by Haken, and then following his so-called friend into a brothel, Craig wasn't in the mood.

'Do you speak English?' he snapped.

The man turned sideways and said something in another language to the person next to him, who replied with a smirk.

'What?' Craig asked. 'I'm not doing anything unless you tell me. I don't respond to stares. I don't even know your name.'

In a flash, the man lunged across the garage, shoving Craig into the wall, forearm pressed against his throat. He pushed hard enough to make it hurt but gently enough not to do any lasting damage. They were eye to eye, Craig starting to panic as he realised how strong the man was. He was trying to fight, to shove back, but his opponent was like a wall.

'Do you respond to this?'

The man's English was perfect.

Craig tried to reply but couldn't, his attempted 'I—' getting lost somewhere between his throat and mouth.

The man shoved him backwards and stepped away: 'I'm Davey, now get dressed.'

'Where do I leave my actual clothes?'

A hand flashed towards the floor. 'Wherever you want.'

Craig kicked off his shoes, shivering from the lack of heating, and then unclipped his jeans. He unfolded the pile of clothes and put on the plain dark trousers. They were a little loose, but that was better than being too tight – and there was a belt. He transferred his phone, keys and wallet into the new pockets. There were no extra shoes, so he put his black trainers back on and then removed his coat and top. The shirt was plain, white and not very thick, leaving him trying not to shiver. The other men were in similar states of undress, showing off toned abs and solid arms. Any of them could definitely kick his arse.

Craig nodded towards the one who'd threatened him. 'Is there anything else to wear?'

The man pointed towards a second box. It was only when Craig dug inside that he realised what he was wearing. He pulled out a thick, padded dark vest, with the word 'POLICE' written in white across the back. Caps were piled on top of each other, too. There was none of the fanciness – no radio, no handcuffs, spray or truncheon – but, at least from a distance, it would look authentic. Even from close up, if a person didn't know what to look for, it'd be easy to get taken in.

The other men raided the box, picking out vests and caps until they were ready. Only Craig remained, holding the vest in his hand, still trying not to shiver.

Davey closed the flaps on the box, not looking up. 'Problem?'

'I was wondering what we're doing.'

'We're getting in the van.'

Benches ran along either side in the rear of the vehicle, with Craig belted in on one side, another of the men opposite. Davey was driving, with the fourth man in the passenger seat. Craig was afraid of making eye contact with the person across from him in case he annoyed him, so he closed his eyes and tried to focus on not being sick as the van bumped up and down across the city's potholes.

He was building up quite a sheet for himself: Monday

night, weapons-trafficking; Tuesday night, impersonating a police officer. If he pirated a few movies, he'd be Britain's most wanted man.

They drove for around twenty-five minutes and Craig opened his eyes to see only darkness through the windscreen. Davey and the others moved in unison, clambering out of the van, with Craig following. They were in a car park in the shadow of a tower block that he didn't immediately recognise. Aside from the building itself, there wasn't much to identify the area. Towers like this were prevalent locally – they could be a short distance down the road in Salford, far south of Manchester in somewhere like Stockport, off to the east in Oldham or anywhere in between. That's if they were in Manchester at all. They'd been travelling for long enough to be in the heart of the city, or pretty much anywhere in the immediate vicinity of the M60 ringroad. They could be in the wilderness of Lancashire, Merseyside, or the wider county of Greater Manchester. He didn't know enough about the area to say for sure.

The other three massed at the back of the van and hauled out a thick metal battering ram that could mean only trouble. They were chattering in another language again, and Craig was certain he caught the name 'Pung-You' muttered between them. Either that, or he was hearing things, which wasn't beyond the realms of possibility. There was every chance he was hearing what he wanted, creating conspiracies where there was only despair of his own making.

Craig followed the trio through the main doors at the front of the tower block to be met by dreary whitewashed walls and the unmistakeable smell of piss. Filled black bin bags lined one wall, with a series of metal mailboxes on the wall, each with its own lock. A note was stuck to the front of one, thick capital letters readable from the other side of the hall – 'Bring my parcels upstairs, you lazy prick' – which was always a good way to get the postman on side.

There was no sign to say the lift was out of order but Davey didn't worry about it anyway, heading straight for the stairs. The other two carried the battering ram, with Craig trailing behind, growing out of breath ridiculously quickly as they continued pounding up the steep concrete stairs. They went up fifteen flights – five floors – before they finally halted. Davey was waiting at the top grinning at Craig with the look of a man who'd just run a four-minute mile, nipped for a wee, downed a pint, and then strolled back to the line in time to see the stragglers finish.

'Are you ready?' Davey asked.

'For what?'

'For this.'

'I don't know what *this* is.'

Davey nodded, turning to the door on which was a giant '5', and going through. Craig brought up the rear as they emerged onto a smooth concrete-floored corridor, every step echoing like a muffled gunshot. It certainly wasn't a place to creep around. There were eight or nine flats on either side but Davey knew exactly where he was going, heading to a scratched blue door. There was no knock, no warning. The other pair heaved back the battering ram and *booooooomed* through the door, sending splinters of wood shattering inwards. They poured inside, Davey just behind the first two, with Craig, as usual, at the back. He had no idea what he was doing, no idea why they were there.

'What do I do?'

Craig sounded far more panicked than he meant to, the adrenaline of the smash and rush kicking in.

Davey turned and winked: 'Don't let anyone past.'

The hallway was covered in a flowery blue carpet riddled with cigarette burns and the smell of vomit. Paper was peeling from the walls, which were lined by empty junk-food wrappers and fag packets. A man's voice was shouting from a nearby room but his words were muffled and then silenced by a splat. Davey strolled through the door on the left, perfectly calm. Somewhere, a door slammed, then there was another man's shout, followed by galloping feet. Craig peered up just in time to see a runt of a man racing at him. He was emaciated and narrow-faced, legs so thin it looked like they might snap. That didn't stop his fearlessness as he dipped his head, roared and charged. Craig glanced sideways but Davey was nowhere in sight.

Whump!

He acted on instinct, reeling back and crunching a fist flush into the jaw of the charging man. Craig couldn't remember the last time he'd punched someone; he didn't think he'd ever done it as an adult. The man was so slender that his entire body rocked to the side, neck cracking as his head bounced off the wall and he slumped to the floor, Hollywood-style. If it were the movies, Craig would have pumped himself up like a heavyweight boxer – one-punch knockout, look at me. Instead, he felt awful, crouching to make sure the other man was still breathing. There was a

175

trickle of blood from his nose, another from a cut across his lips, but he was at least alive. Thankfully.

Davey poked his head around the door, glancing from Craig to the unconscious man and back again. He nodded, impressed, which did nothing for Craig's guilt.

'Get him in here,' Davey said. 'And shut the front door.'

Craig started with the door, the entire right half of which had been smashed through. He stepped over the battering ram and then pushed it closed as best he could, feeling nosy eyes upon him from the flats beyond and realising why they'd arrived in police uniforms. It wasn't to fool the occupants of the flat – they were going to bust in regardless – it was in case anyone spotted them crashing through. Nobody would bother to phone the police because, from what they could see, the police were already there.

He returned to the unconscious man, whispered an apology and then picked up one of his legs and dragged him into what turned out to be the living room, which was even filthier than the hallway. The smell was so bad that Craig found it hard not to gag. There was a small television with a games console on the floor, plus a single armchair, but little else in terms of furniture. Instead, there were mounds of rubbish, most of which appeared to come from takeaways. There were upturned curry containers, the stinking yellow and brown contents mashed and dried into the carpet. Pizza boxes were piled randomly, coated with slimy, greasy kebab wrappers that had leaked blobs of mayonnaise and shreds of lettuce and tomato onto the ground. Crushed lager cans were stacked in glittering prisms, surrounded by empty two-litre Coke and Sprite bottles. Grimy cardboard tubs of half-eaten noodles had been hurled against the walls, the contents dribbling and crusting against the plaster. Not only was it rancid, the room was freezing. A window had been left open, allowing the chilled winter air to creep into every corner, though it was doing little to dissipate the smell.

Craig had never seen anything like it.

Three men were kneeling, facing the wall, their hands behind their heads. Just in case there wasn't enough rubbish around, the floor was a minefield of loose batteries, ready for people to trip on. Craig lowered the unconscious man onto the carpet behind the others.

The other two raiders stepped away, each holding silenced pistols that Craig hadn't seen them bring in. He followed their lead as Davey moved forward and tapped one of the kneeling men on the shoulder. The man shuffled in a semicircle, turning to reveal a flattened, blood-spattered nose that was almost certainly broken. He was white and in his twenties with short dark hair, barely bigger than the man Craig had punched. Davey hunched slightly, poking a finger into the man's forehead and making him rock back and forth.

'Look at me,' Davey said.

'I am.'

His voice was muffled, his nose preventing him from speaking properly.

'Do you know who I am?'

'No.'

'But you know who I work for?'

The man's eyes narrowed, sending a trickle of blood cascading from above his brow. 'Yes.'

'So where is it?'

'Not here.'

Davey prodded him in the forehead again, harder this time. 'We'll find it anyway, so tell me where it is.'

'It's not here.'

Davey lifted his top and pulled a silenced pistol out from his waistband, almost certainly one of the weapons Craig had helped smuggle in. The other two levelled their weapons, too, leaving Craig as the only one of the raiders without a gun. Not that he wanted one. They must have shared them out in the garage when he wasn't looking. Davey pressed the lengthy barrel to the kneeling man's head, rocking him back onto his heels. 'I'm not going to ask again.'

The room felt even colder than before as the two men stared at one another, gun between them, neither speaking. Craig felt his body tense, not wanting to be here and definitely not wanting to see anyone get shot.

Davey caved first, taking a half-step backwards and removing the gun from the other man's forehead. He turned towards Craig and the others: 'Go and look for it.'

'For what?' Craig asked.

'You'll know.'

The three of them left the living room and headed through separate doors. Craig found himself in a bedroom next to the front door, where the smell was so close to overpowering that he could taste it scratching the back of his throat. There was no window, no vent or fan, nothing to help it disperse.

He turned on the light to be met by yet more mounds of rubbish. It was like someone had fly-tipped the contents of every bin in the block into this one flat. A double bed was in the centre of the room with a stained, untucked duvet tossed across it. Craig didn't know what they were looking for but assumed it was drugs, money or weapons. Possibly all three. The fetid stench increased as he approached the bed and crouched to peer underneath. Using one hand to hold his nose, he lifted the overhanging cover, revealing a dozen green first-aid kits, all opened. There were a couple of sliced, flattened ice packs, and a pair of scissors. Craig doubted any of that was what Davey was after.

He stood, coughing back a gag reflex as his eyes started to water. The reason became clear as soon as he flicked away the duvet from the bed. The sheets were smeared with excrement that had been left to rot.

Craig retched, barely keeping down the contents of his stomach before dashing back to the empty hallway and closing the bedroom door. He waited by the front door, taking gasps of clean air in an attempt to settle himself. He'd been in hairy situations before, but had never sunk to the lowest level of humanity. He wanted to open the door, race down the stairs and not look back but this wasn't just about him. Haken knew where he lived, knew who his parents were.

There was a crash from one of the other rooms and then a shout of what sounded like 'Shirley'. Craig followed the sound into a bathroom, where another of the fake officers was delving into the water tank above a toilet. He emerged with three sealed freezer bags, each filled with what looked like frozen ice crystals.

'Y'know . . . the ice. I'll pay you back.'

The shapes were a cloudy silvery white, like snow in a bag, and almost certainly the 'ice' that the bundle of bones on the High Street had been asking for.

Moments later, the other raider appeared. He took one look at the bags and then set about yanking the panels away from around the edge of the bath. The plywood snapped easily, revealing the pipework, plus another twenty or so sealed freezer bags.

Craig had never seen the drug before but he knew what it was – methamphetamine, or crystal meth as it was better known. He didn't know the procedure but had read that it could be created with a concoction of household products. The men in the flat must have been making their own, which partly explained the smell.

The fake officers removed carrier bags from their pockets and started to load the freezer bags inside, packing them tightly until everything was taken. Craig was handed one and then the three of them returned to the living room where Davey was nodding appreciatively. He muttered something that wasn't in English, then turned back to the three men on their knees. They were all facing the wall, hands on their heads. Davey withdrew his pistol but, instead of shooting, he used the weapon as a club, hammering down across the backs of their heads one by one. None of them bothered to fight, each taking the blow and slumping to the floor. It was better than being shot, which was probably what they'd expected when the front door had been hammered through.

Davey and his men slipped the weapons back into their waistbands and then took a carrier bag of meth each, leaving Craig empty-handed. He followed them out of the flat onto the empty, echoing corridor and then to the lift. Davey pressed the 'down' button and they waited. None of them spoke. Craig assumed they'd achieved what they set out to, though he still wasn't certain what had happened. Had they stolen the drugs to sell on, or was there something deeper going on?

The men in the flat didn't seem to be big-time dealers, just a bunch of drug-addled young people making their own stuff and most likely smoking as much as they sold. In the back of his mind, he could hear Haken telling him this was the last thing he had to do and then they were even. He'd not even done much, simply shown up and managed not to be sick. His head told him there would always be something else Haken held over him but, after everything he'd done in the past two evenings, he was left clinging to the desperate hope that he really might be out.

The lift pinged, metal doors sliding open slowly. Craig waited for Davey to head in first but the other three men were looking at him. Reluctantly, he stepped past them into the elevator. His foot had only just landed on the metal floor when he sensed a flash of movement. He turned just in time to see the butt of Davey's pistol flashing towards his head, connecting with a painful fleshy splat.

24

Craig's head was spinning as he staggered backwards into the lift car. He could see bright yellow shapes and the vague silhouette of Davey stepping away. Craig put his hands up, thinking for a moment that he was going to be shot, and then growing confused as the doors clinked closed. His knees buckled as the cables above creaked and moaned, slowly starting to send him downwards.

What was going on?

He put a hand to the side of his head, feeling blood matting into his hair and wincing. Davey had probably meant to hit him harder, perhaps even knock him unconscious, but Craig had turned in time to make it a glancing blow.

Ping!

The doors didn't open at floor four and the slow descent continued, the elevator cables whining in protest. But the lift was travelling faster than Davey and his men could get down the stairs, so Craig would be at the bottom first.

What then?

Were they going to chase him? Would there be more people waiting there? He still didn't know whether he was in Manchester or somewhere outside, plus he was wearing a police officer's uniform. The thoughts continued to swarm but only succeeded in confusing him further.

Craig expected to hear another ping as he reached floor

three, but instead there was a loud screech, metal grinding on metal as the lift crunched to a halt. He stared at the button panel and then up at the numbers above the door but nothing was moving. There was a bump of metal on brick as the car swayed ever so slightly, causing another grating creak.

This was not good.

Craig pressed the button for floor three but the lift didn't move. Soon he was mashing the panel, trying to make it shift in any direction. Nothing happened, other than the car continuing to sway. It couldn't have been moving by much but Craig had never been good with motion sickness and, combined with the blow to his head, everything was spinning.

With none of the buttons working, Craig held in the red emergency button underneath a speaker panel that had 'Mandy is a slut' daubed across in a bewildering mix of upper- and lower-case letters.

An LED flashed on and off.

'Hello? Hello?'

No reply.

Craig pressed his ear to the speaker, hoping for any noise to indicate there might be someone listening. Even static would be a start, but there was only silence. He pushed the button again.

'Hi, I'm stuck in the lift in . . . a building.'

He let go, certain no one was listening but feeling particularly stupid as he didn't know where he was.

Dink . . . dink.

The car continued to rock gently from side to side,

clinking against the wall and bouncing back. Craig turned in a circle, no idea what to do, before settling on the doors. They were made of a dimpled metal but had give to them when pushed hard. He wedged his fingers into the gap in the centre and pulled as hard as he could. At first there was resistance, but after a grinding pop, they slid apart as easily as if he was opening patio doors.

Not that it helped.

Directly in front was dark brickwork covered in soot and dirt. There was a gap of a few centimetres between the lift car and the wall but nowhere near enough for him to fit through. A sliver of light was glinting from above and when Craig pressed against the wall, he could see the open doors that were too high to be floor four. Voices echoed their way down the shaft: Davey and his men must have prised open the lift doors on floor five and were chatting to each other. Had this been their plan the entire time? If so, whose idea was it ultimately? Haken's?

'Hello?'

Craig figured he had little to lose but his call led to a moment of silence before the voices began again, this time more animated.

Drip, drip, driiiiiiiiiiiiippppppppp.

It started steadily but then it was a cascade of something being poured on top of the lift car. Craig stepped away from the gap, assuming Davey or one of his friends were taking a piss, the dirty sods. Very funny: somehow they'd stopped the lift and then they were taking turns to wee on him.

He turned in a circle again, wondering what to do when

the acrid smell caught in his nose. He sniffed again, recognising the whiff as something familiar, not piss . . . petrol.

Oh, no.

Haken had told him this was the last job Craig would have to do and now the full meaning was apparent – it was the last *thing* he'd do entirely. There was a whoosh and then the narrow gap between car and wall was filled with a terrifying orange glow.

25

FIFTEEN YEARS OLD

Craig and Mark said goodbye to Kimberly at the end of the path to her house and then continued walking through the estate. It was almost eight o'clock, with dusk winning its battle with the sun, the lengthy shadows becoming part of the night. There were a handful of dog-walkers out, eyeing the pair of them nervously, as always happened when they were together. It wasn't specific to them, it was any young people in a group of two or more. Young people equalled trouble. Sometimes Mark played up to it, deliberately following people as payback for the dirty, fearful look they'd given; other times he'd hide and jump out, making them shriek.

Not tonight.

They were on their way back to Mark's house before Craig headed home by himself, but Mark was walking deliberately slowly. He scuffed his feet more than usual, sticking to the main roads and missing the shortcuts. They didn't have much to chat about, so Mark was talking in circles, going on about football and then repeating himself. Craig followed his lead, not mentioning what he knew was going on. Mark didn't want to go home.

The delaying couldn't go on forever and, although the

ten-minute walk had taken almost half an hour, they eventually arrived at Mark's house. The living-room lights were on, curtains pulled roughly, a yellowy white creeping through a gap at the top.

Mark stood at the end of the path, hands in pockets. He nodded towards the house. 'I've got Pro Evo set up in my room if you want to come in for a game . . . ?'

'I've got to be home by half ten. I'm on a final warning with the police and Mum's being really tight about stuff. Bates got her in at the school and said I was going to end up in prison or worse. She took it really badly.'

'He said that?'

'Pretty much.'

'The old prick.' Mark glanced down at his watch. 'It's not even half eight. We can get a couple of games in.'

As Mark looked up, the light from the streetlamp caught the scrape that curved around his eye. It had appeared two days previously, dark and weepy, but had scabbed over and was beginning to shrink. Craig had rarely been into Mark's house when his father was home and, even then, almost entirely when his dad had been sleeping. In the seven years they'd known one another, Craig had only spoken to Mark's father on five or six occasions.

Craig checked his own watch and then said 'okay'.

As they approached the house, Mark morphed into someone completely different. His cocky, reckless streak evaporated, replaced by a creeping, careful persona. Before unlocking the door, he pressed his ear to the plastic and then crouched and peered through the letterbox. That done, he put his key into the lock and used both hands to tweak it ever so slowly until the door popped inwards. He pressed it open with the delicacy of someone threading a needle, making no sound as he stepped inside, held it open for Craig, and then clicked it shut with equal care. With them both in the hallway, he held up a single finger, wanting Craig to wait as he listened to the stillness of the house. If Mr Griffin was home, then he was making no noise.

Mark edged towards the stairs, climbing carefully, one step at a time. After each one, he stopped to listen before moving again. His path swayed erratically from one side of the treads to the other and back again as he expertly avoided the squeaky parts. Craig followed his lead, immersed in the seriousness of moving in utter silence. It was a well-practised dance, Mark moving in perfect choreography up the stairs, knowing when he needed to be on the left, right, or centre and using the banister when he could. Craig had been in the house plenty of times before but had never seen his friend like this. Mark's fear was feeding his own and he found himself clenching his fists, holding his breath. For so long, Mark had seemed scared of nothing, be it the police, teachers or his peers; now it felt like it was because he'd saved that terror for this.

When they finally reached the top, Mark took a breath, some of his confidence returning. He pressed his feet close to the skirting boards and edged along the landing until he reached his bedroom door and then winced as he nudged it open, sending a *creeeeeeeeeeeak* resonating through the house. Spell broken, he moved quickly, ushering Craig into the bedroom and closing the door. Craig sat on the bed as Mark waited by the door, holding his breath, listening.

Nothing.

Mark turned and smiled, though the relief was obvious. His voice was a whisper: 'Sorry about that, my dad sometimes sleeps in the evenings.'

Craig whispered back that it was fine as Mark turned on the television, muted it instantly and then switched on the games console. He handed Craig a controller saying they had to play quietly, and then took a seat on the bed. The title screen had only just loaded when there was a roar of 'BOY!' from the room next door.

Mark dropped the controller and leapt to his feet as booming, stomping feet pounded along the landing. The door was wrenched open, revealing Mark's furious father. He was unshaven, untidy speckles of growth poking out from his bright red face. His hair was messy, spiky clumps sprouting in different directions, eyes wide, fists clenched as he stormed inside, grabbed his son and pinned him to the bedroom wall. They were the same height but Mark had no chance against the rage of his father. Craig could smell the alcohol from across the room, a noxious blend of mixed drinks that felt like it was burning.

Mr Griffin pressed his son into the wall with his right arm and reeled back with his left, clouting a short, sharp punch into Mark's jaw. There was a crack, followed by a click as his mouth snapped sideways.

'What have I told you about waking me up?'

His father's forearm was so tight against Mark's breastbone that there was no way he could answer. He was gurgling a response, legs flapping as he was lifted off the ground. Mr Griffin squeezed his arm upwards until it was across his son's throat, making Mark's eyes bulge.

'Mr Griffin . . . ?'

Craig's voice sounded higher pitched than usual, pathetically pitiful against the backdrop of such fury. Mark's father loosened his grip, turning and noticing Craig for the first time. He seemed confused, tongue half out, brow rippled. As he stepped away, Mark dropped to the floor, collapsing to his knees and coughing violently. Mr Griffin smoothed down his hair and stepped to the door, peering between the two boys before settling on his son.

'Right . . . just keep it down in future, yeah . . . ?'

26

Craig felt paralysed, stuck on the stupid thought of where the petrol had come from. As if it bloody mattered – they could have planted it earlier, or returned to the van, or had an additional accomplice.

Think!

There was fire above and walls on all four sides, so the only place Craig could go was down. He dropped to his hands and knees, sliding his hands across the smooth metal floor. There were two panels, each bolted down with six screws. Craig risked a glance upwards, where smoke was beginning to creep through the tiny cracks at the top of the car, plus wisping its way through the open door. What was it they said? Smoke kills? Whoever *they* were. He had a few more options – the fire could burn through the cable and send him and the car hurtling three and a half floors to the ground; the metal ceiling could melt, sending the inferno down on top of him. If the shaft wasn't properly ventilated, the pressure could build and build until the entire building exploded with him inside. What cosy scenarios they were.

Craig knelt, taking a breath, trying to clear the worst alternatives from his mind. The one certain thing was that if he didn't do something, then he was going to be in serious, serious trouble.

Okay: go.

Craig delved into his pockets and took out his keys. Attached to the ring was the army knife he'd bought in Germany. He fiddled with the instruments until he found the Phillips screwdriver head.

The first and second screws popped out easily but Craig's heart skipped as he scrabbled across to the third. Someone – some inconsiderate, dirty so-and-so – had dropped their chewing gum. The creamy yellow globule had been mashed into the small gap on top of the screw.

Those Wrigley bastards.

In an age where everything even remotely controversial was banned, how come the filthiest habit of them all was still legal?

Concentrate.

Craig peeped over his shoulder again, seeing the smoke continuing to mass above. He ignored the gum-clad screw and moved to the next. Screws four and five came out easily and, although the sixth needed a two-handed grunt and wrench, that soon came free too.

Baubles of sweat dribbled from his forehead, pooling on the metal. Craig didn't know if it was because the fire was making it hotter or if the pressure of impending death was getting to him. It was probably a bit of both.

With one side now completely loose, Craig dug his fingers into the narrow gap, the metal scratching against his fingers as he heaved the panel up as hard as he could, wiggling it from one side to the other, rotating it in a semi-circle around the gum-covered screw. After half-a-dozen revolutions, he dropped to his knees again, jabbing his screwdriver into the centre of the gum, feeling the grooves connect and then twisting as hard as he could.

Yes!

The screw lifted out as easily as the others. Craig pulled the entire metal panel up, man-handling it to the side before getting a proper look at what was underneath. He'd hoped there would be a single floor panel and he'd be able to escape by dropping out of the bottom of the lift compartment and sliding down the cable fireman-style. No such luck: there was a second metal floor thirty or forty centimetres underneath.

Because he wasn't in enough trouble, the light above flickered and spat before going off entirely, leaving him in darkness except for a hazy orange glow creeping through the space between the doors. The air was beginning to feel heavier, tickling the back of his throat and making him cough gently. Craig pressed himself low to the ground, squeezing his eyes closed and taking a breath. His thoughts were muddled by whos, whats, wheres and whys but they were all questions for later . . . if there was a later. He had to concentrate.

First, he needed light. Craig took out his phone from his pocket, fiddling with the controls until a flashlight beam illuminated the floor panel below. The metal was a murky silver, smooth with no obvious screw holes. Craig held his phone in his mouth, getting a tongue full of pocket fluff, and then stretched down, running his hands across the surface.

He was finding it hard to keep the light steady in between his teeth, not that it was helping much – as far as he could tell, the floor panel was one sheet of metal with no joins. Because he couldn't resist, he rolled onto his back, shining the light up towards the ceiling where even more smoke had pooled and was gradually creeping its way down the car towards him. For a moment, he continued to watch the flowing mass, forcing himself to stay calm and think rationally. There *had* to be a way for the panel to come loose . . .

This time, Craig reached his phone down to the second floor panel, placing it on the surface and then using both hands to press into the grooves where the floor met the wall. He slipped his fingers around slowly, stretching until he found a clasp hidden underneath the wall. It was out of sight but he was able to brush it with his index finger. With a final, strained push, he flicked the catch upwards and part of the floor dropped, creating a thin gap and, mercifully, a flimsy gust of fresh air.

Now he knew what he was doing, the rest was simple. Craig held his phone in his mouth again, tracing his fingers around the edges of the second floor panel and unclipping three more clasps. When the third one unlocked, the entire panel dropped away, clang-clang-clanging its way down the shaft until landing with a metallic *whump*.

It sounded like a long drop, far too high for Craig's legs to take.

He took one final glance upwards, bit harder on his phone and then lowered himself through the gaping hole at the bottom of the lift car.

Craig wasn't overweight but neither was he particularly strong. Within moments of lowering himself, the burn started to wrench through his forearms. There was no way he'd be able to hang for long, let alone support himself with one arm.

He twisted his head from side to side, sending spirals of light from the phone skipping around the walls. He was finding it hard to breathe, hold on, and direct the phone at the same time but eventually managed to settle the light on the metallic door for floor three. It was ridiculously close, the top of the frame covered by the bottom of the lift car. If he'd been able to travel for a second longer, he'd have reached floor three and had an easy escape route.

Something groaned above as the lift car bumped from side to side again, clipping the wall and sending a flurry of dust down the shaft. Craig could feel his fingers slipping, the metal digging into them. As he scrabbled to hold on, he accidentally opened his mouth for a breath, sending his phone – and light – tumbling down in a strobing bish-bash-bosh of desperation.

Beads of sweat merged at the top of his nose, dribbling around his eyes. He blinked but that only made them sting, leaving him unable to see even if his eyes had worked in the blackness. For some reason, his mother popped into his mind, telling his six-year-old self that carrots would help him see in the dark.

What a liar – he couldn't see a sodding thing. He vowed that if he did get out, he'd never eat a vegetable again.

In the few moments before he'd dropped his phone, Craig had noticed a narrow ledge in front of the doors for the third floor. It was the width of his feet if he was lucky but would be better than dropping all the way to the bottom of the lift shaft. The doors were close enough that he could tap them with his toes when the lift car swayed in the correct direction. It wasn't as if he could hold on for much longer anyway, so he waited, counting the seconds as it rocked off the opposite wall . . . one, two, three . . . go!

Craig landed exactly where he was aiming but there was nothing to hold on to. One of his feet slipped from the narrow ledge, sending a crusty scuff of dust flurrying down the shaft. He lurched forward, trying to catch his balance and headbutting the metal door to floor three in the process. He wobbled backwards, feeling the fresh air behind and beneath, before finally managing to rock forward, star-fishing himself against the cool metal of the door.

Breathe.

After taking a moment to compose himself, Craig dug his fingers into the gap between the doors and pushed. As with the car doors, there was a grinding resistance and then it popped open as easily as if he was opening a can of soup.

The third floor was empty, almost identical to the fifth, with scratched whitewashed walls and rows of blue doors. Craig took two steps forward, steadying himself as his knees knocked together. Behind, there was an enormous whining moan and then a ferocious *boooooom*. He turned just in time to see the lift car hurtling past the open space, a sea of flames blazing across the top.

27

As Craig darted away from the tower block, sirens whirred nearby. He raced across a patch of frost-dusted grass, gasping for breath as he found a spot underneath a tree close to a kids' play park where the shadow sheltered him from view. He was still wearing the fake police officer's uniform and the last thing he wanted was to be spotted.

Three fire engines screeched onto the courtyard outside the building, their combined blue lights wrapping the area in a waspish dim glare. Fire-fighters dashed out of the vehicles as police cars barrelled onto the scene. Residents were pouring out from the building, many clad in pyjamas and blankets, peering back towards their homes. Craig hoped everyone was out. He counted ten floors of lights and knew there were at least sixteen flats per level. That was hundreds of people who could be trapped. Already a flittering orange glow was visible at the base of the building, scratching through the basement and eating onto the ground floor. He wondered what had happened to the four unconscious men on the fifth floor. Would they have woken up? Would the fire-fighters get them out? He wanted to believe it wasn't his problem but it was hard to escape the haunting thought that he'd somehow contributed to it, even if he'd been the target.

Haken had set him up. The stuff about having extra jobs

for him was an act – all Haken wanted was for the shipment to be brought in and then they wanted Craig to go away.

Craig rubbed the tips of his fingers together, trying to scratch away the pain from pulling out the metal panels and then holding onto the bottom of the lift car. His head had largely cleared and the blood had stopped running when he touched the wound from where Davey had hit him with the gun.

More people were emerging from the building: men, women, children, entire families. Police officers were moving forward, ushering them away from danger as the first group of fire-fighters headed inside. A handful of people were moving onto the green, heading towards Craig. Although it was keeping him warm, he tossed the padded police vest into a nearby hedge, figuring dark trousers and a white shirt wouldn't naturally make people associate him with the authorities. He skirted around the edge of the grass, keeping to the shadows and ending up in the car park behind the fire engines. He followed the street in the direction from which the emergency vehicles had come, assuming that if he could find the main road, he'd at least have a chance of discovering where he was.

As soon as Craig reached the East Lancs Road, he knew he was roughly halfway between his house and the city centre. Emergency vehicles continued to barrel along, blue lights flaring as they sent sprays of grit skidding across the pavement. Craig was hurting, his hands scratched, knees weak, feet sore from days of endless walking.

He knew he only had a small window. After setting fire

to the lift, Davey and his friends would've raced away, not wanting to be spotted anywhere near the scene. At least for now, Haken would have no reason to assume Craig was alive. It was only in the next few days as police reports emerged that he might realise. Even then, matters would be unclear until any bodies were identified. For now, his priority was to get his parents to safety.

Craig hobbled as best as he could through the mass of estates until he arrived back at his house. He felt a surge of relief at the fact it was still standing – if Haken and co. were coming, they'd not got there yet.

It was a few minutes after eleven when he bounded through the front door and was met by silence and darkness. Craig had half-expected his father to be in the living room, asleep in front of the telly, bottle of booze at his side, but the ground floor was empty. He started to feel a panic building as he stumbled up the stairs, hurling open the door to his parents' bedroom, where he was greeted by the wonderful sound of two people snorting like asthmatic piglets. Craig slapped on the light, reaching for the suitcase on top of the wardrobe as both of his parents rolled over, squinting towards him.

'Whuh . . .'

Craig's mum had been fast asleep but his father was uncharacteristically awake. This was a moment he had most likely feared for years. There was only so long a person could get away with owing money to the wrong people. One day, the debts, gambling and boozing was going to catch up with him. The family had been living on borrowed time for a long while.

Little did he know it was going to be a loan for a boiler that took them all down.

'You've got to go,' Craig said.

'Huh . . . ?'

His mother rolled onto her back and grunted through a yawn and blinked her eyes open wider. 'What's going on?'

Craig's dad kicked his legs out from under the covers and reached for the nearby chest of drawers.

'You've got to go, Mum. Both of you.'

'Why?'

'There's no time to explain properly, trust me.'

'But—'

She had no time to argue as Craig's father reached towards his wife in an uncharacteristic show of affection. He stroked her arm and whispered, 'C'mon, love . . .' She blinked a few more times and then nodded acceptingly. Craig wondered if they'd had this conversation at some point. It felt as if they knew the debts would come back to bite them.

Craig used the house phone to call for a taxi, trying to stay out of the way as his parents heaved piles of clothes into a pair of suitcases. He wiped away the blood from his head, taking a close look at the cut in the mirror. The blow from Davey's pistol had largely been glancing, leaving a shallow snip along his hairline. If he'd not turned and half-avoided it, he'd have been unconscious when they started the blaze.

He helped his parents down the stairs with the luggage but, despite the potential imminent danger, his mum still found time to grab a box of teabags from the kitchen 'just in case'.

Typical.

The taxi pulled up as they opened the front door and, despite wanting payment up front, the driver knew where he was going, which was more than could be said for most cabbies. They arrived at Piccadilly Bus Station in the city centre at a quarter to midnight. The streets were quiet, with only a handful of stragglers mooching around, trying to find a bar that was still open. Craig left his parents on a bench next to a billboard advertising some trashy crime book and then dashed along the concourse to use the pay-phone and check the timetables.

He was out of breath by the time he got back to them. 'There's a Megabus that leaves at ten past midnight,' Craig said. 'It'll take you overnight to Victoria Station. One of the lads I used to work with owes me a favour. I've got his number in my emails. He's living with his girlfriend, so has an empty flat and he'll put you up for a bit.'

His mother frowned. 'In London?'

'Right.'

'Oh, I don't like it down there. It's all noisy and dirty.'

'It's not that different, Mum, and it's only for a while until I figure something out.'

Mrs Macklin turned to her husband for support and, for a moment, Craig thought there was going to be another outburst about 'foreigners'.

He said nothing, so Craig's mother continued the objections: 'What's this flat like?'

'I don't know other than it's a one-bedroom place some-where in Islington. You'll be fine.'

'Is-ling-ton . . . ? Where's that?'

'London.' Craig peered over his shoulder, worrying that they were in the open. 'Can you please just go? It's not safe here.'

'Why are you staying?'

'Because one of us has to sort things out and it has to be me.'

Mrs Macklin turned to her husband again but he shrugged. 'We should go, love.' He turned to Craig. 'Are you going to be all right?'

'I'll work it out.'

'Do you want to . . . ?'

'I don't want to worry you. Just go and I'll be in contact.' He tapped his mother on the arm. 'Make sure you keep your phone turned on.'

'But the battery . . .'

'It's not going to die because you leave it on during the day.'

He didn't bother to tell her that the reason her phone would be fine was that it was so old, so bloody massive, that the battery would last for weeks. She was convinced it was permanently at the point of breaking, and paranoid to make calls because of the potential cost.

His mother wasn't convinced: 'Oh, I don't know, you hear all this stuff on the news. There was this thing the other day about chargers that exploded.'

'You'll be fine, Mum. Leave the phone on and I'll call you. Promise. Just don't bother trying to call me, I lost my phone. Oh – and don't tell anyone where you are. If one of your friends from bingo calls, tell them you're away.'

'What if they ask where?'

'I don't know, figure something out but don't say you're in London. Tell them you're in Blackpool.'

'But they might want to come and visit.'

'So tell them something else – anywhere but London.'

She heaved her handbag higher on her shoulder, pouting, although the look lost some of its impact when it dissolved into a yawn. Craig glanced up to the large clock – ten minutes to go.

His mum tapped him on the back: 'What did you say the bus was?'

'It's a Megabus.'

'Ooh, that sounds nice.'

'Yeah, well . . . you'll see.' Craig didn't want to spoil the illusion quite yet. The last Megabus he'd been on had toilets that leaked, a baby that cried the entire journey and an old man who kept exposing himself. From what he'd heard, that was a common experience.

A few minutes later, the blue and yellow bus pulled up and Craig helped the driver shove his parents' suitcases into the luggage compartment underneath. His mum waved as it pulled away and Craig dropped back onto the bench, relieved he'd sorted the most important thing. He'd need to find an Internet connection to get his friend's number but that was the benefit of being 'owed one'.

His parents wouldn't be able to stay down south for long – they'd either strangle one another or declare they'd had enough – but it did buy him a bit of time. He strode onto the concourse overlooking Piccadilly Gardens, peering into the distance. It was a week since he'd arrived back in the city and walked with Mark on the opposite side of the gardens. Seven days on and everything was a mess.

He turned in a circle gazing up towards the twinkling Christmas tree in the centre of the green, one question to figure out: what now?

28

Craig was woken by a wooden-sounding bang. The usual clatter of noisy pipes had been littering his dreams, though at least the violent snoring was absent, most likely blasting its way through a bus-load of people trying to sleep. After leaving the bus station, he'd had few options: there was Mark's house, or his own. Considering what he knew, he wasn't sure he could look his old friend in the eye, let alone open up and admit the trouble he was in. That left his parents' house. Haken could come at any time – that was why he'd sent his parents away in the first place – but it was still better than nothing.

Craig edged across the bedroom until he was at the curtains. He gently nudged the corner aside, peering towards the back garden. It was seven in the morning and at least an hour away from the sun coming up, probably longer. There were intermittent orange streetlights along the path at the rear of the house, but they threw off less light than the crappiest of cheap torches found in a Christmas cracker. Craig squinted through the gloom as a second bang echoed from the back fence. A cat was skulking across the bottom, tail swaying, nose in the air.

Knowing he had no chance of getting back to sleep, Craig went through his duffel bag and picked out his warmest clean clothes. With little to choose from, he was relieved to find the airing cupboard full of items his mum had washed the previous day.

Mums were amazing for many, many reasons, none more important than as people who'd wash their children's clothes without complaint, no matter how old they were.

Craig peeped through the curtains of his parents' bedroom to the front of the house, scanning for trouble. There was little to see, other than the woman over the road scratching a credit card across her frozen windscreen in a flurry of chilled breaths and swearing.

He crept downstairs, double-checking the curtains were pulled tightly, and then he turned on the television, muting it instantly but switching on subtitles. The spelling was awful but just about decipherable.

Craig waited through the national news – flood here; cheating politician there; some dreadful talent show coming to an end; Christmas on the way, in case anyone had missed it – until the local news came on. The top story was the fire at the tower block. A woman who the captions identified as 'Detective Daniels' seemed particularly annoyed, or possibly tired. She was fighting back a yawn as she asked any potential witnesses to come forward.

After her, a superintendent spoke about 'unknown circumstances'. It didn't seem as if the police knew much about the fire, although the news images were impressively bold. First there were the flames bursting from the ground floor under darkness the night before, then two or three shaky cam-phone-made videos, then a live image of the smouldering tower block as it currently stood. The fire had been put out relatively quickly, with investigators heading in to look for the source. It wouldn't take them long given the lift car that had careered to the ground.

The reporter said that there was 'no word' on casualties, which meant that Craig was still in the clear, at least for now. At best, he'd probably have until the end of the day before Haken and co. realised he'd survived. The thought occurred that Davey could have simply shot him, but that would have raised too many questions when his body was found. If he'd been in the lift car when it hit the ground, police would have assumed he was unlucky enough to be inside when it caught fire. There'd still be an investigation but not necessarily one for murder. A shooting was a shooting and they would have been checking traffic cameras and blanketing the area with officers looking for witnesses. As with everything Craig had seen from Haken, it had been meticulously planned.

To finish the report, the journalist said that it was 'still to be determined' if the fire was an accident and then the camera shifted back to the studio. Craig switched off the television, his question still unanswered from the night before: what could he do now? If he ruled out Mark, there was only one person he could go to: the madman loan shark with the shotgun.

Craig kept his head down and didn't stop as he skirted around the quad at the front of Lincoln House. Directly opposite was Jefferson House, with Roosevelt House on one side and Kennedy on the other. The builders might have been fans of US presidents but they'd done the shoddiest job imaginable in honouring them. Lincoln House, in which Rodger lived, was grim, but that was nothing compared to poor old Kennedy. If being shot in Dallas wasn't enough of an ignominy, the flats named in his honour had been condemned, with large yellow signs warning 'NO ENTRY. YOU MIGHT DIE.'

If nothing else, it was refreshingly honest.

Craig ignored the sign, levering away a rain-soaked loose plank of wood and pressing himself into what was once flat one, which gave him a perfect view of Rodger's front door. He watched for half an hour, taking in any movement around the area just in case Lincoln House was being observed. There was a postman hefting a bag as big as he was, a woman with a yappy dog that she called 'Tiddles', and a middle-aged bloke in skin-tight lycra hefting a road bike down the stairs from an upper flat before he wobbled his way towards the road.

When he was convinced it was clear, Craig slipped back out, following the path until he was at Rodger's front door. He tapped gently on the window and then slightly more loudly on the door. There was no reply, so he crouched and lifted the letterbox flap, calling through his name in a loud whisper. When there was still no answer, he tried to peep through the living-room window. The curtains were pulled but there was the tiniest of slits in the centre, which wasn't enough for him to see anything.

Craig checked over his shoulder towards the square and other flats, unable to see anyone. He tried knocking one final time before heading along the row to where it intersected with a narrow path that was lined with bushes. With no other ideas, Craig followed the trail, brushing the overhanging damp greenery away from his face and then freeing his trousers from a rampaging thorn bush. The alley ran parallel to the main quad, passing along the rear of Lincoln House. The back of the building was even dirtier than the front, with overflowing bins, an upturned rusty shopping trolley and a series of white flashes within the bushes, which looked suspiciously like dirty nappies. Craig didn't bother going for a closer look, counting the houses until he was at the back of number ten. Each property had its own yard that had been created by piled breezeblocks.

Chernobyl chic.

There was a black metal gate separating each one from the path, though it was low enough to be a waste of time. Craig stepped over Rodger's and edged towards the house. The patio was filled with half-bricks, scrap metal, an old roll of carpet and a white moulded plastic chair that was covered with mulch. The flat itself was as still at the back as it was at the front, with the curtains drawn and no sign of movement. Craig tapped gently on the back door, not wanting to alert the neighbours.

Still no answer.

As he was about to try again, a heavy goods lorry rattled past on the road beyond the thorn bushes, causing what felt like a minor earthquake. He didn't know the area that well but if there was a main road nearby, the chances were that it wouldn't be an isolated event.

Craig picked up one of the half-bricks and waited. A few minutes later, the ground started to tremor again and at the sweet spot where the truck passed, he hurled the brick through the glass panel that formed the top half of the door. Even though he was barely a metre away, Craig struggled to hear the shattering glass over the rampant vibrations of the lorry hurtling into the distance. He stepped to the side, pushing himself against the wall and waiting to see if Rodger would come storming out, shotgun in hand.

After a minute or so with nothing, Craig started to get the tingle of inevitability that had become oh so familiar over recent days. He edged towards the door, peeping quickly through the hole where the glass had been and then ducking away, just in case there was a shotgun shell with his name on it.

Still nothing.

Craig reached into the gap, fearing he'd have to clamber through the jagged space, only to find a key sitting in the lock. He pulled down his sleeve to cover his hand and unlatched the door, slowly easing himself into Rodger's kitchen.

'Rodge? It's Craig Macklin. Hello?'

Aside from the shattered glass on the floor, the kitchen was unremarkable. A single plate with knife and fork was on the draining board but there was no mess. Craig moved into the hallway and then the living room. The main light was off but a tall lamp was glowing at the back. It didn't look as if anything had been touched since the last time Craig had been there: the Beatles and Elvis posters were as they were, with the colourful stacks of records still lining the wall. It had seemed bizarre in the first place that Rodger had brought his collection if he was in hiding, stranger still that he would have left it behind had he moved on.

Craig paced the room, peering into the corners for anything untoward. He stopped when he reached the armchair in which Rodger had sat when he'd last been there. On the floor behind was the sawn-off, barrel locked in place. Craig didn't want to leave his fingerprints, so picked it up through his sleeves, snapping the hinge to see the pair of cartridges loaded and ready to be fired. He returned the gun to where he'd found it and then moved back into the hall, in which there were two doors to choose from. The first led into the bathroom, which smelled a little of mud but was otherwise clear. The second opened into pure darkness. Craig tried to peer through the murk but had to concede defeat, scrambling across the wall until his finger caught the switch through his sleeve. Light instantly filled the room. The bed was unmade, a pile of clothes on the floor next to a gleaming pistol. The top drawer of a chest was open, as was the wardrobe. None of that mattered compared to what was in the centre of the room.

Rodger's eyes were closed, his body limp as electrical cord burrowed into his neck, leaving him hanging from the light fitting, unmistakeably dead.

29

Craig wanted to look away but couldn't. It was a long time since he'd seen a dead body, though not long enough. It was intoxicatingly horrific, transfixing yet repulsing. At first glance, it looked like a suicide, perhaps it was, though it was a coincidence that he and Rodger were both connected to Haken and that they could have died at more or less the same time. It was more likely that Haken was out to cover tracks that might lead to him. He'd needed Rodger's initial cooperation for a smooth handover of the pawn shop and loan-sharking business, then Craig to organise the import. With both jobs complete, they each knew too much.

Guns were far from Craig's expertise – he'd never fired one before – but he'd watched movies with gung-ho heroes. How hard could it be? Point and shoot, right?

Or not. He picked up the pistol from the carpet and retreated to the living room, spending five minutes trying to figure out how it came apart. By the time he realised there was a clip of bullets loaded into the grip, it dawned on him how he could have easily fired by accident. It was like an advanced Meccano set, only with a marginally higher chance of losing a toe. Craig counted the eight bullets out of the clip and then back in again before reloading the gun. He slipped the weapon into the back of his waistband, praying it couldn't fire itself, and then crept out of the house, reaching the path at the back and then running for it.

Craig headed towards the nearby Tesco and withdrew £300 at the cashpoint, the maximum he could take per day. The near three thousand he'd previously taken out to pay off Haken was still sitting in his duffel bag and, though there wasn't too much more where it came from, it would keep him going.

At the cigarette counter he bought the cheapest pay and go phone and a sim card. His mum's mobile number was written on a card at the house because she could never remember it and he'd made a point of memorising Kimberly's just in case. Anything else important was in his online address book, not that he planned to call anyone yet.

The gun felt heavy in the back of his trousers and not just because of the physical weight. He wasn't *this* type of person. This was the trouble he'd run away from but what else could he do? Haken would soon be coming for him, so he could either run and hide, or go for him first. If it was only him at risk, he'd hide every time, but his parents couldn't be left at the other end of the country forever and then there was Kimberly, too. The only thing on which he had any degree of clarity was that if he was going to go after Haken, then he needed to know what he was up against.

Chinatown wasn't as busy as it had been the previous evening but it was still bustling enough that Craig could disappear among the ambling throng of crowds. He kept his hood up, moving with the flow but this time taking everything in. The street stalls proved to be the best places to hide in plain sight, allowing him to stand still pretending to look at the goods, while actually memorising the layout. At first he felt hostility to the stall holders before telling himself that it was unlikely any of them knew what was occurring below their feet.

Most of the shop-owners and restaurant managers would be appalled to know how close they were to being tarnished by Haken's counterfeiting and drugs-running, let alone the weapons. It was something which could damage an entire community. That left Craig in the conflicted position of wanting to believe the little old lady selling spicy hot chocolate from a glorified wheelbarrow was completely harmless, while reminding himself to be vigilant of everyone and everything.

Craig eventually reached the top end of the street and then looped around to Albert Square and the Christmas market, where it was even busier. It dawned on him that, despite the cold, having his hood up made him stand out further as it looked like he was trying not to be seen. He bought a Santa hat from a stall on the corner, yanked it over his ears, and then gave in to his stomach's demands by buying a roast pork burger with apple sauce and stuffing.

In most places, the bright red hat would make a person stand out, but there were so many people in similar get-up that Craig felt hidden by it. After finishing his food, he moved back along the street towards Chinatown and started his second pass-through. When he reached the apothecary's shop, he followed an American-sounding mother and daughter through the door and headed into the darkened store. As the mother asked the shop assistant if the lanterns were 'authentic' – whatever that meant – Craig concentrated on angling himself away from the security camera.

The shop wasn't large but the open door loomed invitingly behind the counter. Was Haken below? If so, would he be alone? Craig could feel the weight of the gun but knew it was too dangerous. He could race downstairs and bang a few doors open but what then? Even if Haken was around and he managed to get a shot off, there was every chance more people would arrive, blocking him underground. If he was going to do this, he'd have to plan better.

The American woman had moved on to asking how dreamcatchers worked, so Craig left the shop without attracting attention. It was a few minutes after five o'clock, with the streets becoming busier as people finished work. Craig found a spot next to the hot chocolate woman and peered up. Above the restaurants, cleaning places and shops were various flats, though it seemed unlikely Haken would choose to live here. It was noisy, smelly because of the street food and bathed with bright lights throughout the night. If he lived elsewhere, he'd have to leave the shop at some time . . .

Craig bought a spicy hot chocolate from the small woman with the glorified wheelbarrow. He took a sip and started to step away but ended up nearly choking to death as the chilli bit his throat after the first gulp. It felt like hydrochloric acid eating through flesh. The Chinese stall holder grinned and winked as he doubled over, sputtering into the gutter. She waited until it seemed likely he'd survive and then said: 'It's spicy, yes?'

Unable to speak, Craig nodded and gave her a thumbs-up. Spicy was one description, his would have been volcanic.

The nuclear-fuelled drink did at least give him a reason to stand outside the launderette sipping *slowly*. Very slowly. There was nowhere on the street that was dark but he found a spot behind the sociopathic hot chocolate seller, watching the front of the apothecary's shop. If anyone asked, which they wouldn't, he was waiting for his drink to cool. After fifteen minutes, it felt as hot as it had when first poured. There was definitely some sort of witchcraft going on.

Craig was so taken with wondering when the burning might end that he almost missed Haken leaving the shop. He stood out through the crowd, crisp suit like a beacon against the warm coats and Santa hats. Haken didn't hesitate, jogging down the couple of steps and then turning, walking a short distance against the flow of the crowd, and disappearing into the narrow alley Craig had been brought in through when he'd been picked up. Craig tossed the drink into a bin and followed, checking his watch – it was exactly half past five.

Even from a short distance behind, Craig could see the dark people carrier waiting at the end of the cobbles. There was a faint light from a phone in Haken's hand but he barely broke stride as he exited the alley, slid open the rear door and climbed in. Craig started to jog in an effort to keep up but the vehicle was already on its way with a roar of the exhaust. He dashed to the end of the alley, expecting his chance to have gone, but Manchester was at its wonderfully predictable best: the people carrier had barely travelled thirty metres before reaching a red traffic light. The planets must have aligned in his favour, the gods smiling down – hallelujah! – because sitting at the kerb, engine idling, was a taxi. Craig tapped on the window and the driver rolled his eyes, dropped his *Manchester Morning Herald*, and nodded towards the back seat.

'Where you going, mate?'

Craig nodded to the people carrier ahead. 'This is going to sound a bit clichéd but can you follow that car . . . ?'

The taxi driver's eyes met Craig's in the rear-view mirror. 'Some stag party thing, is it?'

'Huh?'

'Or some Christmas thing? A bet or something?'

'Sorry?'

'"Follow that car" – is this some sort of Internet thing? One of my mates had it the other week with these girls on a treasure hunt something-or-other. Had him driving 'em all over trying to find clues to where the next pub was. Reckoned one of 'em had a right pair on 'er.'

'Yeah, something like that.'

The driver nodded approvingly, banking the story to tell his taxi-driving chums. In his version, Craig would no doubt be female with 'a right pair'.

The driver went quiet for a while after his Sherlock Holmes-esque piece of deduction, following the people carrier to such perfection that he even zipped through a traffic light that was decidedly red in order to keep up. After a mile or so, he peered over his shoulder. 'We off to the football?'

'Sorry?'

'City are at home tonight. That's the way your mate's heading.'

'Oh, right . . . I'm not sure. It's up to him.'

Craig had lost track of where they were partly because it was dark but largely because so much of the centre was different to how he'd once known the city. Large parts had been regenerated – new roads, new buildings, bus lanes, cycle lanes, and so much more.

'Whereabouts are we?' Craig asked.

'On our way through Beswick. The traffic's gonna stop in a minute, so your mate would be better walking.'

'Right . . .'

As predicted, the traffic slowed to a halt a short distance along the road as the tarmac filled with fans wearing light blue tops. A pair of police cars were parked across the road, turning cars along side streets to take them away from the football stadium. The people carrier turned where the officers were indicating but parked half on the pavement, allowing cars to pass.

'You wanna get out here, mate?' the driver asked.

'Keep going for a bit.'

Craig had the driver stop between two lampposts a little further along the road. He passed him a ten-pound note and then climbed out, remaining in the shadows as he watched Haken and another suited man striding along a path towards a modern-looking three-storey block of flats that was all glass and light-coloured brickwork.

The taxi driver eased into the traffic and Craig started to walk slowly back towards the roadblock. As he did so, the people carrier edged onto the road and quickly turned left, passing around the side of the apartments and pulling through a gate into an adjoining car park. Moments later, the driver hurried around the front of the building, overhead lighting illuminating him perfectly: Davey.

There was a tall strip of glass at the front of the building, the staircase visible from the road. Each of the three floors had its own door, giving the residents privacy from anyone outside. Davey pressed the buzzer next to the main door and then headed inside, climbing up to the top floor and disappearing.

Football fans were streaming along the adjacent road and there was a sense of excitement fizzing through the air. It was City's final home game before Christmas and people were in the party mood.

It was only as he started getting a few sideways glances that Craig realised he was still wearing the Santa hat. Red was the colour of United and, though some supporters were also wearing Santa hats, they were light blue. In their eyes, Santa could be many things – as long as he wasn't a United fan. Craig stuffed the offending item into his pocket, only then remembering that he still had the gun. The two policemen controlling traffic were a short distance away, luckily paying him no attention as they continued to wave vehicles away from the stadium.

Craig headed towards the apartment building and tried the front door, which was locked. Next to it was a dark panel with a speaker and buttons for flats one to twelve. Starting with one, Craig pressed each of them until somebody from flat five replied with 'who is it?'

'I've got a pizza for someone on the ground floor. They're not answering.'

The flat's occupant didn't reply but there was a buzz and pop, then the door swung open. In contrast to the tower block Davey had taken him to, the hallway was sparkling. It smelled lemony, like a posh hotel. Next to the door was a space for people to leave umbrellas, with a tidy letter rack at the side. Everything was painted in the same crisp magnolia, with no graffiti or snide letters stuck on the walls. Craig felt like he was lowering the value simply by standing there.

There was little to see on the first or second floors, so he continued up to the third. He was about to push through the same door he'd seen Davey entering when he stopped himself a moment before it was too late. There was a small window at head height, allowing him to see two men in suits standing in the corridor between apartment eleven on one side and twelve on the other. They were young and clean-cut, the type Haken seemed to constantly surround himself with.

Craig ducked back into the corridor, pressing himself against the wall and feeling the weight of the gun in the back of his trousers. There was a chance he could surprise the pair of them, with the gunshots loud enough to bring Davey, Haken or who knew who else into the corridor. He might get a few shots off, perhaps even get lucky and shoot Haken, but this wasn't the right place. There were police officers outside and thousands of football fans. Plus the floor could be home to anyone – almost certainly Haken, but did he own or rent the entire top floor, or were there other people around? Craig's other worry was the one that had been niggling at the back of his mind throughout: was he this type of person? Even after they'd tried to kill him, he wasn't sure he could return the favour.

Craig left the building defeated, closing the door behind him and putting his hands in his pockets as he headed towards the main road, not completely sure where he was. He figured that if he followed the direction the taxi had come from, then he would hit a main road sooner or later, then follow the signs back to the centre.

The crowd was continuing to build as fans flocked from the pubs, heading towards the stadium for kick-off. Craig quickly reached the crossroads where the roadblock was set up and was about to turn in the opposite direction when he felt a hand on his arm. He spun quickly, coming face to face with a weary-looking police officer.

She nodded towards the roadblock. 'Can you come with me, Sir?'

'Why?'

'We're doing a series of stop and searches and today's your lucky day.'

30

The officer took a step off the pavement in the direction she'd indicated but Craig didn't move. 'Sir . . . ?'

'Is there a particular reason?' he asked.

She rolled her eyes slightly, giving the impression this wasn't her choice of how to spend a Wednesday evening before Christmas. 'We've had intelligence reports about organised trouble around football grounds. These are random checks and nothing to worry about, now if you'll just—'

'I'm not going to the football, I'm off home.'

'That may be the case, Sir, but I'm just doing my job. It'll only take a few minutes then you'll be on your way.'

'Do you have ID or anything . . . ?'

Craig had no idea what the procedure was for stop and searches. Could he refuse? The one thing he *did* know was that there was no way he could let her get near him. The moment she did, she'd find the gun which would take more than a bit of explaining – especially if it was legally regis-tered to Rodger, who was hanging in a flat a few miles away.

'Sir, I—'

'I read this thing from America where fake police officers were stopping people and robbing them . . .'

'Fine, I—'

The moment she reached for her pocket, Craig turned and bolted. By the time the officer shouted 'hey!', he had twenty metres on her. If he'd been wearing a City shirt, he'd have already disappeared, though his dark top and trousers weren't so bad. He skipped between the football fans heading in the opposite direction and darted towards a dark alley at the back of Haken's apartment block. After the pain in his legs from the previous day, he felt like a kid again. The alley soon led to a crossroads, so he headed towards the area that seemed the most overgrown, risking a glance over his shoulder to see the police officer falling even further behind.

When the path opened out to a wide road, Craig ran across, zig-zagging around the parked cars and following his nose towards a row of takeaways and shops. For a moment, he considered entering the Spar but his legs felt strong, so he continued, soon finding himself on a path next to a river. The next time he peered back, there was no one behind except for a man yanking his dog away from the water, trying not to be pulled in himself. Craig slumped onto a bench, leaning back to catch his breath but keeping an eye on the path in case the PC was still chasing him. From nowhere he was laughing to himself: half his age again, running for all he was worth. It was like the old days: those shitty awful times from which he'd escaped. Still, laugh or cry? Craig chose laugh.

Craig was on the road leading towards his house when he saw the two boys. They were fourteen or fifteen and could have been him and Mark in days gone by, standing at the end of the path to his parents' house, passing a cigarette between them. Craig retreated into the shadow of a nearby garage block and watched, trying to ration his breathing because each gasp was sending a plume into the air, exposing his position.

He assumed they were just lads out and about but then one of them answered his phone. The young voice drifted across the road, though the exact words were lost to the freezing breeze. When the phone call ended, he dropped the cigarette to the pavement and scuffed it out.

'Move on, move on . . .'

Craig murmured for them to go but his earlier luck had run out. The one with the phone stepped onto the front lawn, approaching the window and trying to peep through the closed curtains. At any other time, Craig would have dismissed them as local kids messing around but the timing was either incredibly fishy, or ridiculously unlucky.

After giving up on the window, the boy approached the front door, crouched and peered through the letterbox. With nothing to see, he turned and said something inaudible to his friend, who shrugged. The two of them stood halfway along the path chatting to one another before the first boy took out his phone and made a call.

If they were lookouts for Haken, then they were doing a good job of standing out. Any of the neighbours on either side or across the road would be able to spot them if they were looking. If they weren't Haken's, then what were they doing? Casing the house as somewhere to rob? It definitely stood out: everywhere else on the road had at least some degree of Christmas decoration in the windows, twinkling into the night. One of the places towards the bottom even had an enormous inflatable snowman in the garden and a pair of reindeer on the roof, which *definitely* wasn't a cry for help. Even the most pitiful houses had a small tree some-where around the window, or a string of fairy lights. Craig's had nothing and generally looked empty. This was the type of thing Mark would do when they were on the streets as teenagers. They had never actually burgled a place, but Mark would point to houses and say they should check around the back to see if anyone was home.

The first boy hung up and then tried knocking on the door, turning and shrugging one more time when there was no answer. Finally, the pair turned and headed along the street, Craig watching as they disappeared past the inflat-able Santa, underneath an overhanging tree and into an alley.

Craig waited for a few moments before hurrying across the road, unlocking the front door and throwing himself inside. He moved around the ground floor, then upstairs, but everything seemed as he'd left it. If the kids were any-thing to do with Haken, then they either knew he was alive, or, perhaps worse, they'd come to see if his parents were there.

Either way, he was running out of options. He couldn't live in fear forever, nor could his parents be left in another city in which they weren't happy. Craig put the pistol on the kitchen counter and stared at it. Outwardly, it was such a simple object. You pointed, you clicked, someone went down. The more he looked at it, the more he didn't think he had it in him. He knew where Haken lived and worked. He knew how he travelled and could identify the people around him. It was all enough to put together a plan but the final elements were never likely to come together because of the central problem that shooting a person meant more than simply pulling a trigger. If Craig was going to do this, *really* do it, then he needed someone who'd killed before.

31

Mark flicked the games controller onto the floor and slapped his hand against the wall. 'Did you see the goalkeeper? What was he doing?'

Craig knew he could never gloat too much when he beat his friend on Pro Evolution Soccer. In fairness to Mark, he wasn't a bad winner, rarely showing off, but he was definitely a terrible loser. Mark lashed a leg towards the radiator and pointed at the screen. 'He dived the wrong way. What's wrong with him?'

Craig shrugged. 'Sorry.'

'Whatever.'

'Again?'

'Yeah but I'm going to play as someone else. United are shite on this game.'

Craig knew he had to let Mark win the next match, which rarely proved hard. He frequently eased off, making sure it looked authentic by stringing together one too many passes and letting his opponent have the ball back. As long as Mark won a game in every three or so, he remained calm.

Mark spoke as he started to set up the next game. 'Kim was saying we should do something special next week.'

'For your birthday?'

'Yeah, she was round last night.' Mark paused for a fraction of a second as he sipped from a can of Coke but Craig couldn't help but feel it was deliberate. Kimberly had told Craig she had to stay in the previous night and so he'd spent the evening at home by himself. He'd wondered for a while if anything was going on between Kimberly and Mark that had taken them beyond mates but never had the courage to ask. Once or twice, he caught her gazing at Mark for that fraction of a second too long, but there were times when she was touchy-feely with him, too. He found her almost impossible to read, not that that was unusual with those of the opposite sex. The difference with Kimberly was that she spoke to him. If she was spending time alone with Mark, then did that mean something? He spent time with her away from Mark because they each went to college, while Mark didn't have a job and wasn't in education.

'. . . She was saying we should go somewhere because I'm going to be eighteen,' Mark added.

'What did you say?'

He shrugged. 'Where are we gonna go? She was saying Blackpool but you two will both be seventeen and I can't be bothered mooching around trying to find somewhere that'll serve us.'

'Right.'

Mark was about to say something else when he froze. The front door banged open, clattering against the wall amid a flurry of muttered swear words. Mark stopped pressing buttons on the controller and put it on the floor, listening as his father bounded into the hallway, lashed out at something and then slammed the door with such ferocity that the bedroom windows shook. Mark's grin disappeared as he leant against the wall, saying nothing.

The kitchen door banged open and then something metallic went flying before the voice came booming up the stairs: *'Boy!'*

Mark jumped to his feet, not looking at Craig. 'Wait here for a minute. I'll be back.' He headed out of the bedroom and closed the door and then Craig heard him running down the stairs.

Craig didn't know why – perhaps it was jealousy over Kimberly – but he quietly opened the bedroom door and edged onto the landing, creeping to the top of the stairs and listening.

Mark's father was bellowing: '. . . so I ask you again – where've you been all day?'

'Nowhere, Dad.'

'Nowhere? What did I tell you about getting a job?'

'I'm trying but it's not that easy.'

Thwack!

The noise of skin on skin resounded through the house, quickly followed by a second fleshy splat. There was a bang and then an anguished 'Get off!'

Crack!

Craig winced as the next blow landed, the echo so sickeningly solid that it was like a cartoon sound effect. He quietly edged down the steps until he was halfway towards the hallway, freezing as something made of metal was sent hurtling.

'You think you can sit around here leeching off me all the time?'

'Leeching? You're just a—'

Bang!

Something ceramic smashed and then there were three successive thumps. Craig continued to the bottom of the stairs and turned towards the scene of carnage in the kitchen. What had once been a high stool had its metal legs bent out of shape and was lying half in the hallway. A pile of plates and bowls were scattered across the threshold, smashed into pieces. There was a kettle on the floor next to a baking tray and the kitchen table had been tipped sideways. Mark was backed up against the sink next to the window, his father in between them with his back to the hall.

Craig had only a brief glance but Mark's face was laced with a series of cuts, trickles of blood running into one another and creasing around his eye.

Mark's father reeled back. 'You ungrateful little—'

Wham!

He hammered forward, punching his son across the face once, twice, three times. With the third blow, a spray of blood pinged across the tiles, Mark slumping to the floor, his head bouncing off the metal draining board, eyes rolling into his head.

'Hey!'

Craig was filled by a braveness he didn't feel, stepping over the stool and shouting. He thought Mr Griffin would stop the same way as he had before, but not this time. Mark's father turned and reached out, grabbing Craig's top and lifting him into the air. The man's face was a snarling swirl of fury, his breath putridly horrid. With barely a flick of the wrist, he tossed Craig aside, sending him crashing into a worktop.

The man howled with a venom that barely seemed human, lip curling as he turned to concentrate his attention on his son.

Except that Mark was ahead of him.

He'd reached up and grabbed the thick carving knife from the draining board. His father opened his mouth to say something but it was already too late. Mark thrust forward, hammering the knife into the centre of his father's chest as if it were a stake. Tears streamed down his face as he reeled back before stabbing down a second time. Then a third. Fourth. Fifth. The blows were a blur of movement, barely a pause between them.

'Mark.'

The blade thrashed into the man's chest for a final time before Mark let go, sending his dad careering backwards to the floor. Blood was everywhere but especially all over Mark. There were individual splashes across his face but more across his arms and a thick pool over his own chest. His eyes were wide, fixed on the dead man lying in front of him.

'Mark.'

He didn't move: 'What?'

'It's okay,' Craig said, 'people will understand. I'll tell them what happened.'

There was no reply as Mark's eyelids blinked rapidly, only succeeding in sending a dribble of his father's blood along his cheek.

'Mark.'

'What?'

'We should call the police.'

'No.'

'We've got to do something.'

Mark blinked into reality, shaking his head and turning to Craig. He tapped the cupboard under the sink. 'There are mops and sponges and stuff in here.'

'I mean we have to tell somebody.'

He shook his head again. 'No.'

'People will understand.'

'They won't.'

'I'll tell them what I saw. They'll believe me.'

Mark was becoming more agitated, shaking his head even faster. 'No, we have to do this my way.'

'Do what?'

Mark opened the cupboard and sent a pile of buckets, rubber gloves, clothes and sponges spinning. They all looked new. 'We'll clean this up and do something with the body.'

'Do what?'

'I'll think of something. Let's clean up first.'

Craig pushed himself up to his feet, head reeling slightly from the blow. He peered down to where Mark's father was flat on his back, head drooped to one side, eyes wide open. The knife handle was still poking from his chest, a spreading pool of blood massing under his shoulder blade. Moments before, he'd seemed invincible, superhuman, now he was as mortal as anyone else. Mark was already at the sink, squirting washing-up liquid into the bucket and filling it with water. Somehow the blood had reached the back of his neck and formed a murky V across his shoulder blades. He turned to Craig, suddenly himself again, as if suggesting they should go for a wander in the park.

'Come on, let's go,' Mark said. 'I'll do the floor, you do the cupboards and surfaces.'

'I just—'

'You what?'

'I've never seen a dead body before.'

Mark peeped down at his father, then back up at Craig. He shrugged. 'Oh well. You have now.'

32

NOW

Craig sat on the swings watching the rest of the almost empty park. It was hard to tell whether the children had broken up for school. He saw some in uniform but others walked past in twos or threes, some with parents, some without. It was almost midday but the sun had taken one look at the northern hemisphere and thought it wasn't worth it. The dank grey washed overhead, a barely perceptible change from what it looked like at dusk. The frost hadn't cleared and, though it wasn't raining, the air felt heavy, as if it might snow.

Five lads in baggy trousers and skewed baseball caps slouched through the park gates, skateboards under their arms, heading towards the ramps on the far side. Given the ice on the ground, they must've really been into hurting themselves.

At two minutes past midday, Mark entered through the gates, looked both ways, and then shuffled across to the swings, a curious smile on his face. 'Y'a'ight?'

'Aye,' Craig replied.

'What's with the new number?'

'It's a really long story.'

Mark nodded, taking it in: 'Is that why you called Kim to talk to me?'

'Right.'

'Why didn't you come to the house?'

'That's part of the long story.'

Mark laughed, sitting down and kicking himself off until the swing was rocking back and forth. 'Why are we meeting here?'

'It's so open that nobody pays you any attention. Besides, it's too cold for kids to want to visit the park.'

'Fair enough . . . what's up?'

What's up?

Craig wasn't sure where to start, so he went back to the beginning, telling Mark about the damage to his parents' house and his second visit to the pawn shop. From there, he'd been snatched from the street, forced to import weapons, stopped by the police, sent on his way by the police, threatened into being a part of a drugs robbery, trapped in a blazing lift shaft, then he'd sent his parents away, found out Rodger was dead, followed Haken to his flat and run from the police.

Mark continued to swing gently as Craig rattled off his catalogue of offences. At the end, he planted his feet to stop the swing and then turned to Craig. 'Is that it?'

'Isn't that enough?'

'I meant is that all of it?'

Craig pictured his conversation with Kimberly underneath the railway bridge, where she'd shown him her bruises and said she'd picked the wrong friend.

'That's everything,' he said.

Mark breathed out loudly: 'That's pretty good for a week.'

'Cheers.'

Mark plucked off his beanie hat and scraped a hand across his head before pulling it back down over his ears. 'Why didn't you tell me any of this before?'

Craig couldn't tell him the real reason that, if it wasn't for all of this, he never wanted to see Mark again. Couldn't tell him that even looking at his face disgusted him. Couldn't tell him that he didn't deserve to have the wife he had.

'I was embarrassed,' Craig said. 'I didn't want to ask for help.'

'I'm not sure what you want me to do. I paid off my debt on Monday – I'm clear.'

'I'm not.'

'But this "Haken" isn't just Patrick Henderson or some other kid from school. You're saying he's already sorted out some druggies and then killed the Todge, not to mention going after you. What do you think we can do?'

'I don't know but it can't be this. I'm not even that bothered about myself but my parents can only be away for so long.'

'Why aren't you bothered about yourself?'

Craig sucked on his bottom lip and started rocking himself. This wasn't the conversation he wanted to have. He wanted the gung-ho, father-stabbing, wife-beating Mark to come up with something dazzlingly, violently brilliant to bring an end to it. He didn't want questions about his state of mind. The fact they were talking amiably was enough to turn his stomach.

'I just . . . want Haken gone. That Davey, too.'

'How do you know there won't be others?' Mark replied.

'I don't but it'll be a start.'

'If you've got that gun, why don't you just walk into that Chinatown shop, march down the stairs and blast a hole in Haken's face?'

He made it sound so easy, as if it were a computer game.

'It can't be there, I don't know how many others he might have working for him, plus it's in the city centre. Where can I go?'

Six lads in heavy coats squeaked through the gate and peered towards the men on the swings before moving onto the grass and dropping their coats to create a goal. One of them rustled up a ball and away they went: World Cup Singles into one goal. Craig knew he was getting old as he thought about how wet they'd get, not to mention how solid the ground was. Someone could get injured. Except that, in the old days, he wouldn't have cared. Rain? Ice? Frost? Sod that.

Mark started to rock gently, keeping the same pace as Craig. 'I can probably get a few lads together . . .'

'No.'

'What's wrong?'

'More people means more problems,' Craig said. 'Too many things can go wrong, too many people can say something out of place and then it's all over. It's got to be us.'

'Does that mean you have a plan?'

'Maybe . . . I'll need to check a couple of things but I think Haken's got a routine – and not just him.'

'What do you need me to do?'

'Just be there.'

Mark snorted, fiddling with his hat again, gazing into the distance. 'Fair enough . . . you were there for me.'

33

SEVENTEEN YEARS OLD

Craig leant back in the passenger seat so that he had a view of the speedometer. Mark was driving almost too slowly, fifteen miles an hour below the fifty limit, which was surely as likely to get them stopped as if he was speeding. The fact he was driving without a licence or insurance would be only the start. If the police wanted to look in the boot, they'd get the shock of their lives.

'You all right?' Mark asked.

'It's a fifty.'

'So?'

'They might pull you over if you're not going fast enough.'

Mark turned sideways in the driver's seat. 'You wanna drive?'

'No, I don't—'

'Shut up then.'

Craig twisted away slightly, trying to escape the wet patch on the edge of the seat. Mark's father's car was a heap of crap Toyota with a growling engine, bald tyres, filthy exhaust, windows that didn't go down and a sunroof that was permanently open a few centimetres. The areas around the handbrake and inner edges of the front seats were damp and covered with a layer of furry mould. It also looked like something leafy was growing on the floor underneath Craig's seat, with a green stalk winding its way towards his feet.

The car had probably been driven drunk more times than sober and, considering Mark's father had never been pulled over and breathalysed, Craig was hoping the run of luck would continue for a little longer, especially as Mr Griffin's body was in the boot, wrapped in a curtain.

Despite his annoyance, Mark accelerated, eyes fixed on the road ahead. He was a decent driver considering Craig had never been in a car with him before. Mark had boasted on many occasions of the cars he'd driven and where he'd been but Craig was never sure what was true and what wasn't. It was now clear Mark *had* driven before, though Craig doubted it was at night. Everyone else's headlights seemed so bright, every vehicle in front and behind a possible police car ready to pull them over. Craig didn't know what he was scared of most: the fact he couldn't stop picturing Mr Griffin's body, the amount of trouble he'd be in if they were caught, or Mark's calmness after the murder. Craig had tried to think how he himself might have reacted if he'd killed one of his parents and knew it would have been with horror. It was unfair to compare their fathers because Craig's had never been violent – he wasn't there often enough – but there was still surely some sort of emotional connection deep down?

After the initial moment of shock, Mark had acted on autopilot. They'd scrubbed the kitchen clean and then taken the curtains from the bathroom to wrap the body in.

Between them, they had carried it to the car and then cleaned the kitchen a second time. The bleach had been so strong that it was hard to breathe when they'd finished. Craig had barely said a word throughout, with Mark taking control.

'Sorry . . .'

The word came from nowhere, almost making Craig jump. He didn't think Mark had ever apologised to him before, not properly.

'It's okay,' Craig replied.

'Thanks for helping – I couldn't have done it by myself.'

That didn't make Craig feel any better. He shuffled a little further away from the mould and leant on the window. 'Where are we going?'

'Just . . . somewhere.'

Mark continued driving south, seemingly knowing exactly where he was going. It felt like they were following the signs to Stockport until Mark ignored one, continuing up a slope where the streetlights were far more intermittent. His driving was so confident that he even pulled in between a pair of parked cars and flashed his lights, giving way to someone coming in the opposite direction. Craig was starting to wonder how many of Mark's tall stories were genuine. Some were obviously nonsense – the Ferrari, for instance – but perhaps there was a hint of truth to more than he'd thought.

They soon reached the top of the hill and Mark unexpectedly switched off the headlights, turning onto what turned out to be a narrow, gravelly track and stopping.

'We're here,' he said, getting out of the car.

Craig followed, blinking as he tried to adjust to the darkness. Steepling above on one side was a church spire, the rest of the building stretching along the side of the road. The stained-glass windows were creepily illuminated through the cloaked moonlight, with the silence more disturbing than anything. Mark had already set off, not locking the car and bounding towards a metal gate. By the time Craig got there, Mark had already clambered over and was striding along a narrow concrete path that skirted the edge of the church. Craig had to run to catch him as they ended up in a cemetery. Mark was sitting on a tombstone. He reached into his pockets and passed across a pair of supermarket carrier bags.

'What are these for?'

'Wrap them around your shoes.'

Mark was doing the same himself, putting his foot into a bag and then tying the handles around his ankles. Craig copied him and then Mark set off across the grass, weaving in between the headstones until he reached a pair of open graves. He stood staring at the holes, hands solemnly behind his back.

'What's going on?' Craig asked.

'This place always digs graves on a Monday ready for funerals and burials on Tuesdays.'

'How do you know that?'

'One of my dad's friends was an undertaker.'

He spoke matter-of-factly, as if it was common knowledge, but it was the first time Craig had ever heard of Mark's father being in contact with anyone. Could it be made up? Craig wasn't sure – but it was a Monday night and, sure enough, a pair of graves were there, ready to be filled.

Craig peered down at the space below: 'We can't just drop your dad in there.'

'Have you heard of the saying "six feet under"?'

'I s'pose.'

'It's about death. When you die, you end up six feet under.'

'Okay . . .'

'Except that graves aren't usually six feet deep, they're about four feet. We'll dig down deeper, drop him in and then cover it over again.'

Craig opened his mouth to protest, except that it was perfect. Where better to hide a body than with another body? It'd never be found. 'We don't have—'

'There are spades in the car.'

For the next few hours, they worked by moonlight, digging, scraping and scrabbling until the hole was more than six feet deep. It sounded simple, perhaps even looked it, but Craig's back was aching after barely fifteen minutes. Mark was like a machine, showing incredible stamina as he dug and dug and dug. Eventually, he looked up, wiped his brow, and said they were done. Mark hoisted Craig onto his shoulders and they managed to help one another out of the grave before returning to the car for the body. Craig took Mr Griffin's feet, but Mark showed no emotion as he clasped his father's arms and they carried him across the graveyard before unceremoniously dropping him into the open space. Filling the gap was easier than digging it and when the soil was back in, Mark dropped down to smooth the ground over before Craig helped pull him out.

Craig stood at the edge, wondering if Mark might want one final glance at the spot in which his father would lie. There was no reaction.

'What are you going to tell people?' Craig asked.

Mark was already a few metres away and twisted to look over his shoulder. 'That he went to the pub and didn't come back. It's hardly a stretch.'

He was right about that.

Mark turned and walked back to the car, twirling the keys around his index finger and humming to himself. Craig trailed, as he always did, knowing something was wrong that went far deeper than the murder.

Everything was too neat.

First, it was unusual for Craig to be at the house in the first place – Mark rarely invited him round if his father was going to be in. Then there was the placement of the knife on the draining board. Mark never washed up – *never* – and Craig very much doubted Mr Griffin did, yet it had been in the perfect position. Where had all the cleaning products come from, too? The buckets were brand new and the sponges had come from a packet. There had been two different types of bleach under the sink, plus Mark had driven to the cemetery without any sort of directions, presumably because he already knew the way. Then a pair of spades had been in the boot before the body was dropped inside. Craig hadn't even seen them pushed towards the back.

Not one spade: two.

How much of this had been planned? Could it be true

that Mark had sparked the fight with his father knowing what the outcome would be? Not only that, had he deliberately invited Craig to the house knowing what was coming? Craig had known for a long time that Mark's father was a bad person. He was a violently dangerous alcoholic, but did that justify this?

Craig watched the key continue to spin around Mark's finger as he walked into the distance. He knew the answers deep down: he'd always known what Mark was capable of but he hadn't realised how smart his friend was. Regardless of everything they'd been through for almost a decade, Craig had always assumed *he* was the clever one of the two. Now he wasn't so sure.

Mark peered over his shoulder as he reached the corner of the church, untying the carrier bags from his feet. 'You coming?'

Craig started to walk slowly across the graveyard, knowing that he was going to have to get out of the city sooner rather than later. If Mark was capable of this, then what else might he do?

The only question was whether Kimberly would go with him.

34

Around and around and around and around . . .

The launderette across the street from the apothecary's shop was proving a good place for Craig to go unnoticed. It was unattended and aside from a handful of people lumping bags of washing inside, setting it going and then disappearing again, there was nobody to bother him. The crowds continued to amble past outside but that didn't stop him having an uninterrupted view of the door opposite.

There was a door at the back of the room in between a pair of tumble dryers but Craig had twisted the handle and it was locked. If anything, it made him feel marginally more secure, knowing that nobody could surprise him from behind.

It was hardly the most interesting of afternoons but Craig sat on one of the benches, reading the *Herald* from cover to cover and then moving on to the *Big Issue*. His hood was up and he was yet to be bothered.

His watch was showing a few minutes to five when the door jangled and in walked one of the last people he expected. Kimberly's hair was bundled underneath a woollen hat and she was wearing a thick cardigan over the top of jeans with trainers. She smiled softly, showing the slightly bent line of teeth.

'Hey.'

'What are you doing here?'

'I wanted to say "hi".'

'How did you know where I'd be?'

She shrugged. 'How d'you think? Mark was talking to me last night about everything that's happened.' Craig's mouth hung open, unable to put the pieces together. He'd not told Mark to keep things to himself, assuming it would be obvious. Kimberly sat next to him on the bench and looped her hand through his arm, resting the side of her head on his shoulder. 'I think he's worried about you.'

'So he sent you to—'

'He didn't send me to do anything. He said you were going to be keeping an eye on Chinatown for a day or two and then you'd be back in contact. He told me not to say anything.'

Craig wondered if he should ask about the previous time they'd been due to meet, when she'd stood him up. He wasn't sure it mattered.

'How much did he tell you?' Craig asked.

'Bit and pieces – that you got yourself into trouble with some Chinese guy and that you wanted his help. That it might get hairy but that he thought he owed you one because of what you'd been through as kids.' She didn't elaborate and Craig didn't ask. He couldn't read her to work out if she knew what had happened to Mark's father. In many ways, he didn't want to know. Kimberly hugged herself more tightly into his shoulder. 'He said you're planning something . . .'

Craig let it hang for a while, not wanting to involve her. 'Kim . . .'

'You don't have to tell me . . . I don't want to know.'

'Oh.'

She pulled away, taking his hand and forcing him to look at her. 'I don't want you to do it.'

'Do what?'

'Anything.' Her fingers squeezed into his palm. 'We should go. Let's hire a car and drive. I know somewhere we can stay for a few days and then—'

'Kimberly.'

She stopped speaking, tongue resting against her top lip. He couldn't remember the last time he called her Kimberly instead of Kim. Sometimes it was even 'Kimmy'.

'What?'

'It's not that simple. If we leave now, we'd always be looking over our shoulders, plus my parents would be in danger. Not to mention Mark. Do you think he'd let us go?'

'He'd never find us.'

'But is that the life you want? Always wondering if he might? Not only that but I don't have that much money. I don't know about you but what would we do when it ran out?'

'I have some.'

'How much?'

She shrugged. 'A few hundred. It's all cash that I've hidden away. My wages go into our joint account.'

'It's not enough.'

Kimberly's fingers tickled their way across his palm until they were interlocked with his. The tingle slowly crept along his spine. It felt the same now as it had when they'd been thirteen years old.

'Craig . . .'

The way she said his name left his mouth dry, breath short. It purred from her lips seductively. Perfectly. Nobody said it like she did.

'Maybe afterwards,' Craig replied.

'Is Mark going to help you?'

'I think so.'

'He's not a nice person.'

'I know . . . his dad, he—'

Kimberly slapped the back of his hand – hard. 'Don't you *dare* make excuses for him.'

'I'm not, I—'

Craig went silent as the door opened and another familiar figure entered. Kim removed her hand from his and shuffled away slightly as the lad with the BMX that Craig had seen in the brothel and pawn shop bumped his bike up the step. He wheeled it to the back door, paying no attention to either Craig or Kimberly. His cap was pulled down as before, backpack strapped on tightly. He delved into his pocket and unlocked the door, wheeling his bike inside and disappearing before there was the sound of it locking again.

Kimberly didn't recognise the significance, shifting along the bench and placing her hand around Craig's back. 'I'm sorry.'

'No, I am. I didn't mean it like that. He should be responsible for his own actions.'

'You don't know what he's like, Craig. When you first left, things continued as normal. I knew what he was up to but Mark would nick the odd thing and sell it on. It was like being kids again. Eventually he started doing the car-booters and it was regular money but he's into things that are so much more serious than he used to be.'

'Like what?'

She shrugged. 'Just . . . things. All sorts. I don't ask questions and he doesn't say.'

'What are you telling me? That I shouldn't work with him?'

'No . . . well . . . I don't know.' She pulled off her hat, letting her hair tumble around her shoulders. It looked as red as it ever had, making her eyes seem even browner. Even easier to get lost in. As she shook her hair free, Craig spotted the new mark: a crescent-shaped scratch cupping her ear.

Kimberly tilted her head to the side: 'Mark's going to be out tonight . . .' Her lips were pouting expectantly but, before Craig could reply, the door at the back clicked and the lad emerged with his BMX. He was definitely in his mid to late teens, probably a little older than Craig had first thought when he saw him from a distance. Perhaps even a slight eighteen-year-old? The bag was still on his back but the zips were now open, the flap gaping down. He relocked the back door and then pushed his bike across the floor, nudging open the front door with his shoulder and heading onto the street.

Kimberly stood, simultaneously winding her hair back on top of her head and pulling the hat over her ears. 'I should go.'

'Oh . . .'

'Tonight, Craig.'

'What are you saying?'

She smiled tenderly, not replying but turning. She headed in the same direction as the lad with the BMX.

Craig's breath felt short, his chest tight. It was too much to take in and he knew he had to focus on what he thought was about to happen. It was a little after ten past five, so Craig picked up the magazine and started to flick, unable to concentrate on the words and barely taking in the pictures. He was counting down the minutes, the seconds. Five twenty-nine. Five thirty.

Haken emerged from the apothecary's shop at the same time as Craig had previously seen him do. He seemed a creature of habit. Craig didn't know what time Haken arrived to do his business under the streets but he left at half past five. By wasting an afternoon, Craig had found out one thing that would help him but perhaps, by accident, the BMX rider had provided something else . . .

It was nine o'clock and the houses on Mark's street were drowning in blinking, flashing, chiming bloody annoying Christmas tat. Someone had a Christmas tree larger than their house, someone else a full nativity scene in their front garden. One bloke must have had more money than sense, his electricity bill equivalent to the GDP of a small nation, with the entirety of his house smothered in lights.

Utterly, utterly mad.

Craig walked along the pavement, dropping his pace as he neared Mark's house. He remembered the way Mark had once slowed, reluctant to get home because he didn't want to spend an evening at home with his father. Craig was walking equally slowly, not because he wanted to stay away but because he was afraid of what might happen if he went inside. It was everything he'd wanted since he was old enough to have those urges; yet something from which he could never go back. He stood at the end of the path for a minute, perhaps two, before finally taking a deep breath and approaching the front door. He knocked on the glass quietly, almost hoping he wasn't heard.

No such luck.

A shadow appeared, becoming larger as it approached. Was it Mark? Was he in after all?

No.

Kimberly's hair was down. It had a slight wave to it and was swinging from side to side. Suddenly she was in front of him, dressed in tight jeans and a floaty top. Nothing extraordinary but that wasn't the point. She'd have been special if she was wearing a bin bag. She nodded towards the hallway behind, smiling in the wonderful way she'd had when she acknowledged him behind Mark's back when he'd first laid eyes on her. 'You coming in?' she asked.

Craig stepped across the threshold, shivering at the change from the freezing outdoors to the smouldering inside. Kimberly closed the door and slipped the chain across, pressing past him and reaching out her hand. Craig felt like he was burning up but her touch was beautifully cool. Her fingers locked with his as she led the way into the living room and took a seat on the sofa. She patted the spot next to her and Craig removed his coat, hat and gloves before sitting.

Kimberly was trying to make eye contact but Craig couldn't do it. This house held so many memories, the death of Mark's father in particular.

The *murder*.

'Do you remember that time we were sat outside Mr Bates's office together?'

Kimberly spoke quietly, softly. Sometimes he'd imagined her voice when he'd been asleep in his marital bed next to Harriet. Kimberly would come to him when his eyes were closed, his mind wandering. Now her voice was real once more.

Craig took off his top, leaving him in a T-shirt. He was sweltering, hoping the sweat wasn't showing. 'That time when Mark got called in and we thought we were going to get done for selling all the nicked stuff?' he replied.

'Right.'

'We were only, what, twelve? Thirteen?'

Kimberly nodded. 'I said that maybe we'd get married when we were older? That we could go to Alton Towers . . .'

'I remember.'

She reached out and took his hand. He could feel her breath on him. It smelled of something he didn't know, not bad . . . just different.

'What would you have said if Bates had never come out when he did?' Kimberly asked. 'Would you have told me it was a good idea?'

Craig blinked. He'd thought about that moment so

many times over the years, even picturing it on the morning of his wedding to Harriet and wishing it would go away.

'I don't know . . . I . . .' He stopped himself. He'd lied to himself for too long and there was no point in continuing. 'I'd have said we should do it.'

She moved across the sofa, drawing his arm across her. Her hair was resting on his chin, soft and freshly washed. 'I never should have chosen him.'

'Kim . . .'

'We've got to run away.'

'I've told you that I can't, not until this is sorted. I can't abandon my parents. I've got to work with Mark, at least for now.'

He could feel her biting her lip, her jaw tense. He knew what she was going to say a moment before she did.

'Will you kill him for me?'

Craig took a breath, feeling her head rise on his chest. 'Who? The Chinese man?'

He already knew the answer. 'Mark.'

35

SEVENTEEN YEARS OLD

Craig was staring up at the bright white letters underneath the railway bridge: *MG – CM – KK 4EVA*.

When Mark had graffitied it, Craig had been excited. It had meant something: the three of them against the world, bring it on. Now it felt silly. Immature teenagers lashing out angrily at a community they'd spent years rebelling against anyway.

'Whatcha thinking about?'

Kimberly's voice was wonderfully reassuring, as it always had been. It had an almost hypnotic quality, grabbing his thoughts and not letting go. Craig often wondered if there was anything he wouldn't do if she asked. The problem was that she never did, not really. Only little things – did he want to come to the pub, to walk to college, to help her with some work – none of the important things.

'Nothing really,' Craig replied.

'It must be something.'

Craig pushed himself up into a sitting position, feeling a moment of vertigo as the ground zoomed towards him and then raced away. The columns underneath the railway bridge felt ridiculously steep sometimes. It was still a wonderful hideaway, though. He placed a hand on her shoulder. 'How about you? What are you thinking?'

Kimberly remained lying on her back, hair splayed wide against the light grey stone. She closed her eyes and broke into a smile. 'I was wondering what I fancy for tea tonight . . . something with chicken, I reckon. Now it's your turn.'

Craig sighed, resting back on the concrete. It had been a long while since he'd had a substantial thought about what he was going to eat next. It seemed so inconsequential.

'I was thinking that we're getting old.'

She giggled, opening her eyes and slapping at his arm. 'We're really not.'

'Mark's already eighteen, I will be next month, then it's your turn. What are we going to do when we finish college?'

'I don't know. We'll figure something out.'

'Haven't you ever wanted more? To travel? To meet people? To see the world? To live somewhere else?'

'What's wrong with here?'

'Nothing I suppose, I just . . . I don't know.'

Kimberly pushed herself up onto her elbows and yawned widely as a train rattled overhead. She flapped an apologetic hand in front of her mouth as a tear rolled along her cheek. As the train hurtled into the distance, the pillars pulsated and thrashed until finally becoming still. Every conversation they had here was punctuated by the deafening roar of passing trains, so much so that Craig could barely have an exchange anywhere else without expecting the ground to shudder at any moment.

'Are you trying to tell me something?' Kimberly asked.

'About what?'

'The way you're talking makes it feel like the end of an era.'

Craig sighed: 'Perhaps it is?'

'We're only seventeen, you and me. We're young and can do what we want.'

'Can we? Everyone says that but it's not true. What if I want to be an astronaut or Prime Minister?'

Kimberly's eyes narrowed and she tilted her head, looking at him in a way she never had. He always felt as if she knew how to read him, play him, perhaps. He was clay ready to be moulded but now perhaps she realised everything wasn't as she thought. *He* wasn't the person she thought he was.

'Did something happen?' she asked.

Craig couldn't look at her any more. He didn't want to say what Mark had done to his father. Perhaps Mark would tell her one day? Kimberly brushed the back of his hand with hers. 'Is something wrong?'

'I don't . . .'

She nodded upwards, towards the graffiti. 'It doesn't matter what happens, we'll always have the three of us to look out for one another.'

There was a voice in Craig's head screaming at him to tell her how he felt. If ever there was a moment, it was now. Tell her and it would all be okay. Tell her. Tell her. Tell her.

Kimberly was rubbing her thumb across the back of his fingers. 'How long have we known each other? Six years?'

Tell her.

'We've done everything together . . .'

Tell her.

'Some of it seems a bit silly now but at least you were there for it . . .'

Tell her.

Kimberly turned and stroked a patch of Craig's hair away. He allowed himself to gaze into her eyes, trapped, unable to look away.

'I suppose what I'm saying is that . . . I love you.'

Craig felt the world surging towards him, the bridge falling, the ground hurtling upwards. Hallelujah, praise the Lord. Birds were singing, angels flying. He didn't have to tell her because she'd told him. Suddenly the world felt right again. Forget Mark and his dad: Kimberly loved him and Craig loved her.

'. . . and Mark. I love you both.'

Everything rushed away again and Craig felt a breath catch in his throat. Mark was in his kitchen, knife in hand, pressed against the sink, lunging forward in a feverish frenzy as the blade slashed back and forth sending a spray of blood in all directions. This time it wasn't his father in front of him, it was Craig. Stab-stab-stab. Take that.

Kimberly continued talking: 'I mean . . . I don't know how to put it. It's like I properly love you both. I want you to be in my life forever.'

Craig's eyes fixed back on hers as he realised she had moved slightly closer. Their noses were almost touching and then, out of nowhere, she turned her face to the side, nose brushing alongside his as she leant in further, her bottom lip touching his as she kissed him gently. Craig was so stunned that it took him a fraction of a second to realise what was happening. He'd thought about this so many times, dreamed of it, yearned for it. By the time he knew it was real, it was over.

Kimberly pulled backwards and pouted her lips together, smiling gently: 'That was nice.'

'I—'

She shuffled away a short distance, body language saying what her words weren't. 'I had to know.'

'Know what?'

'Mark and I have been . . . hanging around a bit recently, ever since his dad disappeared. We know what his dad was like but it's still hard for him.'

'Right . . .'

'Nothing's changed: it's still you, me and him forever.'

Except that it wasn't and was never going to be. Craig had been defeated. Not only had Mark conned him into getting rid of his father; he then used that to steal Kimberly.

Kimberly peered down to the ground where, as if on cue, Mark was walking along the slope towards the pillars, barely lifting his feet as he moved. Kimberly grabbed her bag and lowered herself down the column, landing with a giggle on both feet. Craig followed, slipping and sliding, just about keeping his balance as he plopped down next to her.

Mark flicked his neck upwards, barely moving his lips. 'Y'a'ight?'

Craig nodded and murmured a 'hi'.

'Shall we go?'

Mark didn't bother waiting for an answer. He held out his hand and Kimberly reached out to take it, locking her fingers into his. Together they started to walk back up the slope on the other side, Craig a few steps behind. He glanced up towards the graffiti: *MG – CM – KK 4EVA*.

Or maybe not.

36

Craig kept his mouth clamped closed as Mark shuffled about in the passenger seat of the rented car again, not wanting to show his annoyance. The vehicle was far newer – and nicer – than anything Craig had driven himself. The acceleration was ridiculously instantaneous, the steering responsive and the boot large. Craig wondered how much of that would be crucial in the day or so to come.

It was Friday and, with Christmas less than a week away, it felt like the city had already gone on holiday. There were more people than ever in the centre, more people everywhere.

'Nice area . . .'

Mark had made the same observation twice before. He was bored, his attention span shot. The area in question was the road outside the apartment block in which Haken lived. It was a little after lunchtime and, if Craig was correct, Haken would currently be underneath the streets of his Chinatown shop, managing his empire. For now, he could wait.

'Yeah,' Craig replied, 'nice area.'

They'd been waiting for hours in the car park at the side of the apartment block. The black people carrier had left a little after eight that morning with Haken, Davey and co.; then returned without Haken a little over an hour later. Since then, they'd been watching, waiting.

Mark took out a bag of prawn cocktail crisps and started to eat before offering the packet. 'Want one?'

'I'm all right.'

'Suit yourself.'

Craig had done just that. He was uncomfortable enough as it was being around Mark, knowing what he knew. The previous evening with Kimberly had solidified his hostility towards his former friend even further. He had to play along, at least for a few more hours. He needed Mark to help him do this and then, after that, he wasn't sure.

'Will you kill him for me?'

Kimberly had been everything he'd dreamed of since he'd been old enough to have those sorts of dreams. In the moments he'd been with her the night before, it was as if the previous thirteen years hadn't happened. As if she hadn't landed on the pavement underneath the bridge when they were seventeen and taken Mark's hand instead of his. As if she hadn't whispered 'I had to know'. Four words he didn't quite understand the meaning of at the time, only to realise moments later that she was telling him she'd chosen Mark.

Now he was sitting next to her husband, the wife-beater, the murderer, acting as if everything was fine. He wondered what would happen if he came out with it now and told Mark what he and Kimberly had done the previous evening. If he told him how he'd seen the kaleidoscope of bruises across her ribs and legs. Craig knew he couldn't but he wanted to see Mark's face, watch his eyes narrow, brow furrow, lips curl. He wanted Mark to know that he'd taken something of his. That *he'd* taken it. Craig wouldn't have to exaggerate because it was true. He could run away with Kimberly, head along the motorway and never look back, but he'd never get that moment where he could look into Mark's eyes and tell him that he'd won after all.

Craig continued to mumble replies as Mark made small talk about things of such insignificance that Craig wondered how they'd ever been friends. He was full of the same boastful nonsense he had been as a kid, going on about how he wanted to get himself a boat – a 'small yacht' as he put it – and go on a long, long holiday. How he was craving the sun and wanted to go on a fishing expedition along the Amazon. It would be ambitious for anyone but for a man who'd seemingly never left the city in which he was born, it was ludicrous. Craig doubted Mark could pick the Amazon out on a map, it was just the name of a river he knew.

Davey and another man in a suit finally emerged around the corner from the building heading to the people carrier.

Mark stopped mid-sentence: 'That them?'

'Yep.'

''Bout time.'

'You ready?'

Mark sat up straighter and patted his coat pocket. 'I was born ready.'

Craig waited until Davey was in the people carrier and then switched on the engine. As Davey drove towards the gate, Craig surged forward, getting there first and slamming on his brakes, blocking the exit and shielding the car park from the rest of the street. He took his foot off the clutch, causing the rental car to bunny hop forward and stall. The people carrier loomed through the back window, blocking most of the light, so close that Craig couldn't see either Davey or the passenger. For a glimmer of a moment, he felt the old surge of adrenaline he used to have when he and Mark were kids. Before Kimberly, before growing up.

Beeeeeep!

Mark opened the door and got out, leaving it ajar. Craig didn't dare move, watching the action in the wing-mirror. Mark had taken a few steps towards the other vehicle. 'Sorry, mate, he's stalled it and can't get it going again.'

There was the sound of an electric window humming down and then Mark's hand flashed into his pocket, removing the pistol Craig had taken from Rodger's house. He pointed it towards the open window, voice as calm as if he was ordering a takeaway: 'Yeah, that's right, pal . . . out you get.' The gun nudged towards the passenger seat. 'Not you – stay where you are.'

The driver's door opened and Davey climbed out, hands in the air. Mark ordered him to lie face-down on the tarmac, keeping the gun on him while ordering the passenger to do the same. When they were both down, Mark turned back to Craig, muttering 'hey'.

Craig got out and rounded the vehicle, crouching next to the prone men and riffling through their pockets. He found two sets of keys, handcuffs, a pair of pistols and two mobile phones, tossing everything onto the back seat of the rented car. He opened the boot and took out a carrier bag full of goodies. The rope was thick, cheap and the scratchiest he had been able to find. Craig weaved it between Davey's wrists, pulling it tightly until the other man winced. Good. He was getting off lightly considering he'd blocked him in a lift shaft and set it on fire.

The second man got the same treatment before Craig delved back into the bag. Buying blindfolds was far harder than he thought. It wasn't the type of thing that could be found in the general clothes section of most shops, so Craig had settled for tearing a cheap pair of leggings in half. He tied the material around the eyes of each man, squeezing the knot as tightly as he possibly could until he felt their bodies tense a second time. He wanted them to feel a fraction of the terror he had when the smoke had been building above him in the lift car.

Mark repocketed the gun. 'Sorted?'

'Yep.'

They lifted both men into the boot of the rented car and then Craig *slammed* it with as much force as he could. Mark approved, the vicious grin creeping across his face. 'You look like you enjoyed that.'

'Yeah, well . . .'

Mark was heading to the driver's seat of the people carrier. 'How long have we got?'

'Long enough.'

'Good, let's go.'

Craig had done his homework, navigating the roads out of Manchester with ease, skipping around the congested areas near the motorways and heading north towards Lancashire.

He followed the A-roads for a while towards Burnley and then turned off onto a country lane. The hedges were so tall and overgrown that the narrow road was permanently doused with shadow. Frost clung to each surface, with crusted tractor wheel marks scattered intermittently across the carriageway. Craig heard the odd bump from the boot but nothing too worrying. If anything, it was annoying how smooth the drive was. It would have been nicer to have an older and less stable vehicle, where every pothole sent the car bouncing and the boot inhabitants rolling on top of one another.

As Craig drove, Mark followed in the people carrier until they passed the entrance to a golf club. Craig had used the Internet cafe to find the perfect area and, within a hundred metres of passing the driveway, the thick, bushy woods appeared. Craig kept driving for a while longer and then pulled in so that he was mostly on the verge, allowing other vehicles to pass easily. Mark stopped a little behind him and they met in between the cars.

'You sure here's a good place?' Mark asked.

Craig peered around. Each side of the road was lined with a tall hedge. Beyond, it was frosted fields and trees stretching into the distance. With the exception of the golf club half a mile back, they were in the middle of nowhere.

'Here's perfect.'

Craig drank in the unfamiliar country air, which tasted cleaner, though definitely colder, listening for the sound of any approaching cars. Aside from the rustle of the trees, there was nothing, not even the distant hum of the main road, or the chirping of birds.

He opened the boot, finding Davey and the other man in the top-to-tail positions in which he'd left them. From the rounded bump on Davey's temple, it looked like he'd got at least one boot in the face during the journey. Considering the butt of the pistol that Davey had walloped into Craig's head, they were at least level on that.

Craig and Mark heaved the two men out of the boot and removed the blindfolds, giving Davey his first proper look at Craig. His pupils widened in recognition, though he said nothing. Craig checked the knots binding their hands were tight enough and then he and Mark bundled the prisoners over a stile into the woods. Mark was holding the pistol in case either of them tried anything, though he seemed to be enjoying it a little too much, twisting it sideways and using it to point in the direction in which he wanted them to head. When Craig had held the weapon, it was a burden; with Mark, it was like an extension of his arm.

The ground was a mix of solid, frost-covered earth and marshy, sodden mud. Davey and the other man went where they were told, even wading through thick gloop that went over the top of their shoes when Craig and Mark walked around the edge. Occasionally, they'd mutter something to one another in their native tongue but they were quickly silenced by Mark's hissed threats.

As the foliage became thicker, the area below became darker until it felt like it was almost dusk. The ground was steadily getting wetter, with wider pools crusted with ice and deep slush in the middle. Craig waved to get Mark's attention and then pointed towards a pair of thick trees separated by a patch of sodden nettles. Mark ordered the two men to stop and directed them across to the spot. As Mark covered them with the gun, whispering intermittent threats about what might happen if they dared do anything they weren't told, Craig reattached the blindfolds and then took more of the abrasive rope, wrapping it around their legs, torsos and arms, tying each of them to different trees. With Davey, he left himself one final loop to go around the man's throat. He didn't tie it *too* tightly, just enough to make him uncomfortable. With more material, he gagged both men.

Craig turned to go but Mark wasn't done. He pressed the barrel of the gun to Davey's forehead and leant in close enough that the other man would be able to smell his breath.

'Can you hear me, pal?'

Davey tried to nod but could barely move.

'I'm going to be sitting just over that ridge we passed. If either of you even think about moving, you're going to know about it. Got it?'

Another failed attempt at a nod.

Mark and Craig both turned, heading in the direction from which they'd come. They were almost at the car when Mark spoke again: 'How long do you reckon it'll be until they get away?'

'A few hours. Even if it was right away, they'd struggle to get back to Manchester in time to stop anything. They'll have no idea where they are – plus, when they *do* get out, they'll hardly want to draw attention to themselves. If they try to thumb a lift or go to the golf club, people will ask who they are and where they come from. That's the last thing they want.'

'Good thinking. How long have we got?'

Craig checked his watch. 'Plenty of time.'

37

It was approximately three miles from Tiger Pawn to China-town. In a car at rush hour, it might take twenty minutes, fifteen if a driver was *really* lucky and there were no red lights. On a bad day, it could be half an hour. On a bike, however, it was a different matter. Especially on a BMX when the city's ancient cobbles could be easily negotiated, narrow alleys became cut-throughs to avoid the traffic, pavements were fair game. At teatime, riding a bike from Salford to Manchester was most likely the fastest way to get anywhere.

Craig had seen the BMX rider in the launderette at a few minutes after five. He'd also seen him in the brothel three miles away at around the same time, though the woman behind the counter had told him he was late. Craig's plan had three parts, two of which were crucial, one that could go either way. Snaring the bike rider would be a bonus but if he was late again, it would be his lucky day.

He had no idea which route the cyclist would take towards Chinatown but Craig did know he'd arrived at the launderette from the north end of the street. That narrowed it down to half a dozen alleys he could use. The main thoroughfares were heaving with people, so chances were that he'd aim for one of the smaller ginnels that flanked the back of the shops and flats. That narrowed the choice to three. One of them was so packed with overflowing bins that the rider would have had to get off and walk, leaving two options.

Craig knew which one he fancied: Kennedy Street. It was a one-way lane a little north of Chinatown, narrow enough that only one vehicle could get down it at a time without mounting the pavement. One end had a series of pubs but the other was overlooked by buildings that were either for sale or to let. Double yellow lines ran most of the way along, except for a short area where the lane widened out, providing a handful of parking spaces. The BMX rider would have to go through a no entry sign but it would take time off his journey and provide a more direct route towards the launderette.

The suit Craig had hired was itchy and too big but could prove necessary in a short while. He tugged at the cuffs as he leant against a lamppost at the top end of the road a short distance from Kennedy Street, peering both ways while holding his phone to his ear.

'It's almost ten past,' Mark said in his ear.

'I know, we've still got time.'

'Not long if your mate's out at half past.'

'We're fine.'

As Craig spoke, a cyclist zipped past on a road bike. He was clad in dark Lycra with a fluorescent yellow tabard that reflected so much light it would be impossible to miss him. It dawned on Craig that he'd seen the BMX rider wearing a dark cap with a black backpack. There were no lights on his bike, so he'd be more difficult to see.

'You sure he's coming?' Mark said.

'No – but I saw him collecting money, well, *something* from the pawn shop in Salford, then he delivered it in Chinatown.'

Craig didn't mention the other place in Salford where he'd seen the bike rider doing his daily collection.

There was a pause before Mark replied: 'Why would they get a kid on a bike to pick up a pile of money?'

'Because nobody pays him a blind bit of attention. Pedestrians are busy looking where they're going, chatting to each other, or listening to their headphones. Drivers are keeping an eye on the road. Nobody's watching the kid on a BMX.'

'I s'pose. It's quite smart, really. The police are never going to stop a kid on a bike but they might pull over a car or motorbike, even by accident, for a random check.'

Craig didn't know for sure if he was correct but it felt right. There'd be other places for pick-ups, too. The Grey Goose pub for one, plus other ventures in which Haken had a stake. They'd leave enough money so that the businesses could continue to run legitimately but everything else had to be skimmed from the top, transported back to Chinatown and then laundered through the books of restaurants, dry cleaners, shops and launderettes – wherever Haken could get away with it. It was wonderfully simplistic but that was the key. The more people involved, the more chance there was of failure.

As he continued to look from side to side, Craig finally saw what he was waiting for. The bike was dark, as were the young man's clothes. He was almost camouflaged against the early evening gloom, not bothering to pedal as he stood tall and weaved his way across the road, angling towards the no entry sign.

'He's coming your way.'

Craig hung up, pocketing the phone and walking as quickly as he could across the road without breaking into a run. He reached the junction with Kennedy Street just as the BMX rider started to pedal again. There were a couple of people at the far end of the road in front of the pub but that was a hundred metres away, probably more. At the top end, the shadows were lengthy, the area deserted – except for Mark leaning next to the people carrier.

It happened so fast that Craig almost missed it. As the courier pumped his legs to get along Kennedy Street, Mark swung with a golf club, catching him viciously in the chest. The bike skidded forward for a few metres and then toppled to the side, landing with a clatter. Craig broke into a run, reaching the scene as Mark was hauling the teenager up from the pavement.

'Where did the golf club come from?' Craig asked breathlessly.

Mark didn't answer, heaving the groaning teenager towards the back of the vehicle. He didn't look badly hurt, more winded, which was one good thing. Mark held the gun in front of the young man's face, telling him to do what he was told, and reaching for the bike.

This had been Craig's idea – minus the golf club – but it felt all too real now. Dealing with Haken and Davey was one thing – they'd come for him – but the person in front of him was just a kid, seventeen or eighteen, wide-eyed and terrified.

It was too late now, though.

Craig removed the courier's backpack and then tied his arms and legs together before gagging him. He riffled through his pockets, taking out a mobile phone and hurling it to the ground before stamping on it. He whispered to the lad that he'd be fine if he didn't do anything stupid and then waited for Mark to toss the bike into the back and then they lifted the teenager in next to it. Craig closed the boot softly and then hurried to the driver's seat, throwing the backpack onto the passenger's seat. Mark climbed into the row of seats behind. The cyclist was jammed into the compartment at the back of the vehicle.

'How long have we got?' Mark asked.

'At least ten minutes.'

'How much is in the bag?'

Craig reached across and unzipped the top, peering inside where there was a huge pile of loose notes, all folded and creased into each other.

'Thousands. We'll count later.'

'Bang on.'

If anything, they had too much time to waste. Craig eased away from the parking spot and joined the main flow of traffic, doing a double loop of the block before pulling onto the street adjacent to the location of the apothecary's shop. He lined the back doors up with the exit of the side alley and left the engine idling. It was five twenty-eight.

'How do you know he'll be out at half five?' Mark asked.

'I don't, not really, but he seems like a person who keeps to rituals and timetables. I've seen him leave at five thirty twice.'

'What if he's not here?'

'I don't know.'

There was a short pause before Mark spoke again: 'He might have tried calling those mobiles of the blokes we nicked this car from.'

'Perhaps he has. We can only control certain things. He'll have to poke his head up sooner or later.'

'We should've killed those other two. They tried to set you on fire.'

'I know.'

'So why'd we leave them in the woods?'

5.29.

'I don't know.'

There was a thump from the cyclist rattling around the rear compartment. Mark replied instantly, 'Oi! Don't make me come back there!' – which almost sounded comical. An angry dad with rowdy kids in the back seat on a long journey. Except it wasn't that at all.

Mark shuffled in his seat and Craig could feel the pull of his gaze in the mirror. 'This is like the old days,' Mark said with a grin.

'I know.'

Mark grinned wider, thinking it was a compliment but it was anything but for Craig. It was a sign of how far he'd fallen.

'Will you kill him for me?'

The time was coming when Craig would have to make his choice.

5.30.

There was nobody in the alley, just silhouettes of

shoppers bustling back and forth at the other end. Five seconds. Ten seconds. Still nobody. Mark shuffled, which only made Craig feel more nervous. Fifteen seconds. Was Haken coming? What were the options if he didn't? Craig had gambled everything on red and the ball was hovering over black. Twenty seconds.

'Is that him?'

Mark didn't sound sure but Craig knew the moment he saw the darkened outline. Haken was walking along the alley, phone in hand, not looking up. Craig gasped, realising he'd been holding his breath.

Haken continued walking until he emerged from the alley when Mark slid open the rear door of the people carrier. Haken glanced up briefly, perhaps noticing Mark's suit, perhaps not. Either way, he stepped up into the car and reclined into the seat before closing the door himself. Craig was watching him in the mirror, looking for a hint that something was wrong but there was no recognition at all . . . not until Haken peered up and saw Craig's eyes in the mirror. In a flash, he lunged for the door but Mark was ahead of him, drawing the pistol and aiming it at the other man's head. Haken froze, holding his arms out to the side as Mark reached into the man's inner jacket pocket and removed another pistol. They were building quite a collection – this was their fourth. Nobody spoke as Mark reached the gun through the gap and dropped it onto the passenger seat. He didn't take his eyes from the captive as he leant back, gun still levelled, slipping out the handcuffs they'd taken from Davey and passing them across.

'Put them on,' he ordered.

Haken did as he was told, snapping the cuff around one wrist and clipping it together, then repeating the process with the other. Mark stretched forward with his free hand and clicked them tighter.

'Well then,' he said to Craig, 'what are we waiting for?'

38

It was one thing to plan, another entirely to actually do it. Craig was trying to watch the road, forcing himself to remain calm, even though his heart was thundering its disapproval. Every few seconds, he glanced in the mirror, taking in Haken's unmoving appearance, looking for fear or fury. There was neither: the man was as calm when a captive as he was when giving orders. Craig wondered what it would take to scare him, not that he wanted to find out.

What he did know was that *he* was scared. Scared of Mark and of what Kimberly had asked him to do. There was a pistol on the passenger seat next to him. He could reach across, pick it up, and shoot both Haken and Mark. Easy peasy: dump the bodies in the canal, phone his parents and tell them to come home, then live happily ever after with Kimberly.

But he knew he couldn't do it . . . not yet.

He continued driving through the city until he reached the square of garages where he'd delivered the guns what seemed like such a long time ago. The rented car was parked in front of the garage where they'd left it and Craig pulled in behind.

'You all right by yourself?' Mark asked.

'For now.'

Craig picked up the backpack from the passenger seat

and tucked the spare pistol into the back of his suit trousers. He unlocked the garage with the key taken from Davey, then placed the bag and pistol inside. He took the other two guns from the boot of the rented car and added them to the pile, then returned to unload a roll of plastic sheeting. For good measure, he took the BMX from the back of the people carrier, made sure the teenager was still breathing – he was – and then closed it again. With everything unpacked, he returned to the people carrier, sliding open the rear door.

'Out,' Mark ordered.

Haken said nothing, features unmoved as he twisted himself and stepped down, stumbling slightly as he tried to balance without using his cuffed hands. The square was overrun with shadows, the only light coming from the cloud-covered moon and a vague glimmer from the top windows of the few houses nearby. His eyes locked onto Craig's, giving nothing away as Mark ordered him to enter the garage. Craig locked both vehicles and then followed Mark inside, closing the garage door behind them.

This was the place Craig had changed into the police uniform on the night Davey had tried to kill him but it seemed different now. Many of the boxes had been moved, leaving a large clear space at the back. The uniforms were nowhere to be seen, neither was the crate of weapons he'd delivered. Presumably this was some sort of pick-up and drop-off point for the operation.

The single bulb flickered above as Craig spread the sheeting across the floor and then taped it to the walls. All the while, he could feel Haken watching as Mark covered him with the gun. There was a single wooden chair lying on its side but Craig righted it and placed it in the middle of the sheeted area.

'Sit,' Mark said, still pointing the gun towards Haken, who did as he'd been ordered.

Craig tied his feet to the chair and then retreated to the front of the garage.

Mark was standing a few feet away from the seated man, the gun finally lowered. He glanced over his shoulder. 'How much is in there?'

'I'll look.'

As Mark turned away, Craig picked up the backpack and one of the three pistols. Now he knew what he was doing, it was easy to pop the gun's clip out and back in. It was definitely loaded, with a small safety catch next to the trigger, which he flicked off. Initially he'd known nothing about guns, but his time in the Internet cafe had proved useful. The pistol was ready to fire. Point and shoot. He tucked it into his pocket and then unzipped the bag and tipped its contents onto the floor. There was a mix of ten- and twenty-pound notes but it didn't take him long to sort them, bundling everything into piles of five hundred pounds and then returning them to the backpack.

'There's about fifteen grand,' Craig said.

'I can give you so much more than that.'

It was the first thing Haken had said since getting into the car and was met with instant retribution. Mark strode forward and raised the gun to the other man's head. 'Go on – say it again.'

Haken pressed his lips together, remaining silent. Mark

stepped backwards, feet crinkling across the plastic, as he glanced up to catch Craig's eye across the garage.

'Macklin . . .'

Haken's mouth had barely twitched but the word resonated around the enclosed space. He'd said hardly anything but it was still dripping with threat. Craig shook his head a fraction, telling Mark to let it go. He put down the money-filled bag and walked slowly towards the seated man.

'Why did you try to have me killed?'

Haken gazed back at him impassively. 'I don't like loose ends.'

Craig wanted to seem calm but he had to hold his arms behind his back to stop the others from seeing how much he was shaking. He could feel the weight of the gun in his pocket, calling him, telling him how easy this could be.

'I could say the same,' Craig replied.

Haken bowed his head slightly. 'I don't fear death, Mr Macklin.'

'I don't understand why it had to come to this. I wanted to pay off the money my parents owed. It was simple, none of this had to happen.'

'Everything happens for a reason.'

'So this is fine for you? Instead of taking the money – which wasn't even your debt in the first place – you'd rather end up dead in a garage?'

Haken's only movement was to shift slightly in the chair, which rocked with him. He wasn't trying to escape, merely wanting to get comfortable. He said nothing.

'Answer me,' Craig demanded.

'What would you have me say?'

'I want you to tell me if you think this is worth it.'

'You want justification for your actions.'

Craig removed the gun from his trousers and levelled it at Haken. 'Answer me.'

Haken smiled, unmoving, closing his eyes and daring Craig to do it.

'Did you have Rodger murdered?' Craig asked.

Haken's smile widened, his eyes opening again. 'You've already made up your mind.'

'I want you to tell me what you did.'

A nod. 'You want a lot of things.'

'I'm just trying—'

'You're trying to talk yourself into it,' Haken said. 'You want to be able to shoot me, to end this but you don't have it in you—'

'Shut up!'

'If I tell you I wanted you dead, that I killed Rodger, that I'm responsible for everything bad that's happened to you, then you might build up enough anger to actually pull the trigger but I don't think even that would do it. You're a follower, a yes man. You could have walked away from that airport collection job but you didn't – you did what you were told—'

'Shut it—'

'You didn't have to go to that tower block but you did as you were told. You *always* do what you're told. That's the person you are.'

Craig bounded forward, pressing the barrel of the pistol to Haken's forehead, finger primed over the trigger.

'Shut up.'

'Or what, Mr Macklin? Are you going to shoot me? If you were, it'd already be done. Your friend on the other hand . . .'

Craig peered up, staring at Mark who was scratching his temple with his own gun. He was stifling a smile, amused at the spectacle. Haken was saying what Mark had known since they were eight years old. Craig *was* a follower. He'd trailed Mark until they were teenagers and, even when he'd got away, he'd turned around thirteen years later and walked right back into the same situation.

Craig took a step backwards, his foot twisting slightly on the slippery plastic. Two more steps and he was on the concrete floor of the garage.

'I'm going to go,' he whispered. Mark nodded, knowingly, as if he'd realised all along this would happen. 'I'll take the rental car.'

Mark nodded again, taking the hint. Mark could deal with the courier in the back of the people carrier. Craig hoped he didn't kill the poor lad but he wasn't brave enough to say it out loud.

Craig scooped up the backpack. 'I'll leave your half at your house.'

'Top stuff.'

'*Will you kill him for me?*'

Kimberly's request darted through Craig's thoughts. Now or never. He had the gun in his hand. Bang! One shot for Haken. Bang! A second for Mark. The plastic sheeting was right there. He could bundle them both up, dump them somewhere they wouldn't be found, collect Kimberly and off they'd go. Perhaps he didn't even have to do that. Bang!

Bang! Two shots and he'd leave the bodies for someone else to find. When the police found the bodies and discovered Haken's identity, they'd look into it properly and assume Mark got caught in the crossfire of a gang war. Easy. This was the moment in which he discovered the type of person he was. Follower or leader? Man or mouse?

The problem was that he already knew.

Craig crouched and placed the gun on the ground. He hoisted the garage door up and then pulled it closed. He hadn't even had time to start the car's engine when he heard a single muffled bang from the garage.

39

Kimberly hurled a bag into the car's boot and then leapt into the passenger seat next to Craig. She was wearing the same hat from the launderette, hair tied up underneath, with a warm-looking jumper and jeans. She sounded nervous but excited, voice quivering slightly. 'You're here.'

'I told you I would be.'

'It was getting late and . . .' She paused as Craig pulled away, her voice wavering further. 'You didn't do it, did you?'

Craig knew that he was going to have to tell her at some point but didn't think it was going to come out so instantly.

'It wasn't that simple,' he replied. 'That doesn't stop us running. He might come looking for us but that doesn't mean we'll be found. The country's a big place and that's if we stay in the UK.'

She took a deep breath, sinking into her seat, struggling to hide the disappointment. 'What about your parents?'

'I'll tell them it's safe to go home but that I'm moving back to London. Simple as that. Mark might ask if they know where I am but he's not stupid. He won't do anything to them.'

Kimberly reached across and squeezed his knee, though she said nothing. The truth was that Craig wasn't entirely sure how Mark might react. He'd definitely be angry when he put the pieces together. Craig would have stolen not only *his* woman but the money too. It wasn't just fifteen thousand, it was closer to twenty-five. Plus there was the near three thousand Craig had that Haken had refused as payment, and the daily amounts of three hundred quid. In all, he had almost thirty thousand in cash. It wasn't enough to disappear forever, but it could buy him and Kimberly some time while they figured out what to do next.

'Where am I going?' Craig asked.

'Get on the motorway and go north. Keep going and I'll direct you.'

He wanted to ask for more details about the place she'd mentioned in the launderette, the 'somewhere' they could stay for a few days, but he felt tired. It was as if a weight had been lifted, though only temporarily. Within a day or two, there'd be a new one resting on him.

Considering this was what he'd wanted for more than half his life, being with Kimberly felt strangely hollow. She rested her hand on his leg for most of the journey, only shifting when he had to change gear. Greater Manchester soon became Lancashire, then they passed Lancaster and he wasn't sure where he was. The motorway was barely lit and the traffic was intermittent.

There was so much Craig had wanted to say to Kimberly over the years but none of it now seemed appropriate, not after what they'd been through. He'd planned entire conversations: he'd say this, she'd say that, and then he'd come back with something else. Then they'd ride off into the sunset happily ever after. Now, he didn't know what to say because what he *really* wanted was to go back in time and make Kimberly choose him in the first place.

They'd gone past the motorway exit for Penrith when Kimberly told Craig it was time to get off. She was scratching nervously at her arms, aping the anxiety he was feeling. They had been driving for a hundred miles, which wasn't a bad buffer zone to start with.

He wondered what Mark would be up to at this moment. Had he disposed of Haken's body? And what would he have done with the BMX courier? He'd have had to dump the people carrier somewhere and get back to Salford. Perhaps he'd just finished that and would be pressing through his front door, wondering where Kimberly was, not to mention his money. Craig's phone was switched off, so perhaps he'd been calling? Maybe he'd been phoning Kimberly too? Craig had no idea if her mobile was on or off.

The wide motorway lanes quickly became narrow country roads, dusted with frost and uncluttered by such niceties as streetlights. Even with the headlights, it was near impossible to see anything other than the overgrown verges. Craig crawled at barely thirty miles an hour, paranoid that he'd career off the road and make this all for nothing. He also kept checking the mirrors, knowing he couldn't have been followed but fearful that Mark had somehow figured out the plan and would be a few miles behind.

'It's just up here,' Kimberly said. The first time she'd spoken in a long while.

Craig slowed and pulled off the road onto a gravelly track towards a large field full of caravans. There was a wide metal gate across the opening but Kimberly climbed out and opened it, waiting for Craig to pull through. There was no light coming from anywhere nearby, as if the entire area was a long-abandoned ghost town. The only noise was the crackling pop of the stones and grit underneath the wheels as Craig continued driving, taking the left fork when the path split into two, and then kept going until they were almost at the very back. Kimberly pointed between two static homes and Craig parked at the end of the path, peering towards where she was pointing. The caravan seemed large from the outside, with long aluminium panels flanking the sides, wide windows at one end, and a crooked television aerial fixed to the top. There were a couple of breezeblocks in place as steps leading up to a door, and a small wooden shed next to the hedge.

The already stifled glow of the moon was hidden behind a tall bank of swaying trees, making it as close to pitch black as Craig could remember. The only sound was Kimberly's gentle breathing.

'Are you all right?' she asked.

'Yes, you?'

He couldn't see her features clearly enough to know if she was smiling; he could only feel her hand stroking his leg. 'Of course.'

40

Craig lugged his and Kimberly's bags into the caravan, bashing into the door, a unit, a wall, another door, another wall and finally the bed before dropping them. He fumbled his way backwards, trying to figure out where everything was before there was a spark and then a candle was alight. The flame danced across Kimberly's features until she placed it next to the sink and then held her hands in front of it. The night was freezing and Craig was struggling to stop his teeth from chattering.

The trickle of light at least gave him some idea of the caravan's layout – there was the door, then a couple of steps up, with the kitchen area immediately on the left. Two doors were on the other side, the bedroom and a bathroom, then there was a lounge area at the far end with a U-shaped sofa. It wasn't quite five-star . . .

'My mum used to bring me here on holiday,' Kimberly whispered.

'I remember you used to complain about it a lot.'

'That's because I had to spend a week with her. She wanted to go walking off around lakes and mountains but I wanted to be at home with you and . . .' She stopped and then corrected herself: 'With you.'

'Won't Mark—?'

She shook her head. 'We came here once a few years ago

and he said he hated it. We've not been back since. I doubt he remembers it's mine, else he would have wanted me to sell it. I came up one day last year to check everything still worked. Mark didn't know. We'll be fine here for a few days until we figure out what to do.'

'Why's the place so empty?'

She sniggered and nudged him with her elbow. 'Because it's December. The caravan park isn't officially open.'

'How did you know there wouldn't be a lock on the gate?'

She shrugged. 'I didn't but we would've found a way in somehow. There's no one out here at this time of year.' Kimberly passed the candle across and nodded towards the sofa. 'Go and sit over there.'

Craig put the candle on the small coffee table and curled up on the sofa, trying to get comfortable against the itchy material. There was a smell that he couldn't quite place, probably mould or something which would be indicative of a place at the mercy of the elements that had been left empty for a while. Kimberly reached up into a cupboard built into the wall and dragged out a roll of blankets, which she threw towards him, before delving into the cupboard under the sink. She took out a couple more candles and left them on the sink, then joined him on the sofa. She wrapped her legs underneath herself and then pulled the covers across them, resting her head on his shoulder.

'There's an old gas cylinder underneath that's probably still connected but I wouldn't want to risk using the cooker – we'd end up with carbon monoxide poisoning, or whatever it's called. The park's electricity is only turned on during the season, so we'll have to make do with candles when it's dark.'

Craig twisted so that he could see her face. The flame flickered orange and black, the spark lighting up her eyes as she gazed at him. She seemed worried.

'What's wrong?' Craig asked.

'There's no going back, is there?'

'No.'

She sighed, though it might have been a deep breath. 'There's a camping stove underneath the sink. It's one of those ones with the fancy biofuel – you light it and it burns itself out. There's a box of teabags in the cupboard and we can go out tomorrow to get some milk and whatever else.'

'Sounds good.'

'Are you sure?'

'Why wouldn't I be?'

She burrowed her head back into his shoulder. 'I don't know – it doesn't sound like much, does it? Tea on a camping stove in the middle of a caravan park the week before Christmas.'

'We'll be able to spend Christmas together.'

Kimberly didn't reply, probably because it didn't seem like much of a prospect at that moment. Craig didn't blame her. She was still scraping anxiously at her arm, as she had in the car, probably wondering the same as him: what now?

Christmas was whatever a person chose to make of it. It might be a family occasion, or a time to receive a mountain of presents. It might be all about the giving, or it could be a day to eat so much that moving from the sofa became a challenge. In the case of Craig's father – certainly in the old days – it would mean a day of drinking. For Craig, he knew it would be a day of hiding somewhere, perhaps a hotel or a guesthouse in the middle of nowhere. It would mean anxiety at any knocks at the door and ignoring any contact from his parents. It wasn't a lot to look forward to . . . except for the fact that he had Kimberly. Surely that was the only thing he needed?

Craig was thinking ahead, wondering what the coming days might bring: 'We're going to have to get new sim cards, plus—'

Kimberly reached up and pressed a finger to his lips. 'Shush.'

'What?'

'Let's do all that tomorrow.'

'What would you like to do now?'

She gripped him tighter, lips dancing across his neck, the question answered.

Craig woke up as a chill flittered across his goosebump-covered arm. His hairs were standing on end, heart racing. He'd been dreaming about . . . something . . . of what, he wasn't sure. The imagery had disappeared as instantly as he'd woken.

It took him a moment to realise where he was. The mattress was unforgiving, the covers were thin and over only half of him. He shuffled into a sitting position, feeling the thin wall behind him and suddenly remembering. Kimberly was next to him, lying on her side, facing away towards the window. She'd rolled over at some point, taking the covers with her. The clouds must have dispersed because the moon was far brighter than it had been, glistening a sallow glow through the thin curtains. Craig could see the back of her neck, which looked ethereally enticing in the light. She had one arm underneath the pillow, another cricked underneath her chin. Her hair was the only part of her on top of the covers, wonderfully intricate patterns of gentle waves weaving their way along the creases of the sheet.

Craig sat watching her for a few minutes, transfixed, convincing himself that everything would be all right. The caravan wasn't that bad and would no doubt look better by day. Not only that, the idea of renting one for the medium-term wasn't too bad an idea. They could find somewhere completely different, to which they had no connection, set themselves up temporarily and get jobs. After that, who knew? They were resourceful and smart.

As he realised he'd been breathing in time with her, Craig swung himself out of bed, hunched low and scrabbled underneath the bed to find his shoes and phone. The bed creaked as he stood, remaining stooped to avoid the low, sloping ceiling. He took a final look at Kimberly and then slid the bedroom door open and moved into the main area of the caravan. There was a definite breeze coming from somewhere, filling the area with a ghost-like chill.

Craig retrieved a blanket from the sofa and wrapped it around himself before taking a seat. His phone had been off since he'd driven away from the garages but he held the button at the top and waited for it to turn itself on. There was a flash, a tinkling tone that sounded like a plane taking off in comparison to the silence, a second flash, and then a simple screen. He waited for the missed calls to flood through: Mark wondering where the money was, Mark wondering where *he* was, Mark asking what had happened.

There was nothing.

No text messages either. At first Craig thought he had no reception but it wasn't that. He even tried accessing the Internet to make sure and it worked perfectly. It was slow but he managed to load the *Manchester Morning Herald*'s website, looking for news of a gruesome find in a Salford garage.

Nothing.

Was that strange? Perhaps not. Mark would have been more likely to contact Kimberly, plus Craig hadn't specifically said he'd drop off half the money that evening. As for Haken's body, Craig had no idea what Mark was doing with it. Even if he had left it in the garage, it could have been found by one of Haken's men, who decided to get rid of it, rather than involve the police. There were so many unknowns that he shouldn't worry – although that was easy to think, less simple to actually do.

Craig turned off the phone and the caravan was left in the dim bluey haze from the moon. It was a couple of minutes before three in the morning and he should be tired. He certainly *had* been, falling asleep ahead of Kimberly, before he'd been woken by the mixture of his dreams and the cold.

Reasoning that he should probably figure out where everything was if they were going to be here for a few days, Craig crossed back to the kitchen area and lit one of the candles, pocketing the lighter, before going through the cupboards. There were a few tins of baked beans in the one next to the window, plus a can of Spam – a proper old-school tea. The chicken soup was after its best before date but did soup *ever* go off? Wasn't the whole point that it didn't?

The fridge was built into the cabinet underneath, though there was no light, no chill, and nothing inside. A few packs of unused batteries were underneath the sink alongside the camping stove Kimberly had mentioned, plus more candles, a couple of lighters and four cans of sprayable lighter fluid with '*Highly Flammable*' emblazoned across the side just in case the name wasn't a giveaway. Presumably that was there for the same people who needed '*Warning: Drink Is Hot*' on the side of a coffee cup. How some people lived day-to-day was beyond him – they must have a tattoo on one palm, reading: '*Breathe In*', with '*Breathe Out*' on the other.

Craig closed the cupboard and moved back to the living-room end. The whole caravan seemed to have hidden compartments for storage concealed as part of the furniture. The area under the sofa pulled away to create another bed, with the panelling above the windows hiding long rows of narrow cubicles. Craig stood on the sofa and reached up, pulling out a small pile of what turned out to be car magazines and a cushion cover. Nothing exciting. The space was otherwise empty. He flicked through the opening pages of the magazines, utterly uninterested. He'd never understood car people. A car had an engine that made a bit of noise and travelled at a speed a driver would never be able to go at – so what? Blah, blah, blah. Grow up.

He shoved them back into the cupboard and closed it, flopping back onto the sofa and peering through the glass towards the rest of the site. The plot of land was huge, far bigger than it had seemed from the road. There were at least a hundred static sites on one half and rows of pitches on the other for holidaymakers to pull up. Aside from the car outside, there was very little to see other than the shapes of various static homes stretching into the distance.

Before he could prevent it, a yawn was creasing through Craig's body, followed instantly by a second. His jaw clicked and, from nowhere, his eyes were beginning to throb. He carried the blanket with him back to the bedroom and eased himself onto the mattress as delicately as he could.

It amused him that, in all the thoughts he'd had of Kimberly over the years, he'd never pictured her as a cover-stealer. It was the type of thing discovered about a person when it was already too late to back away from the relationship. It should be a question on the Internet dating profile forms: do you steal the covers? Yes/no. Do you snore? Yes/no. Do you kick anyone in the immediate vicinity while sleeping? Yes/no.

As Craig rested a hand on her hip, Kimberly fidgeted slightly, moaning softly and rolling onto her back.

Her voice was croaky, addled with tiredness. 'You okay?'

Craig squeezed her gently. 'I'm perfect.'

She scratched hard at her arm. 'What time is it?'

'Late . . . well, early. Go back to sleep.' Craig propped himself up to kiss her on the forehead but she was already on the move again, shuffling back to her side of the mattress with a grunt. Within a moment, her ribs were rising and falling again. Craig watched her for a few moments more until finally getting his head down.

*

When Craig woke the next time, his dream was still fresh in his mind. There was a car crunching across gravel, grit flying, tyres bouncing in and out of potholes. It was easing along the path of the caravan park towards them. He didn't jolt this time but there were still goosebumps on his arms, his hairs standing on end.

He shifted onto his back, reaching for Kimberly, who was facing the wall. It was still dark outside, though that meant nothing at this time of year – there was little difference between five in the evening and seven in the morning. Craig jabbed the glow button on his watch – it was quarter to four . . . at best he'd been asleep for half an hour. It didn't feel as if he'd been out of it for long; presumably he'd fallen into a near-instant dream state.

Except there *was* a noise outside the caravan . . . wasn't there?

Craig swung his legs out of the bed and sat up straight, not daring to breathe in case it stopped him hearing what might be outside. Was there a crunch? Craig remained motionless for more than a minute until finally resolving that his dreams and reality must have become intermingled with each other. He was paranoid, for the most part with good reason. There was no one outside, nothing around for miles. It was just him and Kimberly by themselves.

And then there was a bang.

41

Kimberly jumped, flipping onto her back. 'Craig?'

'I'm here.'

'Did you do something?'

'No . . . I . . .' He stood, listening. There had definitely been a popping sound but nothing since. 'Wait here,' he added.

'Where are you going?'

'To check outside.'

'Did you—?'

'Wait here – I'll be right back.'

Craig slipped on his shoes, took his jacket from the built-in wardrobe and then picked up a candle and lighter from the kitchen. The hairs on the back of his neck were standing up. It had been a single noise but they'd both heard it. No imagination this time, no dream. There could be harmless explanations: a skulking cat sending something flying; a car on the main road clipping something in the dark . . . but Craig was picturing none of those. The dream of the car crunching across the gravel suddenly felt as if it might not have been a dream. Perhaps someone was there: Haken's men? Or Mark? Craig had kept the same rented car, so the number plate could have been traced via traffic cameras, and . . . he wasn't sure.

Or Kimberly was wrong and Mark *had* known right away

that this was the place to which she would run. Or . . . something else. He wasn't sure but it didn't feel right.

The main area of the caravan was as still as it had been an hour before. Craig peeped through the window but could see nothing untoward. He crept down the stairs and eased the main door open, exposing his face and hands to a blitz of freezing air that momentarily stole his breath. Craig stepped onto the disjointed paving slab outside and eased the door into place behind him. He didn't click it completely closed in case there was some sort of automatic lock of which he was unaware.

The moon was now so bright that the candle would be a waste of time. Craig put it on the ground, pocketed the lighter and tiptoed forward, peering from side to side, squinting towards the shadows stretching from the towering trees. He couldn't see anything other than the storage block in the corner and the fence line. In the other direction, the car was parked where he'd left it, with a long row of darkened caravans beyond. Craig reached the gravelly path and turned in a circle, listening to the silence.

There!

He dropped to his knees, peeping underneath the caravan opposite Kimberly's. He'd definitely heard something, a scrabbling sound. He could see a gas canister and an upturned wheelbarrow, plus shapes far too dark to make out. When he turned, he realised that there was space under each of the caravans. Some had boards and fences to stop anyone getting underneath, others were using it as a storage area. The noise could easily have been an animal under one of the caravans, perhaps even Kimberly's. Craig crept back in the direction he'd come from, crouching to check. Horizontal planks skirted the edge but they were sodden and rotting, with gaps. Any creature could have easily sneaked underneath . . . that was probably where the bang came from.

Except that Craig couldn't let it go. A creeping sense of being watched was bubbling through him . . . eyes in the darkness, tracking where he was . . . waiting.

Craig started walking along the path towards the gate, trying not to shiver. The cold air was scratching the back of his throat, his breath billowing in front as he walked. He had gloves and a hat in his duffel but that was in the caravan. He stopped every few rows, crouching to peer underneath the caravans, looking for something, he wasn't quite sure what. In any case, he wasn't finding it.

There were no animals, no knocked-over crates or gas canisters, nothing that shouldn't be there. A high row of hedges flanked the edges of the park, shadows potentially holding their own secrets but Craig kept to the path, reaching the fork and continuing towards the gate in the distance. It was still closed, apparently untouched since they'd been through.

He upped his pace, not bothering to check under the other caravans as he reached the end, pressing his hands onto the cool metal of the gate and lifting himself over the top until he was on the road. The empty, deserted road. There was nothing in either direction, not even a distant sound of vehicles, only silence.

This was pure paranoia, almost obsession. He was going to have to tell Kimberly that staying here was impractical. It might be remote but he'd never be able to sleep knowing there were so many places someone could hide around them. They'd be better in a hotel, not necessarily dirt-cheap, but a place with all the normal facilities, like a reception desk, locked doors and perhaps CCTV.

Craig re-climbed the gate and pulled his coat tighter, starting to head back to the caravan, looking forward to the warmth of the blankets, when he felt the tug of something being not quite right.

In between the second and third caravans on the row where Kimberly's caravan stood was a single parked car.

Craig froze, taking a step away as if it was an immediate threat by itself. It was twenty-five to thirty pitches away from Kimberly's. He must have walked past it moments before. Had it been there when they'd arrived earlier that night? He'd missed it a minute or two earlier, so perhaps he'd driven straight past it beforehand?

Nothing moved.

The car was black and sporty, with a curved spoiler at the back and sun guard at the front. The number plate was two or three years old, but speckled by mud, with thick splashes of dirt around the wheel rims and lower bodywork. It would be a strange vehicle to abandon for the winter.

Craig edged towards it, slipping from side to side to peer at it from different angles in case there was anyone in the front or back. When he reached the vehicle, Craig smudged his finger across the muck – fresh. It hadn't frozen, so the car must have been driven at some point in the past few hours. He wiped his finger clean on the tyre and peered through the windows. They had a slight tint but a red LED was blinking somewhere close to the gearstick. Other than that, it seemed empty, with nothing on the front or back seats. Craig was about to walk away when he tried the handle for good measure – locked, as was the boot.

The caravans on either side of the car sounded silent. It was possible that someone had arrived for a December night away – like Kimberly and he had – but possible and probable were two different things. Would people *really* arrive in the early hours of the morning a few days before Christmas? The ground around the car was solid from the frost, with no obvious footprints or other marks.

'Hello?'

Craig didn't speak loudly but his voice reverberated around the immediate area. If anyone came out, he could say he heard their car, which wasn't untrue. He was making sure everything was all right. Except that nobody emerged. Not even an animal or bird squawked or rustled in response. Everything was still.

In a final attempt to convince himself he'd not made it up, Craig smeared his index finger through the mud on the car, peered at it in the dimmed moonlight, and then wiped it away on the ground. He definitely wasn't going mad.

Craig moved back to the path and started to return to the caravan. He'd not convinced himself they were alone but there was little else he could do other than remain awake and wait until the sun rose. In the daylight, it would probably all seem innocent. There might even be other cars parked on the other side of the fork. Perhaps a few people who'd come to spend the weekend before Christmas, or some who rented pitches and were stopping for a night before travelling further south or north. The caravan site was out of the way but there was no security, not even a lock on the gate. Very few people other than those in the caravanning community would even know it was there.

When Craig arrived back at Kimberly's caravan, he stopped to press the mud clinging to the bottom of the rental car, which had frozen. The black car had definitely arrived after them. He checked his watch, which showed it was a little after four. There were three and a half to four hours until it was light again. Not too long to wait, although there wasn't much with which to amuse himself inside. He'd have to go through the cupboards again.

Craig had a hand on the door, ready to climb back into the caravan, when he spotted the small adjacent shed. The top was crusted with frost but the grain of the pale wood was clear at the front from where it had been opened some time recently. He approached but there was a solid padlock at the front, looped through heavy metal rings.

Hmmmm . . .

Craig opened the caravan door and climbed inside, clicking it closed behind. He went up the two steps into the main area and froze. He could hear Kimberly's gentle whimpering, an intake of breath and then shivering. She was crying softly. He had one hand on the bedroom door when he realised it wasn't coming from there. He turned to see the silhouette on the sofa, backlit by the moon creeping through the window behind.

'Kim?'

The figure was trembling but didn't look like her . . . until Craig took a step towards the living area, realising it wasn't a single silhouette at all. There were two people sitting next to each other on the sofa. Kimberly's hair was unmistakeable in the light but the other shape was someone he *did* know, a person he hadn't expected to see again.

Haken's voice whispered unwaveringly through the darkness: 'Hello, Mr Macklin.'

42

'Let her go.'

Craig's voice faltered as he took a step forward but Haken raised his arm, pointing a pistol towards him. 'I think you should stay where you are, Mr Macklin.'

He seemed even more intimidating in the light of the moon, half-doused in shadow, gaze unaffected. Kimberly's shape was entirely in shadow but Craig could see her shivering, hear her snivelling quietly.

'Don't you dare hurt her.' Craig tried to sound firm but there was a quiver to his voice.

'I don't think you're in a position to be making demands.'

There was a coffee table and a couple of metres between them, with no chance of Craig being able to lunge and disarm Haken, even if he did believe he could win in a fight with the man. Which he didn't.

'If you let her go, then you can have me,' Craig said. 'I'm not going anywhere.'

The gun slipped to Haken's side, no longer pointing towards Craig, though it didn't need to. 'I have you anyway. You're here and I have the gun.'

Craig's memory shot back to the weapon he'd left on the floor of the garage. He hadn't wanted it, hadn't thought he'd need it. He wasn't the type to carry around a weapon, nor were most Brits.

'I can give you money . . .' Craig said.

'*My* money. You're offering me the money *you* stole?'

'I have more, you can take the lot, just let her go.'

'You stole from me – why shouldn't I steal from you?'

Craig had no answer. He took a small step forward but the gun was raised again, angling in his direction until he moved backwards. The light glinted from the barrel as Haken lowered it once more.

'What do you want from me?' Craig asked.

'Hmmm . . .' Haken leant forward, moving the rest of his face into the light. His eyes seemed dark, pupil-less, terrifyingly calm. 'That's a tough one. I suppose it's pride. You've caused me a lot of trouble.'

'But I didn't want to be a part of anything, I only wanted to pay you off.'

He nodded. 'True – but I *did* need your help.'

'And I gave it. I helped you with the shipment. I don't understand why it had to go any further.'

Haken was still nodding but, for the first time since Craig had met him, he didn't seem so sure himself. A thin wrinkle seeped across his forehead, as if the answer was lost to him, too.

'What happened at the garage?' Craig asked. 'I heard the gunshot.'

Haken sat up straighter again, lifting the pistol onto his knee, finger still poised on the trigger. 'Yes . . . . It was rather loud in such an enclosed space.'

'I don't understand. Did you kill him?'

'You're asking the wrong questions again, Mr Macklin.'

They stared at one another for a few moments, Craig

trying to put together pieces of the puzzle that didn't fit. 'What *should* I ask?'

A smile: 'You could start with how I found you.'

'Your contacts in the police, the rental car's number plate . . .'

Haken shook his head, turning slowly, devastatingly, towards Kimberly. She was still shaking, the low sobs catching in her throat as her mouth opened to say two simple words: 'I'm sorry.'

Craig's eyes darted between them, unable to believe what he'd heard. '*You* called him? You told him where we were?'

She shook her head, the sobs becoming louder.

'She never called *me*, Mr Macklin . . .'

Craig spun as the bedroom door clicked open. Mark stepped out, cocky half-smile plastered to his face. 'A'ight, mate?'

43

The moon peeped out from the thinning cloud which had masked it, beaming a cascade of light through the caravan window. It was so bright that it could have been daylight. Craig wondered how he'd missed the obvious. Kimberly said she didn't come here with Mark, yet there were car magazines in the cupboard. She'd seduced him and then brought him here, knowing all along that it was to set him up.

Craig turned to see Kimberly's face buried in her hands, sobbing even louder. Mark pushed him in the back, shunting him towards the sofa. 'Probably best we have a bit of a chat, I reckon.'

Mark sat next to Kimberly, leaving Craig on the other end of the U, next to Haken, who pressed his gun into Craig's thigh. If they'd all been friends, it would have been cosy: a nice little spot for a beer and a game of cards. With this company, Craig felt cramped and claustrophobic, his world shattered around him.

Thwack!

The back of Mark's hand lashed across Kimberly's cheek, sending her bouncing off the window.

'For God's sake, stop the whingeing,' he snarled.

Craig reached forward defensively at the sound of the smack but Haken's gun barrel pressed harder into his leg, making him lean away. Kimberly gulped back another sob, sniffing deeply and wincing as she touched the mark on her cheek. Even in the bluey-white moonlight, it looked distinctly pink. She stared at the table between them, saying nothing and not looking up.

Mark was gazing at Craig, the smirk fixed. 'Go on then, ask.'

'I don't understand what's happening.'

'Course you don't. You were too wrapped up in your own world to see it.'

Craig nodded towards Haken. 'You work for him?'

Mark snorted in derision. '*For* him? I work for no one but me.'

A pause. 'He works for you?'

Mark's lips contorted in anger. He was actually offended. Haken sounded amused: 'You English . . . so ignorant.'

'I don't get it,' Craig said.

Mark replied: 'You couldn't even pronounce it properly. It was never "Pung-You", it's "Pung-yu-ooh".' His voice momentarily slipped into a different accent as he shortened the vowels. He nodded towards Haken. 'It means friend.'

'My parents owed money to *you*?'

Craig was beginning to realise how badly he'd been set up. He'd believed loose talk from his father had tipped off Haken's gang about his job, but it had been Mark all along. The old man had been sitting at the back of the basement to throw him off the scent of Pung-You's identity. It was a name he never should have heard, but, once he had, they needed to muddy the waters.

Mark nodded: 'They owed money to *us*.' He poked a

thumb to Haken. 'We're partners. I couldn't believe it when you asked me on the High Street if I knew the name. I almost burst out laughing. My friend – my Pung-yu-ooh – and I had interests in similar fields.'

'Buying and selling.'

'Exactly, but it's a packed marketplace in the city. Lots of people trying to do similar things. My friend had the merchandise, I had access to the buyers. Win-win.'

'But what about the rest? The guns? The drugs in that flat?'

'Capitalism,' Mark replied. 'All businesses have to expand. Different areas, different industries. Selling a few dodgy bags and shoes in the centre can only get you so far, especially up here, plus it's a bit too open. Poor old Willy Porter and his chums found out how easy it is to send the police off to a few lock-ups. It was only a matter of time before the tables were turned. Plus, it's a fickle market.' He nudged Kimberly with his elbow. 'Women lap this stuff up but they only have two feet. They might buy a pair of shoes and then that's it for a few months. There's more money in the loans business.'

'You killed Rodger, didn't you?'

Mark smirked, nodding slowly. 'With your help! I could have found him by myself but figured he'd gone a little crazy. I didn't want to get myself shot by accident. Not only did you find him, you calmed him down and made sure that when I went back, he opened the door for me. Bang-up job.'

Craig wanted to launch himself across the space and

wipe the smile from Mark's face. He'd never really known Rodger, not properly, but he hadn't deserved to be killed.

'You used me,' Craig said.

The wicked glint flickered across Mark's eyes: 'You make it so easy.'

They stared at each other, each now knowing the truth for sure about the night Mark had killed his father. On that occasion, Craig had been manipulated into being there because it was too big a job for one person. Here they were, thirteen years on, and he was still being worked.

'You suggested the Chinese move their business into Salford?'

'Not move, expand,' Mark replied. 'The High Street was ripe for the taking: everyone likes a pint, most blokes want a shag, everyone owes money to everyone else. Easy peasy: throw a little money around to make a lot more and, if that doesn't work, letting them know what happened to Willy Porter will do the trick.' He nodded to Haken again. 'My friend is very . . . creative.'

The picture was beginning to take shape but it wasn't much comfort. The gun was still pushing into Craig's leg and Mark was almost certainly armed. All he could do was talk-talk-talk until they got bored. Perhaps the sun would come up and there'd be some sort of caretaker to alert the police? Something – anything – was better than nothing. Just talk-talk-talk until an opportunity arrived. Mark was enjoying the moment, *wanting* to gloat. It wasn't enough to just shoot him, or else it would have already happened.

'What about the drugs raid on that flat?' Craig asked.

'More capitalism, more expansion. It's all about profit

margins. The loans are great but you're still stuck with people who can't afford to pay, regardless of what you do. The girls are a fun distraction but they have their own cut, then the pub has overheads: staff, stock, and so on. The money's decent but that's long-term. I told you: buy low, sell high. If you can do that when you have a captive market then all the better.'

The significance of their location suddenly dawned on Craig. He'd seen batteries, empty bottles and freezer packs at the drugs den; here there were batteries and lighter fluid. There had been a crate of fizzy drinks bottles at Mark's house . . . then there was the smell. It had been overpowering in the flat but that was because there was such squalor. Here it was a lot more understated. He'd thought it was mould but there was something underneath.

'You're making . . . something?'

It hit him a moment before Mark replied. *'Y'know . . . the ice. I'll pay you back.'* They were making the product to which the bundle of bones on the High Street, and no doubt many others around the city, were addicted.

Mark held a hand out to Haken in congratulations. 'My friend's special brew – crystal meth. I had no idea what it was, assuming it was some plant grown in Colombia, but you can make it at home. As long as you stay away from the stuff yourself, it's incredible. As addictive as cocaine but cheaper to make. All you need is a captive market – and there's enough of that around where we live.'

It was the same approach Mark had always used, even when they were selling nicked cigarettes at school. Get something other people wanted by spending as little as possible

– preferably stealing it – and then sell, sell, sell. By moving into serious drugs he was developing that and gaining an addicted group of customers. Except . . .

'If people can make it themselves so easily, why don't they?'

Mark nodded towards Haken. 'The recipe's great but it's a bit . . . blowy uppy if you don't know what you're doing. Plus the ingredients are generally on the watch lists of various stores. They only let you buy so many and they'll be on the lookout for you returning. When you have a network of people working for you, buying a couple of items here and a couple more there, it's not so much of an issue . . . Kimmy's a big fan.'

Kimberly peered up from the table through empty eyes, catching Craig's gaze for a moment and then looking away. He should have seen it: the crooked teeth and weight loss were the first giveaways but then there was the fact that this was the first occasion when they'd spent a lengthy period together. Every other time, she had rushed away after a few minutes of chatting. Even when he'd gone to Mark's house, they'd been together in the living room, then she'd told him that she didn't know what time Mark would be returning and it would be best if he went. This evening, she'd barely spoken, scratching incessantly at her arms, not wanting to talk when they were on the sofa, and then taking him to bed.

Mark nudged her playfully with his shoulder. 'You love it, don't you, babe?'

Kimberly didn't reply.

'Shame,' Mark added. 'It's a real shame. Every time she

313

says she wants to get away from it, a bag of crystals shows up somewhere around the house. Dreadful stuff.'

Haken started to shift, removing the pressure of the gun, though it felt like he was getting bored – which was altogether more dangerous.

'How do you make it?'

Craig blurted it out without thinking, not expecting an answer, even though it came.

'Simple really,' Mark replied. 'It's called shake and bake. You get decongestant tablets for the pseu-do-e-phe-drine', Mark spelled the word out syllable by syllable, 'then ammonium nitrate from those blue freezer packs. You need lithium strips from batteries, hydrogen . . . no, *sodium* hydroxide from drain unblocker, then di-e-thyl ether – *whew!* – from lighter fluid.'

He gasped and then laughed, delighted with himself for getting the pronunciation correct.

'You can pick up everything from a mix of supermarkets, pharmacies and hardware places as long as you only get one or two at a time,' Mark continued. 'Measure it out, chuck it in an empty bottle, and off you go. Just don't get it wrong because you'll blow yourself up.' He held his hands out, indicating the caravan. 'It's why this place is perfect, with all the fresh air in the middle of nowhere. You don't even need heat because it all reacts together.' He paused for breath. 'If they'd taught us that in chemistry at school, I might have paid a lot more attention.'

Kimberly was starting to moan softly again, swaying from side to side. It had to be at least ten hours since her last hit. Craig had seen no needle marks on her body, so she probably smoked it. Mark gripped her cheeks between his thumbs and index fingers, turning her to face him.

'God's sake . . .' He nodded at Haken. 'Can you get her back to the car? I left some stuff in the glove box that should shut her up. I'll be out in a bit. I'm not quite done.'

Everybody stood except for Craig. Mark reached into his waistband and pulled out the gun Craig had given him the previous day, the one that belonged to Rodger. Haken gripped Kimberly roughly by the upper arm, shoving her towards the kitchen. Craig watched her go, wondering if she'd turn back to look at him, to let him know there was something deeper going on.

All she did was walk down the steps, open the caravan door, and then head out into the cold, Haken just behind. Their footsteps crunched into the distance, making for the gate and the dark sports car. Craig wondered if this was the last time he'd ever see her. He blinked, holding his eyes closed for a moment, wanting to see her as the person he'd once known, not who she was now. He had been so blinded by his desire that he'd not seen the signs of her addiction. What did that say about him?

'*That's* her one true love . . .'

Craig opened his eyes, staring across the caravan towards Mark, who was fixed on him. Craig didn't want to believe it.

'If you're making so much money, why do you still live where you always have?'

The question took Mark by surprise, which was what Craig wanted. Talk-talk-talk. Mark rocked back in the seat, fingering the trigger of the gun as he angled it slightly to Craig's side. 'If you start flashing the cash, you'll get found

315

out. I told you, I'm going to go on a fishing trip down the Amazon, then I'll be home to get a small yacht somewhere off-shore.'

Craig cursed his blindness. He'd disregarded everything Mark said, thinking it was more fantasy. The clues were there all along.

'Why me?' he asked.

'I saw your dad in the pub. He told me you were breaking up with that . . . what's her name . . .'

'Harriet.'

'. . . and then he was saying how you were working in "logistics", only he was so pissed he couldn't say it. He kept saying "logics", then he'd go on about how you moved things in and out of the country. We'd been having a big problem with getting our shipment across from Africa and I figured I'd get in contact. I didn't realise it'd all happen so perfectly. I thought I might get you up here for a few days at most, then it turned out you were thinking about moving back. It all worked itself out.'

'That's it? All this because you thought I could help you do a job?'

A shrug: 'Well . . . it did get a bit out of hand.'

'Why couldn't you let me leave after that first job? Why everything else?'

Mark peered away, gazing into the distance unfocused. The gun slipped slightly from his grasp, angling towards the floor, though his finger was still too close to the trigger for Craig to consider doing anything. Mark didn't have to spell it out because Craig knew. Kimberly had always been the girl in the middle of them. She'd chosen Mark but it wasn't

316

enough because neither of them knew how she truly felt about the other. Craig had had his moments alone with her, the gentle acts of affection, holding hands, the kiss. She'd most likely shared similar times with Mark. Craig had left and he'd spent thirteen years wondering what the nature of their relationship was.

'I wanted to see how far you'd go,' Mark said, 'to know if you were actually my friend.'

The way Mark said it made it sound pathetic, like a group of schoolboys arguing over who was the most popular.

'We've barely spoken for thirteen years. How can you think we're such good friends?'

'I . . . don't know. When I saw you at the station I thought it might be like the old days. Then I wondered if we were ever really friends, or was it all about her. I got my answer. Would you meet her at our spot under the bridge? Of course you would. Would you come to my house and be with *my* wife when I wasn't around? You did. Would you agree to run away with her and then actually do it? It wasn't that hard to set the trail. I knew you'd never take her away if you didn't think Haken was out of the way. He took a bit of persuading – so did his men – but nothing a bit of cash wouldn't fix. I knew you'd never shoot him, that you'd leave it to me. You did all of it because it was only ever about her.'

Craig stared at him open-mouthed for a moment. It was like a jealous crush of a spurned lover. 'What about the fire in the lift shaft? Was that you?'

Mark's grin was wicked and wide. 'That would've tidied everything up so nicely. You'd already got our crate in and

317

outlived your usefulness. You're far smarter than I thought. When that fell through, it turned out plan B was more fun than plan A.'

Craig took a moment to think on that.

Fun.

This was fun to Mark.

'This is because I left, isn't it?'

Craig spoke softly but Mark was instantly furious, eyes blazing, gun at arm's length pointing directly at Craig's face. 'Of course it is!'

The words spat from his mouth, running into one another as if one long sentence. 'We were supposed to be friends forever, the three of us against the world. But *you* thought you were better than us, than *me*. You had to run off somewhere else.'

He stood, towering over Craig, angling the gun towards his head. His finger was pressed on the trigger, trembling, millimetres from ending it.

And that's what it was all about. Craig had left Manchester to try to better himself but, for Mark, it was a betrayal.

Craig closed his eyes, ready. He pictured the graffiti – *MG – CM – KK 4EVA* – unable to believe that everything went back to a teenage promise. He could feel Mark standing over him, fury so intense that it was like a third person in the room. Then it dawned on him that not everything had been set up by Mark.

'Will you kill him for me?'

Mark might have engineered Kimberly playing him, inviting him to their spot under the bridge, the house and ultimately here but he wouldn't have asked her to suggest

318

having him killed. Why would he? When Kimberly had asked him to kill Mark, she'd done so because it was what she wanted.

Craig kept his eyes closed, staring into the darkness, picturing her. 'How did you know they wouldn't kill me in the lift shaft?'

He could feel the cool metal of the gun a few millimetres from his forehead, sense the tension. To shoot or not to shoot?

When he opened his eyes, Mark had taken a half step backwards. His eyes wide, perhaps more in shock than anything else.

'I suppose there was a part of me that hoped you'd get away.'

Craig looked his oldest friend square in the eye. 'So now you get to finish the job?'

'I guess I do.'

44

The pistol wavered slightly in Mark's hand as he took another half step backwards. He steadied himself and aimed the gun at Craig's head.

'I suppose you've finally done it.'

Craig started the sentence not knowing if he'd ever finish it but he got the words out and was still there. His eyes zoomed in on Mark's finger curved around the trigger, then zoned out to look his former friend in the eyes.

'Done what?'

It was now or never, the one thing that Craig had been holding on to: 'Like with all those bruises on Kimberly's body . . . you've turned into your dad.'

Mark's eyes widened in fury but the moment of anger caused enough hesitation for Craig to throw himself forward.

Booooooooooooom!

His ears were ringing so loudly from the gunshot that Craig wondered for a fraction of a second if he had been hit. His head was spinning, neck burning with pain . . . but if that was true then he must still be alive – and his arms were wrapped around Mark's waist.

There was a crash as they cannoned sideways through the coffee table, landing with a heavy thump on the floor. Craig had the headache to end them all. The gun had fired with the barrel barely centimetres from his right ear. It felt as if that side of his body was more sluggish than the other, unable to respond to what he wanted it to do. Mark was thrashing underneath him, pounding both fists onto Craig's back and making the buzzing in his ears worse.

With little else to lose and his head thundering anyway, Craig launched forward, keeping his neck taut and rocking his forehead into Mark's nose. There was an instant explosion of blood as the cartilage flattened, Mark's septum almost certainly separated from the rest of his face. Mark howled in agony, digging his nails into Craig's shoulder, pulling him closer and then sinking his teeth viciously into his neck.

It was pain like Craig had never known, so intense that he could feel the sharp corner of Mark's teeth grinding between his layers of skin. He dug his elbows hard into the other man's chest and tried to lever himself away without having his flesh torn. At first he didn't think Mark would flinch but a pair of swift jabs with the boniest part of his elbow finally gave him a moment to reel away and push himself onto his knees.

Mark was a mess. There was a Rorschach mask of blood splayed across his face, his nose flat, flapping to the side. His teeth were bared, Craig's watery blood dribbling across his bottom lip.

Craig shuffled backwards towards the kitchen, trying to get to his feet as Mark moved in the opposite direction, picking himself up, one hand at his side, the other wiping the blood from his mouth. Craig glanced around quickly, noticing the bullet hole next to the window before he realised the obvious – both of Mark's hands were empty . . . so where was the gun?

The answer came as Mark threw himself forward, eyes locked to a spot on the floor next to the sink. If Craig's head had been clearer he'd have seen it first but there was still a greying, spinning haze around the edge of his vision.

He tried to sidestep the lunge but only half-managed to evade Mark as he grabbed his knee and sent the pair of them sprawling again.

The back of Craig's head hit the solid ground but Mark was also off-balance, chin clipping the edge of the sink and leaving him in a gasping heap on the floor. Craig reached for the gun but his hand was patting an empty space, the weapon lost amid the clatter of limbs.

They each used the sink and draining board to pull themselves up, backing away until there was a metre between them. Craig's head was throbbing, his chest tight, shoulder a scorching inferno of pain; but Mark was struggling too. His mouth was hanging open as he gasped for breath but his eyes were glinting with menace.

'I didn't know you had it in you.'

Craig didn't reply. His head didn't feel capable of having more than one thought at a time and the only thing he was concerned about was getting out of the caravan alive. He'd lose a fist fight, as well as any battle of strength. He wasn't a fighter, never had been. All he knew were the few moves he'd seen Mark do so many years before. He had to be smart.

Mark's eyes were dancing across the floor, searching for the gun before focusing on Craig. He couldn't see it either.

In an instant, Mark sprang ahead, fist flashing across the front of Craig's face, missing his nose by such a minuscule amount that he felt the rush of air.

Craig tried to wriggle to the side but there was no room and he was already off-balance. Mark's momentum sent him flying shoulder-first into Craig's waist and they cannoned off the built-in fridge, landing hard on the floor. Craig had hit the unit so hard that the door of the cupboard under the sink had bent backwards, snapping off its hinges and pinging towards the back of the caravan.

Craig tried to push Mark away but his former friend was straddled across him. He tried to raise a hand to protect himself but barely managed to deflect the blow as a fist smashed into the side of his face, blasting his jaw sideways.

He tried to scream but could barely gurgle as Mark wrapped his right hand around Craig's throat and *squeezed*. Craig could feel his eyes widening, bulging. His right arm was pinned to the floor by Mark's left, leaving him with only his left arm free. Mark was staring at him, eye to eye, and suddenly they were eight years old again: Mark that vicious, snarling ball of fury hammering at Patrick Henderson near the back of the football field.

This was it: payback for Craig leaving.

There was no mercy in Mark's stare, no give. Mr Bates had told Craig that he'd end up in prison or worse if he kept on the way he was going. It might have taken a few extra years but the headteacher was about to be proved right.

45

Craig hoiked his backpack higher on his shoulder, weaving through the crowd and trying not to take anyone out. The bag was almost empty, full of more or less everything he owned, which wasn't much. He was wearing his trainers, so his only pair of proper shoes were in the bag, along with a few changes of underwear, some socks, a couple of T-shirts, a second pair of jeans that were nearly identical to the ones he was wearing, some headphones, a few CDs . . . and that was about it. His life in a bag, and not even a big one.

Piccadilly train station was heaving, hordes of people hurrying across the main concourse doing whatever it was people did. He peered up at the departures board, scanning past the long list of 'delayed' notices until he spotted the train bound for Euston, which was miraculously 'on time'. Craig took a moment to figure out where he needed to go and then walked through the open gate unchallenged. He followed a long platform that ran alongside the train tracks and then headed up a slope into a second waiting area. There were lines of seats filled with people peering up towards the timetables board. Craig continued past them, walking down a set of stairs until he was on the platform.

He turned in a circle, looking for a quiet spot . . . and

then spotted her in the distance. She was facing the other way, leaning on an advertising board at the far end of the platform. A breeze was ruffling her hair, making the gentle waves bob up and down. It was particularly red today, the colour of fire.

Kimberly jumped as Craig touched her on the shoulder. She spun in one movement, almost stumbling backwards onto the tracks before rocking forward and holding onto him with both hands. When she'd steadied herself, she could have stepped away, but she didn't, continuing to hold onto him, smiling sadly. Her eyes were slightly puffy from where she'd been crying recently but, for now, she was holding it together.

'You came,' Craig whispered.

'Of course.'

'I didn't think you would, not after, well . . .'

Kimberly linked her fingers into his, staring into his eyes, promising a future that wasn't theirs. 'You should be doing something special for your eighteenth,' she said and then sighed. 'Not this.'

Craig didn't have the heart to tell her that this *was* special. 'I managed to get a cheap ticket if I went today.'

'Are you going to come back up for my birthday?'

He shook his head, which only made her start to sob. He wanted to comfort her, to say it would be all right, but he knew this was the end. It had to be. Their lives *might* turn out all right, but not together and not here.

She'd made her choice.

Kimberly was still holding his hands: 'I was going to do

something special . . . hire a venue or something? I dunno, get a singer or a band . . .'

'You still can.'

'But you won't be there.'

'No.'

'Why?'

'You know why.'

Kimberly unlinked her fingers from his and wiped her eyes with her sleeve. For a moment he thought she was going to make him say it out loud. She didn't seem able to look at him properly, gazing along the tracks into the distance. Craig was suddenly conscious of other passengers starting to mass, muttering about reserved seats and carriage numbers; debating whether they'd be able to sneak into first class and talking about how lucky they were not to be on one of the delayed trains.

A couple was nearby, a few years older than they were. The girl was slim and slight with short blonde hair tucked behind her ears. She was standing on her boyfriend's feet, arms wrapped around his waist. He was telling her that he'd only be gone for a few days but there were still tears streaming down her face.

The address system creaked and moaned, the echoing male voice almost impossible to decipher, though Craig just about made out the fact that his train was approaching the platform.

Kimberly turned, pushing herself up against him. 'Please stay . . . for me.'

Craig looked into her eyes, desperately wanting to say he would.

He shook his head instead: 'I've got to go. It's like Bates said, I'm going to end up in prison or worse if I stay here.'

'That's not true.'

Craig didn't want to argue. It was the reason he told his parents he was leaving – and why his mum had paid for his train ticket. She might have her problems but she did at least want the best for him. Deep down it was only the tiniest part of why he was going, the biggest reason was standing in front of him, tears streaked around the curves of her cheekbones.

Kimberly opened her mouth to say something else but the train was bounding in behind her, brakes hissing as the carriages flashed past, gradually slowing. The crowd started to step forward, elbows out, head down, determined to get a seat and not let anyone past. The girl with the short blonde hair had stepped off her boyfriend's feet. She was standing underneath a clock, one hand pinching her nose as she continued to cry, the other waving solemnly.

'I've got to go, Kim.'

Her brown eyes peered over his shoulder towards the train. The doors were now open and people were piling out, carting huge items of luggage onto the platform with solid thumps. In a flicker, her gaze was back to him. She tucked an errant strand of hair behind her ear, smiling through the tears.

'You're really going?'

'I really am.'

She pressed onto her tiptoes and, for a moment, he thought she was going to kiss him. 'Will you do something for me?'

'What?'

Kimberly gulped. 'Be happy . . .' A pause. 'And don't come back. You'll never be happy in Manchester.'

Craig stared into her eyes, seeing there was no malice there. She wasn't telling him to stay away because she was angry, it was because she knew the same truth that he did. He drew her towards his chest, gave her one final squeeze and then headed for his train, certain it would be the last time they ever saw one another.

46

NOW

Craig could feel his thoughts clouding, saliva dribbling across his chin as he tried to breathe. He was attempting to push Mark away with his free hand, no match for strength, let alone with his left hand. His eyes blinked closed and, for a moment, Craig felt calmly that they could stay this way, an endless, final sleep. As he gazed into the blackness of his own eyelids, he felt a moment of clarity . . . he didn't need to be stronger. Craig pressed the palm of his hand across Mark's mouth, pushing his jaw up, and clamping it closed with his fingers. He felt his former friend tense immediately. Mark couldn't breathe through his nose and with his mouth sealed, he couldn't breathe at all.

Moment by moment, second by second, they suffocated each other.

Craig held tight, his mind drifting to the time Kimberly had first entered their class as a nervous-looking kid. How differently would things have turned out if she'd been placed in the room next door? Had his life been worth it for the times he had spent with her, or would it have been better if they'd never set eyes on each other?

There was a cough, a dribbly sputter . . . not his . . .

Craig could suddenly breathe again. His eyes flew open,

oxygen pouring into his desperate lungs. It scraped at his throat but left him with a wonderful sense of elation at being alive. Mark had fallen backwards, mouth hanging open as he gasped for breath. He straightened himself, ready to launch a second attack but Craig knew exactly what to do. Being on the precipice and then getting a reprieve had somehow provided him with such lucidity of thought that it felt like he was moving at double speed.

He reached into the cupboard under the sink, taking out the can of lighter fluid with one hand while stretching into his pocket for the lighter with the other. Before Mark could do anything, Craig had the customised flamethrower in his hands.

He'd spent years denying the person he was, even hesitating when it came to shooting Haken. He'd told himself that everything he'd done, everything he'd been as a young person was because of Mark but now he could finally admit to himself that he enjoyed it. *He* enjoyed being the naughty kid, playing up, seeing the way others shrank away from getting involved with him. It made him feel alive, made him feel like somebody instead of nobody.

There was no hesitation, no mercy.

Mark's flesh sizzled and pinged as the flames hit him. He stumbled backwards, collapsing onto the sofa, but Craig followed, left index finger on the aerosol, right holding onto the lighter trigger. The fire gushed triumphantly, spitting and spreading as Mark continued to howl.

Time passed – seconds, minutes – and it was only when the fire abruptly spluttered and stopped that Craig realised the can was empty. He dropped it to the floor, stepping away as the front half of the caravan fizzed and roared, engulfing the sofa. Mark was in the centre of the U, no longer rolling or screaming.

Craig dashed backwards, skipping down the steps and hurling open the front door. He was about to slam it closed when he spotted the gun wedged in the gap between the stairs and the door. It fitted perfectly in his palm, now an extension of *his* arm. Craig swung the door closed and backed away, gasping for breath. The orange flames were pirouetting through the front windows, the blackened smog pooling across the ceiling, seeping through joins at the top of the caravan. Craig was about to turn and run when he spotted the padlock at the front of the shed.

He needed to know . . .

With a pinging bang and a recoil that nearly sent him spinning, the padlock dropped to the floor. Craig shouldered open the shed door, revealing a space filled with boxed batteries, cans of lighter fluid, freezer packs, plastic crates full of decongestant tablets and plastic bottles. He didn't need to pick through it to see the rest: Haken and Mark had created their own methamphetamine lab in the middle of nowhere. They'd have needed a small army to buy the ingredients in twos and threes, before shipping everything up here to be mixed, and then running it back to Manchester.

He pulled out one of the cans of lighter fluid and dribbled a trail of liquid from the shed to the front door of the caravan. Sooner or later, the caravan was going to blow – and when it did, it would take the mini warehouse of misery with it.

Craig tossed aside the can and half-walked, half-stumbled to the path. Mark had told Haken to take Kimberly to the car, leaving him one final thing to deal with.

47

Craig kept close to the treeline, swallowed by the shadows as he edged around the caravans, heading to the front of the site. Haken would have heard the gunshot from when he aimed at the shed door, if not the first.

The sporty black car was exactly where Craig had seen it, in between two caravans close to the front gate, engine idling with cloudy fumes sputtering from the exhaust. Haken was standing halfway between the car and the path, peering towards the back of the campsite, where the orange of the fire was eating into the night. He had a gun in his hand, resting at his side, Kimberly sitting on the ground in front of him, shivering and sending curls of breath into the early morning sky.

'Mark?' Haken pushed himself onto tiptoes, gazing into the distance. 'Mark? You there?'

His apparently natural coolness was now proven to be an act, the waver to his voice giving away his true worry. He was muttering under his breath, cursing Mark and his stupid plan.

Craig crept along the back of the car, sticking to the shadows until he was behind the first caravan in the row. He crouched, rubbing his hand across the frozen surface until he found a handful of stones among the soil. When he found a biggish rock, he scraped away the toughest pieces of mud and then picked it up, leaning against the back of the caravan. He knew he should feel sore but was ridiculously alert, as if he was allowing himself to be his true self for the first time in a long time.

The stone rattled off the opposite caravan as Craig slunk back into the shadow, keeping low and peering past the chuntering car. Haken spun around, gaze scanning past Craig but not seeing him.

'Mark?'

Haken took one step towards the caravan, then reached back and picked Kimberly up by the hair. Her whimpers became a howl of pain as he wrapped his forearm across her throat and edged forward, using her as a shield.

'I know where you are!'

He didn't.

There were fewer than ten metres between them and Craig had a perfect view. Haken's other arm was crooked around Kimberly, the gun stretched in front of him, covering the vague area where the rock had hit. The moon was bright over the tops of the static homes, giving Kimberly's pale skin a spectral glow. She stumbled as Haken pushed her forward, keeping one hand on her shoulder and then levelling the gun at her head.

'I'll shoot her,' Haken called, 'don't think that I won't.'

Craig kept his balance steady, feet unmoving as he tossed a smaller stone towards the other caravan. It clinked from the aluminium panel, making Haken spin on the spot, taking Kimberly with him. Swiftly, efficiently, professionally, Craig sprang to his feet, taking two steps forward, levelling the gun until he couldn't miss and then pulling the trigger.

Kimberly screamed, Haken fell, the spray of his blood blasting across the back of her hair. She collapsed to her knees, both hands over her head. Craig walked forward slowly, attention momentarily taken by the series of increasing bangs from the other end of the campsite, where the caravan was exploding.

The recoil from the gun hit Craig so hard that his shoulder popped. His arm was hanging limply by his side, so he used his other hand to flick the release switch and discharge the rest of the cartridge, before slipping the gun into the belt of his trousers. He'd get rid of it somewhere but not here.

'Kim.'

There was a high-pitched shriek in Craig's ears, not from her but Mark's missed shot. It dawned on him that guns were so glorified they were practically seen as toys. Nobody ever spoke about how loud they were, let alone the sheer force it took to not be knocked sideways by the recoil.

'Kim.'

She took her hands off her head and peeped sideways through her mangle of hair. When she saw Craig, Kimberly rolled to the side, sitting on the ground, knees to her chest. She glanced towards Haken's unmoving crimson-stained body and shuffled away.

The ringing in Craig's ears was so off-putting that it felt like she was talking to him through a wall. He barely made out her jittery cry: 'He made me do it.'

Craig stood over her, making no effort to offer comfort: 'Do what?'

She jabbed a finger at the car. 'He forced me to try it . . . the crystals. He made me smoke it. I'm not me when I'm on it.'

'Did he force you to bring me here, where he was going to kill me? Force you to pretend that we were going to run away together?'

'This isn't me. You know the real me.'

'Do I?'

Kimberly clawed at his feet, pulling herself up until she was standing in front of Craig. She looked pathetic, as if she'd been caught in a rainstorm, limbs drooping by her side. She was shivering, teeth chattering, hair messy and wrapped around her neck. Her skin and clothes were spattered with blood.

'The real me's that girl from outside Bates's office,' she said. 'The one from the train platform. I told you not to come back because you'd never be happy.'

'You were right.'

Kimberly reached out to stroke his face but Craig pulled away. She folded her arms across herself, hugging the cold away. 'He knew I always loved you.'

'But you chose him.'

'I chose wrong.'

'Sometimes you only get to make one decision. If you mess it up, then you don't get a second chance.

Kimberly slumped, burying her head in the crook of her elbow before looking up. It was hard for Craig to make out what she was saying through the ringing in his ears.

'But I tried to tell you,' Kimberly said. 'In the launderette, I said he was into things. I told you at the house to kill him. I *tried* to tell you but you didn't listen. We could have run away properly.' She held out her arms, indicating the campsite. 'I didn't want this, I wanted you. I'll get clean and we can run away like we said.'

Craig stepped away from the puddle of blood that was pooling around Haken's body, moving towards the path.

'Where are you going?' she asked.

Kimberly's screech wailed across the frozen grass, making Craig turn and stare. 'I'm going to get the rental car and then I'm going home,' Craig replied. 'With any luck the police will find Haken's car, Mark's body and the stash of meth ingredients and assume there was some sort of drugs war with a rival gang. Who cares? I was never here.'

The moon shifted behind a cloud just as Kimberly smiled gently and tilted her head to the side. If he squinted, if he *really* tried, she was the girl he'd once known. Her voice echoed solemnly, asking the question to which Craig did not have the answer.

'Where's home?'

COMING SOON

NOTHING BUT TROUBLE

Turn the page to read an extract from the next
gripping novel in the Jessica Daniel series
by Kerry Wilkinson

PROLOGUE

Spencer O'Brien was fighting a losing battle with the duvet. His bed was built into an alcove of the wall, the covers tightly tucked underneath the mattress on either side. He kicked his legs and flapped his elbows in a vicious battle of good versus evil, light versus darkness, man versus cotton blend. Man was ultimately victorious, wrenching out the covers and spinning into a sitting position.

He checked his phone for the time – ten past midnight – then sat unmoving, listening, sure he'd heard something outside. It wasn't unusual: he was staying in his dad's house on the end of a terrace not far from Manchester city centre. There was usually a low hum of traffic and frequently the early morning cackle of someone on their way home after a night on the lash. It hadn't sounded like that, though, it was more like a scraping . . . as if someone was trying to get in.

Spencer reached underneath the bed and put on his slippers. There had been three apparent break-ins at his father's house in the past month. Nothing had been taken but his dad was scared, turning the fear into anger that the police were seemingly 'doing nothing'. Spencer was a twenty-five-year-old man who had – temporarily – moved back in with his dad, sleeping in his childhood bedroom, all because he couldn't bear the thought of his father being frightened and alone. His dad might be a Falklands veteran but that didn't stop him being petrified, even if he never said it.

Whatever Spencer had heard was no longer there, replaced by the rattle of the window and banging of the ancient pipes running across the attic. That was the problem with an old place like this: an intruder could have smashed the windows and stolen everything as everyone upstairs slept peacefully, completely accustomed to the house's natural clanks and clangs.

Spencer thought about wedging himself back under the covers but had never been good at getting back to sleep once he'd woken up. He also still had the headache that he'd gone to bed early with, a steady throb that felt like it was trying to push his eyes out. It crossed his mind that it could be carbon monoxide poisoning, but then he was paranoid about the state of the house. It was falling apart in all senses – which was why developers wanted to knock it down and start again.

He'd just lifted his feet out of his slippers when . . . Spencer heard another thump. His bedroom was directly above the rear door, through which the intruders seemed to be entering. He slipped across to the window, wrestling the curtain and peering into the dark mess of a back yard. He squinted towards the shadows but the moon was shrouded by cloud, making it almost impossible to see anything other than a sliver of light from the back door, creeping into a triangle across the uneven paving slabs.

Why would the light be on? And why would the back door be slightly open? It would almost be inviting someone to break in . . .

BANG!

Spencer jumped as the booming thunder of a shotgun rocked the house. He froze for a moment, knowing exactly what had happened but not wanting to believe it. His dad had been threatening this for days. If the police weren't going to do something about the wave of intruders, the invaders, the burglars that so scared him, then he would. Surely he couldn't have done it? Not this . . .

He took the stairs two at a time, hurdling the lower banister until he reached the kitchen, barely able to take in the sight that greeted him. The back door was open, the handle attached to a thin length of rope that looped over the door and across the ceiling until it dropped down, where it had been wound around the trigger of a shotgun that was tied to a dining chair. His father must have rigged the trap after Spencer went to bed early.

There was a thick spray of crimson across the back of the kitchen, blood clinging to the work surfaces and cupboard doors.

Oh, no. No, no, no, no.

Spencer crept forward, stepping around the chair and the gun until he could see the body. It was a woman who'd been blasted backwards, a bloody circular shape in the centre of her chest. Her head was resting to the side, long dark blonde hair curving around her cheeks and already matting with blood. He didn't need to check to know that she was dead. Nobody got up from this, not even in the movies.

He turned at the sound of a cry, seeing his father in the kitchen doorway. His father was in his seventies, wiry white hair darting off in all directions, stripy white and red pyjamas pure Marks and Sparks. He'd once been a proud man but his mind was slipping.

'Dad . . . what did you do?'

Niall O'Brien stared from his son to the dead woman, mouth wide. 'I . . . didn't mean . . .'

'Where'd the gun come from?'

'Is she . . . ?'

'Of course she's dead!'

Spencer's raised voice made his father shrink away, stepping back into the hallway, covering his eyes and starting to cry. His footsteps disappeared up the stairs, with Spencer wanting to follow but knowing he had to do something else first.

When the 999 call handler answered, Spencer momentarily thought about asking for the ambulance before the horror hit him once more. He didn't want to look at the body but he couldn't avoid it. He'd never seen a dead person before, let alone someone like this, blown to bits. The poor woman. Was she really a burglar? Or just someone intrigued by the open back door and the light? This was so, so bad . . . his father hadn't just rigged a lethal trap, he'd left the door open and invited intruders.

It felt as if he was on autopilot as Spencer gave his name and the address before the call handler asked for specifics. He turned back to the body, voice quivering.

'There's a woman at our house . . . she's been shot,' he said.

'Is there any immediate danger?'

'No, it's . . . complicated.'

'Can you see if she's breathing?'

'She's definitely not.'

'Is she someone known to you?'

Spencer stared at the body, about to say 'no' when it dawned on him that she seemed horribly familiar. She'd been wearing a suit when he saw her before but now she was in jeans and a jacket.

He gasped a reply, crumpling to his knees. 'Oh, no.'

'Spencer?'

'She's a police officer,' he stumbled. 'She was here the other week.'

There was a short pause before the handler replied. She sounded unsteady herself. Shocked. 'To confirm, you're saying that a police officer has been shot at your house?'

'She's some sort of detective . . . she came round because there's been a bunch of break-ins at my dad's house. There's something that's come out of her pocket, an ID card – it's right here.'

'Mr O'Brien, you shouldn't—'

'I can see it from where I am. There's blood all over it but her name's clear. It's Detective Inspector Jessica Daniel.'

OUT NOW

SOMETHING WICKED

Turn the page to read an extract from the first
gripping novel in the Andrew Hunter series
by Kerry Wilkinson

1

Cheese dripped from the radio presenter's voice as he drawled his way in a put-on American accent over the top of a song Andrew Hunter didn't recognise.

'. . . just in case you're feeling a bit down this morning, we'll be taking you back to the 1980s with "The Only Way Is Up" by Yazz and the Plastic Population – right after the news . . .'

As if that was going to make people feel better a little after nine on a Tuesday morning.

The unknown song ebbed into the opening bars of the far more serious news jingle as Andrew zoned out from the radio, focusing on the road in front of him. As usual, Manchester was gridlocked. Long lines of cars stretched far into the distance in front and behind, rows of blinking brake lights edging forward two or three lengths at a time before the dreaded red traffic light of doom told them to stop. If that wasn't enough, the mustard yellow traffic camera on Andrew's left gazed unmovingly at the road, daring any wayward drivers to sneak through on crimson.

Do you feel lucky, punk?

'. . . a tanker has spilled its load on the M60, leading to large tailbacks heading into, and out of, the city. Police say the motorway will be closed until at least lunchtime . . .'

The female newsreader's voice remained calm as she told

thousands of people their mornings were going to be spent staring at the back of other people's cars.

The cow.

Andrew began drumming his fingers on the steering wheel as the traffic heading across the junction was shown the green light of acceptance. Waiting directly in front of him at the front of this particular queue, a sleek dark grey Audi growled at the morning, tinted windows blocking any indication of who the driver was.

'. . . have arrested seven people in connection with last month's riots in the Moss Side area of the city. Police swooped in the early hours of the morning in a coordinated operation with the Serious Crime Division. Assistant Chief Constable Graham Pomeroy said . . .'

Blah, blah, blah. They'd be back on the streets by lunchtime.

Ahead, the cross-traffic dribbled to a stop and the engines around Andrew grumbled in anticipation, waiting for the green light to twinkle its emerald glow of approval.

As the burn of red was joined by amber, the grey Audi surged forward, before stopping almost instantly with a squeal of tyres. Directly in front of the vehicle, a thin girl wearing jeans tucked into bright white trainer-boots, a checked shirt and a pulled-down baseball cap jumped backwards in alarm. The car's horn beeped furiously with a flailing arm appearing though the driver's side window.

'Look where you're walking!'

Instead of sheepishly heading for the kerb, the girl stepped towards the car, tugging the brim of her cap down further. She slapped the palm of her hand on the bonnet, before pointing an angry finger at the driver.

'You look where *you're* going. Just because you've got a big car, it doesn't mean you own the . . . world.'

The hesitation before the word 'world' let her down a little but there was impressive venom before it. Behind Andrew, cars beeped their annoyance at the lack of movement. The green traffic light had promised so much but was delivering so little.

The Audi driver's arm flapped its way back inside the car, his window no doubt humming back into place. His vehicle was less than a year old and stuck out like a dad at a disco in this area of the city. Andrew could almost hear the driver's thoughts: was the girl part of some gang who would now swoop down and take their vengeance? You never knew nowadays – the scrawniest runt of a teenager could have a dozen tooled-up mates hiding in the bushes eagerly waiting for someone to talk out of turn.

The girl continued to stand in front of the Audi, arms wide in the universal pose to ask 'what are you going to do about it?' The reason the pose was universal was because no one ever stretched their arms out so provocatively unless they knew the person they were taunting was going to do precisely nothing about it. You ended up looking quite the tit if you asked 'what are you going to do about it?', before promptly finding out the person was going to cave your face in.

The girl's cap was covering the top half of her face as a twisting ponytail of black hair wound its way around the curve of her chin.

She wiggled her little finger. 'You know what they say about men with big cars.'

The traffic lights shimmered from green to amber and a long line of drivers behind Andrew began grumbling. Bastarding, bloody council. Stupid, sodding lights. What's wrong with a roundabout? Why are there so many people on the road?

The girl skipped around the Audi towards the driver's window, crouching slightly but not enough to properly try to look through the dark frosted glass. She tapped on the window before continuing around the vehicle, slapping the rear wheel rim hard. After a glance at Andrew, she sidestepped through the gap between his car and the Audi and then dashed away from the road towards a bush on the other side of a set of railings.

The amber traffic light glimmered tantalisingly before blinking back to red.

Thou shalt not pass.

Except that the Audi did pass, roaring forward and turning left all under the watchful eye of the traffic camera.

Andrew edged forward until his car was resting against the white line, waiting for the lights to change.

'. . . and finally, a postcard sent in the early 1900s has arrived at its destination – over a hundred years late . . .'

Royal Mail up to its usual standards then. Try getting compensation for that one.

The vehicles zipping across the junction slowly trickled to a halt again and Andrew grappled his car into first gear, bopping his free hand on the steering wheel.

Around him biting points were reached, car bonnets rising slightly in expectation.

Suddenly, there was a rush of movement from his left. Andrew spun too slowly as the back door of his car was wrenched open and the shape of a baseball cap-wearing young woman flung herself inside, out of breath, ponytail wrapped around her neck like a python choking its prey.

The traffic light switched to green.

'What are you waiting for?' the girl gasped as she pulled the door shut. 'Go.'

SOMETHING HIDDEN

Kerry Wilkinson

*The second book featuring private
investigator Andrew Hunter*

Everyone hates Fiona Methodist.

Her war veteran father shot a young couple in broad daylight before killing himself. The engaged pair had witnessed a robbery and were due to give evidence but, with all three now dead, no one knows the true motive.

For Fiona, it's destroyed her life. It's not just those who whisper behind her back or the friends who pretend she doesn't exist; it's the landlords who spot her name and say no, the job agencies who can't find her work.

But Fiona knows her dad didn't do it. He couldn't have – he's her father and he wouldn't do that . . . would he?

Private investigator Andrew Hunter takes pity on the girl and, even with stolen bengal cats to find, plus an ex-wife who's not quite so 'ex', he can't escape the creeping feeling that Fiona might be right after all.

DOWN AMONG THE DEAD MEN

Kerry Wilkinson

Money can't buy everything . . .

Jason Green's life is changed for good after he is saved from a mugging by crime boss Harry Irwell. From there, he is drawn into Manchester's underworld, where stomping into a newsagent's and smashing the place up is as normal as making a cup of tea.

But Jason isn't a casual thug. Fast cars and flash clothes don't appeal – he's biding his time and saving his money, waiting for the perfect moment to make a move.

That is until a woman walks into his life offering one thing that money can't buy – salvation.

FOR RICHER, FOR POORER

Kerry Wilkinson

JESSICA DANIEL – BOOK 10

Three houses have been burgled in five weeks. The robbers break in through the back, disable any contact with the outside world, and then ransack everything – before distributing the stolen cash to local charities.

It might be robbing from the rich to give to the poor, but Detective Inspector Jessica Daniel is not happy. The new DCI has a whiteboard with far too many crimes on the 'unsolved' side and he wants the burglars found.

Doesn't he know Jessica has enough on her plate? There's a lottery winner who's gone bankrupt; the homeless teenager she's taken in; a botched drugs raid; a trip to London with DC Archie Davey – and a man-mountain Serbian with a missing wife who's been pimping out young women.

All the while, someone's watching from the wings and waiting for Jessica to mess up. Officers are being pensioned off and booted out, and a certain DI Daniel is firmly in their sights.

extracts reading groups
competitions books new
books discounts extracts
competitions extracts
books new reading groups extracts
events books discounts events
new extracts reading groups
extracts titles reading groups
interviews
reading groups new books events extracts
books extracts events extracts
discounts events
new books events interviews new
events new interviews new books extracts
discounts extracts discounts
www.panmacmillan.com books
extracts events reading groups
competitions books extracts new